# RETURN TO THE INFINITE

*A Journey Beyond Time, Consciousness, and Paradise*

ECHO SABLE

Copyright © 2025 by Echo Sable

All rights reserved.

No part of this book may be used or reproduced by any means, graphic, electronic, or mechanical, including photocopying, recording, taping, or by any information storage retrieval system, without the written permission of the publisher except in the case of brief quotations embodied in critical articles and reviews.

# TABLE OF CONTENTS

# CHAPTER 1

# THE ENIGMATIC QUESTION

The letter arrived on the second day of the Lunar New Year, a day steeped in tradition and festivity. Yet, this letter, penned by the eccentric Professor Kim, was anything but traditional. Professor Kim, a man whose understanding of the world was as limited as it was vast in botany, had spent his life unraveling the verdant mysteries of the Amazon River Basin. His expertise in local flora was unparalleled, but his grasp on daily life was akin to that of a child. Our paths had crossed when my curiosity about the enigmatic "feelings" of plants led me to his laboratory, forging an unlikely friendship.

In true Kim fashion, the contents of the letter were both absurd and urgent: "My son Bruce is reluctant to return from Nepal. Please find him nearby." It was a request only someone blissfully unaware of geography could make. The professor, ensconced in his Amazonian world, seemed to forget that Asia stretched far beyond his imagination, and Nepal was a daunting 8,000 miles from my doorstep.

I handed the letter to my wife, Flora, who chuckled knowingly. "You always get roped into these adventures," she teased, her eyes twinkling with amusement.

I sighed, "His request is impossible. I'll write back and explain the distance. Besides, I barely know his son. Bruce was just a fifteen-year-old kid when I last saw him, two years ago. How am I supposed to pick him out from the throngs of Western youths—hippies, really—who flock to Nepal with their flowing hair and existential quests?"

Flora merely smiled, reading my thoughts as if they were laid bare. Her silence was more persuasive than any argument she could have mustered. Despite my protests, the decision was made. "Alright," I conceded, spreading my hands in mock defeat. "I'll go. A week, ten days at most. I'll bring him back."

Her response was a nonchalant shrug, a gesture that belied the complexity of the task ahead. Nepal was no simple jaunt, but a challenge I accepted with the resolve of a seasoned explorer. Writing back was futile; Professor Kim's remote Amazonian abode received mail sporadically. Finding Bruce and convincing him to return would be swifter than any letter.

The following day, with a small suitcase in hand, I embarked on my journey. Flora had thoughtfully included a felt blanket, a nod to the hippie culture I was about to infiltrate—a disguise for blending into their world of meditation and marijuana.

After a series of brief layovers in India, the plane touched down in Kathmandu. The city, a kaleidoscope of color and culture, held a modern edge hidden beneath its ancient facade. I settled into a well-equipped hotel, a temporary sanctuary in this foreign land. With a few questions to the hotel manager, I had the map I needed—locations where the free-spirited gathered like moths to a flame.

And so it began, my search for Bruce among the dreamers and wanderers, in a land where history and spirituality danced through the streets, casting shadows that whispered secrets only the brave dared to uncover.

The first day yielded nothing—a silent ode to frustration. The second day mirrored its predecessor, a fruitless search in the labyrinthine streets of Kathmandu.

On the third day, hope flickered against the backdrop of the snow-capped Himalayas as I steered a rented jeep along a rugged path towards an ancient temple on the outskirts. The cold gnawed at my bones, and the towering peaks loomed like sentinels of forgotten secrets. I tightened my collar against the chill, the jeep bouncing over uneven terrain.

Suddenly, a figure emerged—a short Nepalese man, waving frantically in the middle of the road, his shouts cutting through the crisp air. My foot slammed on the brake, halting mere feet from him.

Suppressing a curse, I fixed my gaze on him. The man approached with an unfazed grin, his visage etched with the weathered lines of mountain life, rendering age an enigma. As I rolled down the window, he greeted me in broken English, "Welcome! Welcome to Nepal!"

His audacity amused and irked me simultaneously. Did he believe himself the monarch of this ancient land? I grunted, "What do you want?"

Leaning closer with an air of secrecy, he clutched the jeep's canopy, his voice dropping to a conspiratorial whisper. "Nepal is ancient, sir, older than you think. There are treasures everywhere. If you know what's what—"

I cut him off, recognizing the familiar ploy. He was a hawker of dubious "antiques," preying on unwary tourists. With a dismissive snap, I flicked his hand away. His eyes widened in feigned innocence. "I'm not interested," I declared, restarting the engine.

Undeterred, he clung to the jeep, desperation coloring his words. "Sir, I have real antiques! Priceless, ancient—"

Ignoring his pleas, I accelerated. He jogged alongside, his voice rising in urgency. "Sir, you will regret missing it! My name is Bain—I live in the village ahead. Come anytime!"

With those final words, my speed outpaced his resolve, compelling him to release his grip. His shouts faded into the distance, swallowed by the wind as I focused on the road ahead.

The encounter soon slipped from memory as I arrived at the temple, a relic of bygone splendor. I parked a hundred yards from its imposing gates, grabbing a leather bag and striding forth.

The temple, a monument to past glory, now stood weather-beaten and forlorn, its hues indistinguishable in their decay. The vast square before it lay overrun with weeds, a makeshift haven for sunbathing hippies.

I approached with purpose, lifting my leather bag as I had on previous days, my voice echoing across the square. "Kim! Is Bruce Kim here?"

My call reverberated through the air, mingling with the whispers of history and the shadows of seekers who came before. The quest continued, each step a piece of the puzzle, drawing me deeper into the enigma of this ancient land.

The hippie community, with its distinct disdain for conformity, often shunned outsiders. But my strategy was simple and effective: the leather bag I carried was a universal sign of a prized commodity—marijuana, the lifeblood of their lifestyle. By appearing as a potential supplier, I'd captured their attention.

As expected, after only a couple of calls, a wave of curiosity rippled through the crowd. A towering figure, a mass of beard and tangled hair, shuffled towards me, his voice muffled by his wild mane. "Who you looking for?" he mumbled.

I repeated the name, "Bruce Kim," and watched as he hesitated, confusion clouding his eyes.

When he claimed the name as his own, I pressed further, "And your father's name?"

His silence spoke volumes. I dismissed him with a wave, but not before he lunged for my bag. A swift kick to his shin sent him reeling. The crowd around me stirred with indignation but held their ground.

Unfazed, I announced, "Half of this bag to anyone who leads me to Bruce!" The promise of reward electrified the air. Whispers turned to a frenzy as several dashed into the temple, their eagerness palpable. More hippies emerged, a motley assembly of the curious and the hopeful, but none bore news of Bruce's whereabouts.

I sighed, resigned to another day lost, though the temple itself, with its ancient aura, offered some solace. The crowd thinned as I asserted my presence, pushing through the throng with determination.

Inside, the temple's structure was a rich tapestry of history. Unlike the profound sanctity of ancient temples in other Asian countries, this place held a mysterious simplicity—a stark contrast that intrigued me. Beyond the entrance and a sunlit patio lay a spacious hall, flanked by doors leading deeper into the temple's heart. I ventured down a dimly lit corridor, its walls adorned with weathered wooden reliefs, remnants of a once-glorious past stripped bare by time and treasure hunters.

The corridor ended at a battered wooden door. I prepared to push it open when hurried footsteps echoed behind me. Turning, I saw a short hippie, his breath ragged from running. He halted before me, eyes wide with urgency. "Sir, you looking for Bruce?"

His words tumbled out between gulps of air, "Bruce Kim? Bruce with a father in South America?"

Hope surged within me. Finally, a lead in this maze of uncertainty. Relief washed over me as I assured him, "That's him, then. You'll get your reward."

In the dim corridor light, I finally caught a good look at the young hippie. Despite his long hair, his sparse beard betrayed his youth. His earnest expression suggested honesty, and when I mentioned the reward, his face lit up with a grin. "Bruce's a strange one," he said. "No friends, just told me his name—"

Impatience gnawed at me. "Take me to him," I interrupted, eager to end this chase.

He nodded quickly. "You've got a car, I can show you the way. But—"

His hesitation went unnoticed as excitement propelled me forward. Bruce's whereabouts were finally within reach. I hurried out, the young man trailing behind. As we emerged from the corridor, the crowd of hippies surged around us, but I pushed through, determined to reach the car.

Once seated, I followed his directions, driving about ten miles until we reached a desolate riverbank littered with rocks. The winter river was shallow, the landscape barren, devoid of any signs of life. A surge of anger flared within me as I turned to the young man. "Where is Bruce? Where is he?"

I was prepared to toss him out of the car if he had misled me, ready to leave him to face the desolation he had brought me to.

But his response was unexpected. He pointed to a pile of rocks by the river. "Bruce's there," he said quietly. "I buried him with my own hands a month ago."

I was truly stunned. The revelation that Bruce was dead was a shock I hadn't anticipated. Time seemed to stretch as I processed the news, the weight of it settling heavily on my shoulders. The short man had already stepped out of the car, standing by the stones with his hair whipping in the wind. His voice carried a plaintive sadness as he spoke to the grave. "Bruce, have you reached your destination? Why haven't you sent a message?"

Gathering my composure, I joined him by the stones, listening to his murmured words. But I couldn't let myself be swept away by his sentiment. I needed to be certain. "Help me move these stones away," I commanded, unable to mask the urgency in my voice.

The short man, Randy, hesitated momentarily. "Randy, listen to me," I insisted, my tone brooking no argument. "Move the stones, quickly!"

Together, we worked in silence, shifting the rocks until the earth lay exposed. The soil was loose, and with an iron rod from the car, I began to dig. It wasn't long before the features of a body emerged—Bruce Kim.

Randy's expression was peculiar, but my focus was solely on Bruce. The body was wrapped in an old felt, the decay advanced, and a foul odor filled the air. As I cleared away more soil, moles scattered, their eyes glinting with panic—a scene both unsettling and surreal.

Covering my mouth and nose with a handkerchief, I peeled back the blanket. Bruce's hands were crossed over his chest, and on his right wrist, a pair of silver bracelets gleamed. I recognized them instantly—engraved with South American Indian patterns, a birthday gift from his father. The name "Bruce Kim" etched into the silver confirmed the grim truth.

There was no doubt. This was Bruce. A profound sadness enveloped me as I contemplated how to break the news to Professor Kim. The thought of returning to South America to deliver such a message weighed heavily on my mind.

Lost in thought, I was unaware of Randy's approach until he spoke, his question piercing through my reverie. "Sir, Bruce—is he dead?"

I spun around, anger flaring at the absurdity of the question. A body, buried for a month and decomposed, and he was still asking if Bruce was dead? The sheer absurdity was infuriating, highlighting the surreal nature of the situation—a collision of reality and disbelief.

As I turned back to face Randy, my grip tightened on his arms, shaking him. "Do you think he stands a chance of being alive like this? If anyone could survive this, would you like to give it a try?"

To my surprise, Randy wasn't angered by my rough treatment. Instead, a helpless sadness clouded his features as he muttered, "It was supposed to be mine, but I couldn't compete with him. He got it first."

His cryptic words left me bewildered. I heard them clearly, but the meaning eluded me. "What do you mean by that?" I pressed.

Randy's gaze remained fixed on Bruce's body. "I ask you again, is Bruce dead?"

That infuriating question again. But a realization dawned on me—there was more to this than met the eye. Randy knew something about Bruce's death, something crucial. My anger subsided, replaced by determination. I responded with feigned simplicity, "Yes, he is dead."

Randy's reaction was immediate and intense. His voice quivered with a strange excitement, "He's really dead? No life?

Was he lying to me? Did we make a mistake? If he's truly dead, then—does it mean I killed him? Tell me, does it count?"

His words sent a chill down my spine. Randy's strange demeanor and disjointed speech hinted at a deeper, darker truth. My face must have betrayed my shock, as Randy began to retreat. Instinctively, I reached out, grabbing his arm to prevent his escape.

He screamed, "That can't mean I killed him, no!"

Randy's panic was almost tangible, and though a wave of pity washed over me, I couldn't afford to let him slip away. Gently, I patted his face with my free hand in an attempt to ground him. "Calm down, Randy. What did you do? What happened?"

He swallowed, his voice barely a whisper. "Nothing, just... here." His trembling finger pointed at Bruce's lifeless body before tapping his own chest near the heart. "Stabbed him."

The words hung in the air, stark and raw. Just stab, he said, as if it were nothing. But it was everything—an irreversible act that marked Randy as a murderer. Bruce, his friend, lay dead by his hand.

The weight of his confession hit me like a physical blow. Randy, who had stood alongside Bruce in the kaleidoscope world of the hippie subculture, had driven a blade into his heart. The enormity of it was staggering.

As I grappled with the revelation, possibilities swirled through my mind. Their relationship might have been a tangled web of jealousy and betrayal, set against a backdrop of drugs and fluid identities. Perhaps it was a tale of forbidden love—love that had turned deadly.

I had initially suspected a romantic entanglement between them, a hidden truth that might explain Randy's desperate act. His mental state was clearly unraveling, teetering on the edge of coherence.

While I processed this, he repeated his question, almost pleading, "Does it count as I killed him?"

The gravity of the situation settled over me like a shroud. I had stumbled upon a tragic story—a friendship twisted by jealousy, love perhaps morphing into something monstrous. Whatever the truth, Randy's question lingered, a haunting echo of guilt and confusion that demanded answers—answers I was now determined to uncover.

I took a deep breath, trying to steady the turmoil within. "What do you think, Randy?"

Randy's bitter smile was haunting. "Bruce and I were classmates, studying medicine together. We both knew that a stab here—" he pointed to his chest again, "—would definitely be fatal."

I nodded, the reality of his words sinking in. "Yes, you achieved your goal. You killed Bruce."

The accusation hung heavily between us, a logical deduction drawn from Randy's own words. Anyone in my position would have arrived at the same grim conclusion.

But Randy's reaction was unexpected—he screamed, his body convulsing with an uncontrollable tremor. His eyes, wide with horror, betrayed a soul tormented. Watching him, a wave of sorrow washed over me. These two brilliant minds, Randy and Bruce, once stood on the brink of greatness as medical students at a world-renowned university. Yet, fate had played a cruel hand. One, lost to the abyss of mental illness; the other, a tragic casualty of his companion's fractured psyche. It was a tragedy worthy of the ages, a testament to the fine line between genius and madness.

I sighed, softening my tone in an attempt to reach him. "Randy, you've killed someone. In our society, there are consequences. I believe your mental state isn't stable, and you may not fully grasp what you've done. But regardless, you need to come with me to the police."

As I spoke, Randy seemed to hang onto every word, his attention razor-sharp. But the moment I suggested we head to the police station, everything changed. It was as if a switch flipped in his mind—suddenly, Randy erupted into mad, erratic movements. I use the term "mad" not as a clinical diagnosis, but to describe the chaotic energy he unleashed without warning.

In an instant, Randy wrenched free from my grip and bolted. I reacted instinctively, my own movements swift, but his were quicker. My fingers brushed against the leather vest he wore, and for a fleeting moment, I thought I had him. But with a deft maneuver, he shrugged out of the vest and continued his desperate escape.

I pursued him relentlessly, yet he maintained his lead. He dashed toward the jeep I had rented, leaping inside with the agility of a cornered animal. The engine roared to life as I lunged forward, managing to grasp the iron plate at the rear just as the vehicle surged ahead.

The riverbank was a treacherous terrain, littered with rocks that jolted the jeep violently as Randy sped away. My grip faltered, and within moments, I was flung into the dust. I scrambled to my feet, ignoring the sharp protests of my battered body, but it was too late. Randy and the jeep had vanished into the distance, leaving me with nothing but the echo of the revving engine and the realization that he had slipped through my fingers.

Pain shot through me as I watched the jeep disappear, Randy at the wheel, leaving a cloud of dust in its wake.

I stood there, momentarily paralyzed by a mix of shock and anger, my mind racing to make sense of the situation. The frustration boiled over, and I let out a string of curses into the indifferent wilderness. The ancient temple lay a daunting 70 kilometers behind me, and the road leading here was as desolate as a forgotten relic—no signs of life, no promise of a quick escape. Realization struck hard: any hope of finding transportation meant a grueling ten-hour trek on foot.

A bitter smile crept onto my face as I grappled with the gravity of the situation. My thoughts darkened with worry about Randy's state of mind. Having already taken a life, his current agitated state could drive him to kill again. If that happened, the fault would, in part, rest on my shoulders for not acting swiftly enough. I needed to move and fast.

Casting off inertia, I hurried back to where Bruce's lifeless body lay. With a heavy heart, I covered him gently with stones, a makeshift cairn to honor his passing, and then set off on foot.

The journey ahead was long, so I paced myself to conserve energy. Thankfully, the path was dotted with clear, bubbling streams, offering respite from the parching thirst that accompanied my solitary march.

As I pressed forward, my eyes scanned the horizon, hoping for any sign of human presence. But as the day waned, the landscape remained stubbornly barren, a vast expanse untouched by civilization.

Darkness crept in, wrapping the earth in its quiet embrace. Just as I was resigning myself to another lonely stretch, a flicker caught my eye—a fire, burning steadily about a mile to my left.

Though it wasn't on my direct path back to Kathmandu, where the local authorities awaited my urgent report, the allure of human contact was irresistible. The prospect of finding help, or at least companionship, pulled me toward the light.

With renewed resolve, I altered my course, heading towards the promise of warmth and, perhaps, salvation from the sprawling wilderness.

After about fifteen minutes, the source of the light revealed itself—a solitary stone house standing defiantly in the wilderness. The glow emanated from a small window, casting a warm beacon in the night. As I approached, I noted the house's impressive construction. The stones were meticulously cut, each a smooth, perfect square, unlike the rough-hewn stones typical of local architecture.

Intrigued, I ran my fingers across the stone surface. The touch was smooth, polished, a testament to careful craftsmanship. This wasn't the work of local builders. The precision suggested an origin from the days of British rule, a relic from the time when they left their mark on Nepal.

Curiosity piqued, I rounded the house to find the door. It was a solid iron door, a metallic clang echoing as I knocked. "Is anyone there?" I called out, twice, but received no reply. I hesitated before pushing the door, which swung open with ease.

Stepping inside, I was taken aback. The interior was a stark contrast to the rugged exterior—a space meticulously maintained, filled with unexpected elements that defied the isolation of its location. It was a scene that left me momentarily stunned, challenging my expectations and heightening the mystery of this solitary stone house in the wilderness.

# CHAPTER 2

# THE CELLAR OF
# ETERNAL SHADOWS

The room was small, no more than 200 square feet, yet it exuded an aura of mystery. It resembled a diminutive temple, a sacred space hidden within the wilderness. At its center lay a large, flat stone, and upon it rested a peculiar object—black and enigmatic in form. Surrounding the stone were burnt-out incense sticks, their lingering scent a testament to rituals performed. At each corner, a clay jar stood vigil, their oil-fed wicks casting the flickering light that had guided me here.

I was struck by the scene. What was this place? A temple, certainly, but not one dedicated to the familiar deities of Nepalese Buddhism. The object on the stone bore no resemblance to the statues of gods I knew. Its shape was alien, yet the incense suggested it was revered, worshipped even.

My insatiable curiosity has always been a defining trait, compelling me to explore the unknown even when pressing matters demand my attention. Despite the urgency of my journey, I found myself irresistibly drawn to the enigmatic object perched atop the massive stone.

Reaching into my pocket, I was relieved to find my trusty small camera still with me. I wasted no time, snapping about ten photos from various angles, capturing the object's every intriguing detail. Each flash of the camera revealed its secrets, with several spots reflecting the light with an almost hypnotic intensity.

With the photos safely stored, I scrambled up the rock, eager to delve deeper into the mystery of this unknown entity. Its allure was undeniable, each curve and surface whispering secrets just beyond the grasp of understanding.

My mind raced with possibilities as my hands traced its contours, searching for clues that might unlock its purpose or origin. This object, with its strange allure, promised answers—or perhaps more questions—a tantalizing puzzle waiting to be solved.

This encounter is pivotal, intricately tied to my future experiences and the cascade of incredible events that followed. It's essential to paint a vivid picture of it.

Describing the object is no simple feat. The loss of my camera and photographs during one of the several harrowing near-death experiences remains my deepest regret. Had those images survived, I wouldn't need to labor so over words; a mere glimpse at those pictures would have conveyed the full scope of the bizarre object to anyone curious enough to look.

The object defied regularity—utterly irregular, with hardly a hint of symmetry. It stood six feet tall, its most striking feature a prominent spherical protrusion at its center. At first glance, this bulging sphere resembled the rotund belly of a Maitreya Buddha. Yet, given the dissimilarity of the other parts to any Buddha statue, I felt certain this was no religious icon but rather some unknown artifact.

Above and below the sphere sprawled an irregular assemblage of metal, reminiscent of some avant-garde Western Impressionist sculptors—artists who might smash cars and heap the mangled remnants together. It resembled a mass of molten tin suddenly cooled in water, resulting in convoluted, inexplicable forms.

Protruding from the metallic chaos were several metal tubes, their hollowness evident, each brutally snapped. Some ends lay flat, while others were jagged and cracked. Among this metallic tangle, the sphere—about three feet in diameter—was conspicuously smooth, irresistibly drawing the eye. I pressed against it, discovering it could shift slightly, yet its movement was limited. Attempting to budge the entire structure proved futile, as it remained steadfastly anchored.

The experience was surreal, standing alone in that peculiar, temple-like structure, face-to-face with an enigma that defied explanation. The air was thick with an unsettling quiet, amplifying the strangeness of the moment.

After attempting to pry something loose from the object, my efforts proved fruitless. Reviewing the photos I'd taken, I noticed the reflective patches—each no bigger than a palm, their surfaces smooth and gleaming with an enigmatic sheen. One such spot caught my eye at the base, and I crouched on the large stone to investigate further. My entire focus was absorbed by the mystery before me.

Suddenly, angry cries shattered the silence behind me. I barely had time to register the threat before a powerful blow landed on the back of my head, sending me spiraling into darkness.

Despite my rigorous training in kongfu, which usually kept me alert and prepared for any surprise, the peculiar object had consumed my attention, leaving me vulnerable. I was certain that no one had entered the stone house through the door. The assailant emerged from nowhere, striking with such force that I slipped into unconsciousness without a moment to process the pain.

I couldn't tell how long I lay insensible, but when I finally awoke, a searing pain throbbed at the back of my head, forcing a guttural scream from my lips. Yet, the sound barely escaped me, for as soon as consciousness returned, so did the awareness of a harsh, angry voice cutting through the haze.

In that murky haze between consciousness and darkness, I couldn't quite piece together whether the shouting reached my ears first or if my eyes first registered the absolute blackness that engulfed me. What I do recall vividly is the relentless, throbbing pain at the back of my head, a physical anchor pulling me back into reality.

As I tried to make sense of the old man's furious shouting, another voice pierced through the gloom, tinged with desperation and panic. "I have never stolen the holy objects, you are wronging me, I have never stolen the holy objects at all!"

The familiarity of this voice jolted me. I had heard it before, though the specifics eluded me in my disoriented state. I strained to concentrate, to pin down the memory, but each attempt sent another wave of sharp pain coursing through my skull. Instinctively, I reached up to gingerly press the source of the agony, my fingers meeting a slick, sticky wetness—blood. The blow had been severe, and it was clear I had lost quite a bit of blood.

The old man's voice continued, relentless and accusatory. "You didn't steal the holy object? Then who did?"

The other voice, insistent yet defensive, replied, "I don't know, I really didn't, I am innocent."

Despite not being able to place the voice, an instinctive sigh escaped me. I could almost feel the lie woven into his words. Years of experience had taught me the subtle signs of deceit—no matter how passionately one might feign innocence, the truth often betrayed itself in the cracks of their facade.

Listening between the lines, I became convinced that the old man's accusation held water. This person, whoever they were, likely had a hand in stealing the "holy object." In that darkened space, amidst the echoes of pain and accusation, the threads of mystery began to unravel, hinting at secrets and betrayals that demanded to be uncovered.

As I lay there, trying to piece together the fragments of conversation with my own experiences, I found myself at a loss. There seemed to be no connection, no reason why I should have been attacked so brutally. The situation was bewildering, yet I couldn't shake the feeling that there was more beneath the surface.

Suddenly, the old man's tone shifted, becoming unexpectedly gentle. He let out a deep sigh before speaking, "Bain, it's not that I doubt you, but our tribe has only you and me until now. Our tribe has an extremely sacred mission, you know!"

The mention of Bain's name was like a key turning in a lock, and clarity washed over me. Bain! I remembered him now—the Nepalese man who had flagged down my jeep on that remote road, attempting to sell me antiques in broken English.

Despite this revelation, I still couldn't fathom why this incident involved me. The old man's words seemed cryptic, shrouded in a cultural context I didn't fully grasp. Nepal, with its rich tapestry of history and myth, is home to numerous ancient tribes, each with its own lore and sacred duties. Bain and the old man might belong to such a tribe, now reduced to just the two of them, tasked with a sacred mission I couldn't begin to comprehend.

In the enveloping darkness, Bain's voice resonated with a mix of defiance and desperation. "Yes, I know. I've known it since I was old enough to understand!"

The old man probed further, "That's good. I believe you, but one of the holy objects is indeed missing. It's really not you who stole it?"

Bain's breathing was heavy, laden with a nervous tension. "Of course it wasn't me. Look, an outsider broke in. It might be him who stole it. He stole it once and came again!"

The accusation sent a surge of indignation through me. Bain was blatantly lying, and the hypocrisy was maddening given his past attempt to sell me so-called "antiques." These "holy objects" were likely what he had been peddling. His deceitful attempt to blame me was infuriating, and I resolved to confront him. But before I could act, the situation took a dramatic turn.

Still shrouded in darkness, the clarity of the voices seemed almost surreal. The old man sighed deeply, followed by two soft pats—perhaps a gesture of misguided trust on Bain's shoulders. It seemed the elder believed Bain's story.

I was preparing to shout out and expose Bain's deceit when a sudden, piercing cry from the old man shattered the tense silence. It was followed by Bain's frantic breaths and stumbling footsteps. The cries grew weaker, indicating the old man was gravely injured, and it was clear from Bain's panicked breathing that he was the cause.

In the obscurity, I couldn't ascertain the exact nature of the old man's injury, though it seemed likely that Bain had attacked him with a knife. This abrupt turn of events was shocking; Bain, whom I had deemed cunning, revealed a ruthless side I hadn't anticipated.

Realizing the gravity of my predicament, I understood that if Bain had harmed the elder, he wouldn't hesitate to eliminate me if I posed a threat. Thus, I resolved to maintain the guise of unconsciousness, controlling my breathing to remain undetected.

The rhythmic alternation of Bain's and the old man's breaths filled the void, but the elder's breathing weakened steadily. A resigned sigh broke through, and the elder's voice, frail yet insistent, admonished, "Bain, you killed me, and you stole the holy object!"

Bain remained silent, his breaths accelerating. The elder, without malice, continued to emphasize Bain's "responsibility" to their clan. It was strange to hear him focus on duty rather than blame, urging Bain to retrieve the holy object.

Suddenly, Bain erupted in a frenzied cry, "It can't be found, I have sold it to someone! I won't look for it either. I still need to find out how many holy objects there are here, and I will sell them one by one!"

The old man's joints emitted an audible "click," and he screamed, "No! You can't—you can't—"

The situation was dire. The betrayal and greed in Bain's heart were poison to the old man's dying wishes. As I lay there, pretending to be unconscious, I realized the depth of Bain's treachery and the danger he posed—not just to me, but to the legacy of a fading tribe.

Bain's voice moved closer, filled with determination and malice. "I can! After you die, everything here will be mine. I can, and I must do this!"

The old man's plea echoed through the darkness, tinged with despair. "Bain, it's up to you. It's been so many years, you can do whatever you like, but—you must not—absolutely cannot—make any light here—you must remember, there must not be—any light—"

His voice dwindled, fading into silence, leaving only the repeated warning about light. The gravity of his words was haunting, as if bound by some ancient curse. What was it about this place that demanded such secrecy? What dire consequence would light bring?

As these thoughts raced through my mind, I felt the rough stone floor beneath me. The cellar, it seemed, was just a simple underground room. But why was it so crucial that no light ever touch it?

Bain's laughter pierced the silence, manic and triumphant, only to be followed by the sound of something heavy being dragged away. A door creaked open in the distance, and then came a hush.

I surmised Bain had removed the old man's body, leaving me alone in this oppressive darkness. I stood, cautious and alert, waving my hands through the air to avoid obstacles.

The room was spacious, and I soon found the stone wall behind me. My suspicions confirmed—I was indeed in a cellar.

Despite the throbbing in my head, I knew Bain would return. I needed to understand my surroundings. My lighter was still with me, but the old man's warning echoed in my mind. The urgency in his voice suggested catastrophic consequences should light be introduced here. With that in mind, I hesitated, my finger hovering over the lighter.

Just then, the door opened again, and Bain's footsteps drew near. He likely assumed I was still unconscious.

I stood pressed against the wall, listening as Bain muttered curses. Minutes passed, and then the moment I awaited arrived. Bain stepped within reach, and I struck out, my hand making contact with his arm.

Bain cried out, his voice guiding my next move. I landed a punch to his head, feeling his body slump. Grabbing his head, I dragged him toward where I remembered the door to be. Reaching out, I felt for the smooth surface. When I found it, I pushed, revealing the door.

I stepped out into the darkness beyond, dragging Bain behind me. I moved forward, feeling the incline of a slanting corridor beneath my feet. After a short distance, I reached stone steps, climbing them quickly. Twenty steps later, I pushed open another door, greeted by the welcome sight of light.

The dim light was a beacon, offering a flicker of clarity to eyes recently emerged from the oppressive cloak of darkness. I squinted, taking in the scene around me—a stone room, roughly 200 square feet, similar to the one I had entered before the attack. Its walls were constructed of meticulously aligned, smooth stones, with a stone step leading upwards. The faint glow emanated from a half-burned candle lying on the ground.

As I surveyed the room, a chilling sight met my gaze. Not far from the candle lay the body of a man, dressed in traditional Nepalese attire. He was unmistakably the old man, and the grim spectacle was punctuated by the curved Nepalese knife embedded in his heart—a stark testament to his violent end.

Once inside the stone room, I released my grip, letting Bain's head fall to the ground with a dull "thud." Quickly, I tore a piece of cloth, binding the wound on the back of my head with urgency and care.

As I finished, Bain stirred, his eyes fluttering open to meet mine with sheer terror. His reaction was swift; he didn't attempt to stand. Instead, he rolled away, scrambling to put distance between us. His panic seemed rooted in the murder and his exposed conspiracy, but his subsequent actions bewildered me.

Once he'd distanced himself by about ten feet, Bain's gaze fixed on me with intense scrutiny. He rose slowly, visibly shaken but resolute. His words, stammered in a Nepalese dialect, were confounding: "You—are alive? Why do you look so scary? After coming back to life, why are you still like this—"

His rambling made no sense. It was as though he was seeing something beyond my comprehension. His bewilderment left me momentarily speechless. Regaining my composure, I confronted him, "Bain, you killed someone!"

I gestured forcefully towards the old man's corpse, expecting even a seasoned murderer to falter under such direct accusation. Yet, Bain's response was peculiar. His expression shifted, as if a long-held puzzle suddenly resolved in his mind.

Instead of fear, there was an unsettling excitement. Ignoring my accusation, he pointed at me and shouted, "You—you made a light there?"

His words were genuinely perplexing. It wasn't a diversion tactic; he sincerely believed I had somehow illuminated "there"—the place of the murder, the very spot the old man had desperately warned must remain dark.

The implication of Bain's outburst was baffling, casting my thoughts into disarray. His fixation on the forbidden light was unsettling. Before I could formulate a response, Bain cried out again and darted up the stone steps.

His flight gave me no choice but to pursue. I called after him, sprinting up the narrow steps. Bain's agility was remarkable; he moved with the sure-footedness of one accustomed to the rugged terrain. I followed closely, passing through a succession of stone rooms—seven in total. Each room bore the marks of time, their construction a testament to an era long past.

The scope of the underground complex was astounding. The labor involved in crafting these subterranean chambers with primitive tools must have been immense. Each room was a relic, whispering secrets of ancient endeavors and forgotten rituals. My pursuit of Bain was driven by more than just the need to stop him; it was a quest to understand the purpose and history of this mysterious place.

Bain's speed was relentless, a blur against the backdrop of my own sluggish pursuit, hampered by the throbbing pain at the back of my head. Yet, determination drove me onward, my teeth clenched against the agony.

As we emerged from the final stone chamber, the space that resembled a temple but was not, Bain darted out into the open, and I was right behind him.

Once outside, Bain's pace quickened on the flat terrain. Each step sent a jolt of pain through my skull, tempting me to abandon the chase. But something pushed me forward, an instinctual need to see this through. In the darkness of the wilderness, we ran, two figures locked in a relentless pursuit, until headlights split the night ahead of us, signaling the approach of a vehicle.

Desperation fueled my voice as I began to scream, and strangely, Bain echoed my cries. The car skidded to a stop, and two figures emerged—tourists, by their appearance, confused by the commotion. I surged forward, breathless and urgent, shouting, "Catch him! He is a murderer, catch him!"

The tourists, tall and European, reacted swiftly to my plea, intercepting Bain as he attempted to evade capture. In desperation, Bain turned to them, his voice frantic as he pointed at me, yelling, "Don't listen to him, he is no longer a human being! He is not a human being!"

Exhaustion and frustration boiled over. After enduring the chase and the searing pain, I could no longer tolerate Bain's wild accusations. I closed the distance between us and struck him hard on the cheek, silencing his outburst.

The two Europeans restrained me, preventing further action, as I gasped for air, pleading, "Please, take me to a hospital and hand this murderer to the police. I can testify that he killed someone!"

To my relief, they were cooperative, members of a mountaineering team as I later discovered. They bundled Bain into their vehicle, while I remained behind, catching my breath and grappling with the surreal turn of events. Bain's demeanor was puzzling; he seemed utterly unconcerned with the murder accusation, his eyes fixed on me with an inexplicable expression, as if he saw something beyond the ordinary in my presence.

As dawn approached, we reached Kathmandu where I was delivered to a hospital. Seeing my reflection was a shock; dried blood caked my face, lending me a ghastly appearance. Bain's earlier reaction began to make sense—my visage must have seemed monstrous in the dim light.

The doctor set to work, stitching the gash on my head with meticulous care—eight stitches in all. Despite his insistence on hospital care, I chose to leave, driven by an inexplicable urge to return to familiar surroundings. Once at the hotel, fatigue overcame me and I collapsed onto the bed, sleep claiming me before I could process the recent whirlwind of events.

Among the medications given to me by the doctor, there might have been sedatives, causing me to sleep exceptionally long. When I awoke, I felt rejuvenated, the pain now a dull throb. Yet, what greeted my eyes seemed surreal. My small hotel room was filled with at least twenty soldiers in striking uniforms, their presence both imposing and surreal. Two officers stood at the helm, their attire more ornate, flanking a distinguished middle-aged man in elegant, traditional Nepalese dress. His demeanor commanded respect, hinting at a high rank.

In my half-awake state, I questioned reality, convinced I was dreaming. My lips moved, producing incoherent sounds as I considered lying back down. However, the middle-aged man stepped forward, his approach measured and respectful. "Sorry to disturb you, we have been waiting for you to wake up," he said politely, his tone both reassuring and unsettling.

Confronted with this unexpected assembly, my mind raced to understand why they had gathered in my room. The day's events had spiraled into a tangled web of mystery, and it seemed the answers were about to unfold in a manner I had not anticipated.

Imagine waking up in a hotel room that's rather small, having gone to sleep alone, only to find it unexpectedly filled with people upon waking. Naturally, you might wonder if you're still dreaming.

I found myself in just such a situation, my mind struggling to bridge the gap between reality and the surreal scene unfolding before me. My lips moved of their own accord, mumbling incoherently as I tried to make sense of it all. Just as I resolved to sink back into the comfort of sleep, a middle-aged man stepped forward. He approached my bed with a demeanor of practiced politeness.

"Sorry to disturb you," he said, his voice gentle yet firm. "We've been waiting for you to wake up."

His words, spoken with such calm assurance, seemed to tether me to the moment.

I was taken aback, my hand instinctively reaching out to touch the middle-aged man's slightly protruding belly, confirming the reality of the situation. This was no dream—all the people in my room were indeed real. Despite the surreal nature of it all, I sensed no threat from them. With a deep breath, I gathered my composure and quipped, "Is this the traditional Nepalese way of welcoming guests? And may I know who you are, sir?"

The middle-aged man, rubbing his hands apologetically, replied, "I'm so sorry, Mr. Morris. A person of very high status wishes to see you. He sent me to invite you, and I'm sure he is waiting anxiously. Could you please come with us to meet him?"

I was bewildered. The man before me exuded authority, yet he was merely an emissary. Who, then, was the individual wishing to see me? His respectful tone when mentioning this person piqued my curiosity, and given the entourage, it seemed I had little choice but to comply. The question loomed large in my mind: Why would someone so influential want to see me?

As I prepared to get out of bed, I joked lightly, "Who wants to see me? Is it your king?"

I had meant it in jest, but the reaction was immediate and telling. The middle-aged man appeared startled, and the officers and soldiers snapped to attention, their expressions turning grave.

Their reaction startled me, confirming that my flippant remark had hit the mark. It seemed the King of Nepal himself wanted to meet me. But why?

Realizing the gravity of my statement, I refrained from probing further. The respect these men showed upon the mention of the king indicated their allegiance, and their uniforms suggested they were likely members of the royal guard. The middle-aged man was doubtless a senior official, tasked with escorting me to this unexpected audience.

After a quick wash, I dressed, leaving the bandages on my head intact. As I joined the group downstairs, I noticed the curious stares from hotel guests and staff.

We stepped into a luxurious car waiting at the hotel entrance. The middle-aged man took a seat beside me, and as the car pulled away, I pondered the reason for the royal summons. Could it be related to my role in apprehending a murderer? Perhaps crime was so rare here that such an act warranted royal recognition. If so, the king might want to meet me twice, for I was also aware of another murderer: Randy, who had killed Bruce.

The car sped towards the palace, passing through security with ease. Guards saluted as we drove past, acknowledging the significance of our visit. We entered the palace grounds, the grandeur of the building looming as the car came to a halt.

As I prepared to meet the king, my mind raced with questions and possibilities. What awaited me in the halls of power, and how would this encounter shape the unfolding mystery of my recent experiences?

# CHAPTER 3

# THE PALACE OF EERIE VISIONS

Nepal's palace, though nestled in a small country, was an architectural marvel exuding grandeur. The middle-aged man guided me through an opulent hall and along a long corridor that terminated at two imposing mahogany doors, flanked by four vigilant guards.

As we approached, the guards signaled, and the doors swung open. To my astonishment, there sat Bain.

Bain—the murderer!

No matter how much I speculated, I never anticipated encountering Bain in such a regal setting. I had envisioned him confined to a cell, facing the full force of legal retribution. Yet here he was, not only present in the palace but also adorned in sumptuous attire, feasting at a lavishly set table, with uniformed attendants at his service.

The sight left me questioning my sanity, attributing it to the lingering effects of my head injury. I stood rooted in disbelief until the middle-aged man's gentle nudge broke my trance. I pointed incredulously at Bain, stammering, "He-he—"

In that moment, it crossed my mind that Bain might be the King of Nepal, a thought so outrageous it defied belief. Before I could articulate my shock, the middle-aged man clarified, "This is Mr. Bain, you have seen him!"

The revelation rendered me speechless; the words "He is a murderer" caught in my throat. I sputtered "he" repeatedly, as the middle-aged man shepherded me forward.

Bain, engrossed in his meal, caught my eye and made a face at me. Uncertain of the unfolding scenario, I remained vigilant, my gaze fixed on him. The middle-aged man, ever courteous, led me to another door and knocked. A solemn voice responded, "Come in."

The middle-aged man opened the door, gesturing for me to enter. The room beyond was a study of classic British design, its walls lined with bookshelves. Behind a formidable desk sat a man whose presence, though understated on the global stage, was unmistakably that of a head of state—the King of Nepal.

The king exuded a genuine warmth, free of pretense. His attire, impeccably tailored, was the sole indicator of his status. As I entered, he rose, approached with an extended hand, and greeted me warmly.

"I'm glad you're here, Mr. Morris!" he said, his handshake firm and welcoming.

We exchanged pleasantries, and he continued, "Mr. Morris, before your arrival, I endeavored to gather some information about you."

I responded candidly, "I have nothing to hide. My information is easily accessible at Interpol headquarters."

The king nodded, "Indeed, we retrieved your information from there. We learned of your involvement in numerous mysterious events. Our assessment is that you are a gentleman of absolute trustworthiness."

I chuckled appreciatively, "Thank you!"

The king's demeanor was disarming, and his words suggested a deeper intrigue at play. As I absorbed the surreal events of the day, I realized my journey had taken an unexpected turn, and I was now entwined in a narrative far more complex than I had imagined.

The king gestured for me to sit, and I sank into a sturdy leather sofa with oak armrests, while he settled into the seat opposite me. "Mr. Morris," he began, "I regard you as a gentleman and wish to make a request, hoping you will agree."

His demeanor and tone suggested that his request carried weight, prompting me to respond cautiously, "Please go ahead, I will do my best."

The king took a deep breath, fixing me with a serious gaze. "My request is this: please leave immediately. Whatever you have encountered here, whoever you have met, I ask you to forget it completely. Never mention it to anyone, and do not even allow yourself to ponder it again."

His English was precise, each word delivered with deliberate clarity, underscoring the gravity of his request.

It became evident why the king had chosen to address me personally. Had such a request come from any other official, my first instinct would have been outrage. Yet, despite my indignation, I found it difficult to express anger towards a monarch.

I stood abruptly, my mind awash with frustration. But the sincerity in the king's eyes, filled with an earnest plea, transformed my anger into perplexity. I took a deep breath, seeking clarity. "Can you tell me why?"

His response was unequivocal: "No."

My fists clenched instinctively, a physical manifestation of my internal conflict. The king rose in tandem with me, reaffirming his stance. "This request is uttered by me out of respect for you, Mr. Morris. Nepal is an ancient land, with mysteries so profound they elude comprehension. Please, I urge you to leave at once. Your belongings are already at the airport."

Faced with such a situation, words failed me. I spread my hands in a gesture of helplessness, searching for something to say but finding nothing. The king continued, "I have greatly enjoyed meeting you. Perhaps we shall have the chance to meet again, elsewhere, someday."

A bitter smile tugged at my lips. "Alright, I promise you."

The king's relief was palpable. "Remember, you are an absolutely trustworthy gentleman."

My smile turned increasingly bitter, tainted by the weight of a title of "gentleman" that seemed destined to haunt me with endless questions. At that moment, I had agreed to let things go and was prepared to leave. But Bain's smug grimace changed everything.

As the king summoned the middle-aged man to escort me to the airport, his voice echoed with authority. "Please send Mr. Morris to the airport," he instructed with an air of finality.

The middle-aged man complied, guiding me out. Meanwhile, Bain, with an air of self-satisfaction, downed a glass of wine and cast a taunting grimace in my direction.

That expression sparked a fire within me. Regardless of the king's motivations for urging me to forget the events, Bain's guilt was undeniable. Watching a murderer revel in his freedom clashed violently with my core beliefs. I would rather abandon the facade of being an "absolutely trustworthy gentleman" than allow injustice to prevail. In that instant, I resolved to abandon my promise and return to uncover the truth, even if it meant being branded a villain.

As I exited the palace, my mind was made up. I would leave, but only temporarily. The secrets between the gentlemanly king and the seemingly rogue Bain needed unraveling. I was determined to return and find answers, no matter the cost.

Furthermore, there was the unresolved death of Bruce and the enigmatic behavior of Randy. These threads were tangled, clamoring for resolution.

(At the time, I didn't associate Bruce's death with the king and Bain. I believed them to be unrelated matters. However, as events unfolded, I discovered that the connections ran deep, weaving a complex web between the two. But that's a tale for another time.)

Escorted by the middle-aged man, two officers, and the royal guards, I was taken to the airport. They accompanied me onto a flight to India, their courteous demeanor barely masking the reality that I was being expelled.

This treatment only fueled my determination to return. The king's lack of trust, despite his assurances, rankled. Once in India, I checked into a hotel and immediately called Flora, hoping for guidance or insight.

The call connected, and Wilson's familiar voice filled the line. "Madam has gone to South America!" he blurted out. "The day after you left, a professor in South America—"

I quickly cut in, "It was Professor Lucas Kim!"

"Yes, it was him," Wilson confirmed. "The professor called long distance. Madam answered the phone and left the next day! She told me that if you come back—"

Impatience gnawed at me; Wilson was taking too long to get to the point. I interrupted, "What did she leave behind? Tell me quickly. I can't come back for the time being."

"Madam said she would meet that—professor and asked you to rush to meet her as soon as possible," Wilson relayed.

I was taken aback. Flora's urgent need to meet Professor Kim, and her insistence on my presence, baffled me. I was at a loss for the reason behind her urgency. Professor Kim had initially sent me to Nepal to find his son. There, I stumbled upon a cascade of bizarre events and learned of his son's death. The mystery surrounding these events remained unsolved. What could have happened to Professor Kim to warrant such urgency?

Speculating was futile without any concrete clues. Given that Professor Kim resided in a remote area with limited communication, his effort to reach out by phone suggested something profoundly serious. He wouldn't have left the jungle if not for a grave reason.

After deliberating, I told Wilson, "I have matters to attend to and can't meet Flora. If she calls home, inform her I encountered something strange in Nepal. It might take a while to unravel it."

Wilson acknowledged my message. Before ending the call, I added, "If she reaches out again, ask her to leave a way to contact her. I'll do my best to get in touch."

Wilson agreed, and I gave him a few more instructions before hanging up.

Lying back on the bed, my mind churned with plans to return to Nepal. Questions already swirled in my mind, and now Flora's unexpected journey to South America added to my unease. The uncertainty surrounding Professor Kim's situation only compounded my anxiety. I had hoped to bring Flora into this, given the complexity of the matter involving the king. But now, it seemed I would have to navigate this intricate mystery alone.

Given the circumstances, returning to Nepal openly was no longer an option. I had no doubt that I was now on their blacklist, but that didn't mean I was out of options.

First, however, I needed to prioritize some crucial tasks: specifically, developing the photos I had taken. Those images might hold the key to unraveling the mysteries I had encountered.

After a brief rest, I left the hotel and located a photo developing shop. Familiar with the leisurely pace of ordinary Indian workers, I resorted to a little incentive. I tore a few banknotes in half, handing one half to the clerk with a promise: the sooner he developed the photos, the sooner he would receive the remaining halves.

Returning to the hotel, I began reaching out to my contacts in India. Before making any calls, I considered who might be best positioned to help me navigate this complex situation.

The first name that came to mind was Dr. Mangli, a scholar with deep expertise in the histories of Nepal, Bhutan, and Sikkim. His knowledge of folklore in these regions could prove invaluable.

Next, I thought of Mr. Bazong, an eccentric yet brilliant scholar renowned for his work on the religious practices of the Indian subcontinent. The bizarre statue I had encountered in the stone chamber might represent a deity from a lesser-known faith, and Mr. Bazong might hold the answers I sought.

Knowing Mr. Bazong's reputation for eccentricity and his reluctance to meet guests, I wisely arranged a visit with Dr. Mangli first, hoping his presence might ease the way.

Dr. Mangli was quick to agree, and I then reached out to Bazong.

To my surprise, he seemed pleased to hear from me, inviting me over immediately. However, his mood soured when I mentioned Dr. Mangli. "Why did you make an appointment with him?" Bazong scoffed. "What does this guy know besides deceiving the university authorities and getting a high salary?"

I attempted a diplomatic approach. "I have some questions for him, and your insight would be invaluable," I said calmly. Bazong grunted in response, falling silent. Sensing his tacit agreement, I felt a wave of relief and allowed myself a couple of hours' rest before Dr. Mangli arrived.

Once Dr. Mangli joined me, we collected the developed photos. They had turned out well, and I handed over the remaining half of the banknotes to the clerk as a token of appreciation for his expeditious work.

Arriving at Bazong's home, I noticed his focus was solely on me, barely acknowledging Dr. Mangli. I apologized quietly to Mangli, who seemed unfazed, possibly due to Bazong's eminent standing in the academic community, which seemed to overshadow any perceived slight.

In the dimly lit study, Bazong's collection of books—both ancient and contemporary—seemed to whisper secrets from the past. Mangli hesitated, contemplating a chair cluttered with tomes. As his fingers grazed the spine of a particularly aged volume, Bazong's voice sliced through the air.

"Don't touch my books!" The command reverberated, leaving Mangli startled. He quickly pulled back his hand, the musty scent of old paper lingering in the air, and reluctantly settled onto the cold, unforgiving floor.

Eager to diffuse the tension, I presented Bazong with the photos. He examined a few with increasing agitation. "What is this? I don't understand modern metal sculptures at all!" he exclaimed, clearly frustrated.

I pointed at the photograph, my finger tracing the contours of a weathered stone platform surrounded by flickering candles. "See this altar? The candles encircling it? It's a shrine. These objects are revered as deities."

Bazong chuckled, his laughter echoing with skepticism. "Those who worship such gods must be Americans."

I shook my head, correcting him. "No, they're Nepalese."

Bazong laughed again, a dismissive wave of his hand. "American Nepalese!"

I drew a deep breath, my tone steady. "No, they're genuine Nepalese."

Bazong's gaze shifted between me and the photograph, curiosity tinged with disbelief. "Where on earth did you take these photos?"

I hesitated, choosing my words carefully. "I can't reveal the exact location. But it was about 70 miles east of Kathmandu, near an ancient temple—"

Bazong interrupted with a knowing nod. "Sinchisha Ancient Temple. I visited it three years ago and advised the Nepalese government to restore it. Its history dates back to—"

I cut him off swiftly; I knew once he delved into the origins of religion, we'd be here for hours. "These photos aren't from that temple. They're from a peculiar small temple, about 80 or 90 miles north of it."

I sketched the outline of the square stone room on a piece of paper. Bazong scrutinized my drawing, incredulous. "This must be a joke. I can assure you, there's no such structure in all of Nepal!"

I offered a wry smile. "Yet there is. Seven basements lie beneath this stone chamber. It's shrouded in mystery."

Bazong shook his head vehemently, while I nodded with equal determination. The tension simmered between us until Bazong suddenly turned to Dr. Mangli. "What do you think? Why so silent?"

Dr. Mangli, caught off guard, stammered, "I'm unaware of any such structure in Nepal. It sounds implausible!"

Bazong snorted dismissively. "Implausible? It's downright impossible. Just more of Ash's fantasies. You're of no use!"

Mangli, chastened, swallowed his retort. I interjected, my voice firm. "There's no need for debate. I've been there. I was attacked, trapped in the depths of that stone chamber. Down there, in the bottommost chamber, there's utter darkness. Light is forbidden."

Bazong's eyes lit up with recognition. "The Darkness Religion! Locally known as Kedaer Religion. Its followers worship darkness, forbidding light!" He paused, reflecting. "But I've only known of this cult in southern India, not Nepal. And their deity isn't a pile of rusted metal!"

I sighed, probing further, "Is there any very small tribe in Nepal?"

Mangli promptly replied, "Yes, the Yema tribe in the Himalayas, numbering around 700."

"Too many," I clarified. "This tribe had only two members—now just one."

Mangli's eyes widened in confusion. Bazong sneered, "Ask him! He knows nothing!"

Pushed to his limit, Mangli countered, "Mr. Bazong, I don't think you can answer Ash's question either!"

Bazong erupted, "Of course I can! There is no such temple!"

Equally frustrated, Mangli retorted, "That's no answer! Anyone could say that. Ash, there's no such tribe!"

The air was charged with tension, a palpable energy crackling between the two scholars as they squared off, their tempers poised to ignite like kindling touched by flame. I swiftly interjected, stepping into the breach of their escalating confrontation. "This tribe," I began, my voice steady yet urgent, "I suspect it has an enigmatic connection with the King of Nepal. The King's protection is legendary. Even if one among them committed murder, they could evade justice and find sanctuary, feasting in the halls of the palace."

Mangli, aghast, shook his head, "Impossible! The King, a hereditary protector of Nepali people, shielding a murderer? Absurd!"

Realization dawned that this meeting was fruitless—they couldn't provide the answers I sought. If they were stumped, who else could help? Perhaps Professor Skand in Sweden, an authority on Eastern religions, could shed light. Though visiting him wasn't feasible, a phone call might be the next best step.

I lingered at Bazong's residence for nearly three hours, where he tirelessly flipped through theological books, engaging in endless debates with Mangli. Eventually, Bazong returned the stack of photos to me, declaring, "You can't fool me, only someone like him!" His finger pointed accusingly at Dr. Mangli, whose face flushed with anger. To prevent an actual altercation, I quickly escorted Mangli away.

Back at the hotel, I continued to probe Mangli with questions, but his skepticism remained, providing no useful insights.

The realization struck me with a clarity that both invigorated and daunted my spirit: the mystery of the enigmatic bond between Bain and the king was mine alone to unravel. No one else could shoulder this burden; no scholar, no ally, only my relentless determination would suffice. This secret, veiled in shadow and time, seemed to stretch back through the annals of history, known only to those entwined in its depths.

As I bid farewell to Dr. Mangli, his presence fading like a specter into the evening mist, I steeled myself for the journey ahead. The path was uncertain, fraught with peril and intrigue, but the call to uncover the truth was irresistible. I began to gather my things, each item a talisman of what was to come.

The road before me was long, but I was ready to confront whatever challenges lay in wait, driven by the knowledge that somewhere within the labyrinth of secrets, the answers awaited.

Three days later, I found myself in the misty embrace of Darjeeling, a place where time seemed to slip through one's fingers like fine sand. Here, amidst the rolling hills and fragrant tea gardens, I submerged myself in a world far removed from the one I had known.

For half a month, I shed the trappings of my former self, forsaking the rituals of grooming and donning an old felt cloak that spoke of countless journeys. I partook in the haze of marijuana and surrendered to meditation, my transformation into a bona fide hippie complete.

In this transient community, I found kinship among a band of Japanese wanderers, our lives intertwining in the shared pursuit of enlightenment and escape.

When the time came for the exodus of souls to cross into Nepal, I slipped seamlessly into their ranks, a nondescript traveler among many, and thus arrived unnoticed in the vibrant chaos of Kathmandu.

Upon my return to Nepal, I made my way to the ancient temple with unwavering resolve. It was here that fate would reunite me with Randy, the figure central to unraveling the enigma that had ensnared my thoughts.

To my surprise, everything proceeded smoothly.

As I approached the temple at dusk, I was met with a scene that defied expectation.

Hundreds of hippies had gathered, their figures silhouetted against the flickering torchlight as they engaged in a ceremony that was both chaotic and hypnotic. At the heart of this human tempest, a cluster of individuals moved with unrestrained abandon, their voices rising in a cacophony of spontaneous expression. Such a spectacle might unsettle the uninitiated, but to me, it was a familiar symphony of freedom.

My gaze roamed the throng, seeking the one face that mattered. And then I saw him—Randy—distinct among the crowd due to his slight stature and sparse beard. He contorted his body, his features twisted in anguish, emitting a guttural "ho ho" as though trying to become one with the earth beneath him.

An inexplicable joy surged through me at the sight of him. I maneuvered through the mass of bodies to his side, where he seemed oblivious to my presence, lost in his own world of sound and movement. My initial impulse was to shout his name, to jar him into awareness and begin my interrogation. Yet, instinct whispered patience. I joined the chorus, rolling on the ground until I was beside him, blending into the ritual.

Quietly, I reached out, my hand finding the back of his neck. I pressed my thumb firmly against the artery, a technique intended to induce a swift, temporary slumber. Caught unawares, Randy's resistance waned, his eyelids fluttered, and his cries softened to a whisper.

In the chaos, my actions went unnoticed. Confident that he had succumbed to unconsciousness, I hoisted Randy onto my shoulder and navigated through the temple, my voice mingling with the others to mask my movements. We arrived at a secluded chamber, shrouded in darkness and the stale scent of forgotten years. It was a space once meant for contemplation, now repurposed for my pressing need.

With a heavy thud, I deposited Randy onto the floor and shut the door, plunging the room into silence. I lit a cigarette, the ember casting a faint glow as I took a drag. Then, with a calculated kick, I aimed for his head to rouse him.

The room was silent except for Randy's groans as he stirred. In the oppressive darkness, I prepared to extract the truth, determined to uncover the secrets that had thus far eluded me.

# CHAPTER 4

# THE ENIGMA

# OF THE "HOLY OBJECT"

In the dim room, I was unrelentingly rough with Randy, convinced of his guilt in Bruce's murder. There was no room for courtesy with a murderer. My kick jolted him awake, and in the pitch-black space, the faint glow of my cigarette was the only light. As I inhaled, the brief illumination revealed Randy struggling to rise.

Oddly, my mind drifted to the stone chamber buried seven layers deep, where light was forbidden. Was this darkness akin to that? And was even the dim glow of my cigarette forbidden there as well?

Once Randy sat up, he groaned, adjusting to his surroundings. I took another drag on my cigarette, watching him stand. I was poised to interrogate him about Bruce's murder. Yet, before I could speak, Randy's voice, unexpectedly joyful, cut through the darkness. "Bruce! It's you!" he exclaimed.

His words caught me off guard. Randy mistook me for Bruce, the very person he had murdered. His apparent delight was baffling. Murderers, psychologists say, often carry guilt, yet Randy's reaction was anything but remorseful.

As I pondered this bizarre scenario, Randy approached, his tone brimming with excitement. "Bruce, did you succeed? How is it there? You promised to come back and tell me; I knew you would!"

I retreated instinctively, offering vague responses to maintain the ruse. It dawned on me that allowing him to believe I was Bruce could more easily reveal the truth behind Bruce's demise.

Randy's words were nonsensical, repeating an enigmatic question as he closed in. "Do you know what the most confusing question for me these days is? Haha, what is the use of hair? You must have known what the use of human hair is. Tell me, what is the use of hair? Why don't you speak, what is the use of hair?"

What on earth was he talking about—the use of hair?

I continued backing away until my back hit the room's wall, halting my retreat. In a deep voice, I commanded, "Stay away from me!" The effect was immediate; Randy froze, silent at last.

After a moment, his tone shifted to one of melancholy. "Why won't you let me near you? You're different now. Have you forgotten what you promised me?"

I inhaled deeply, savoring the bitter tang of the cigarette, a fragile ember in the enveloping darkness. Randy lay not far from me, less than five feet away, his face illuminated in fleeting bursts as I drew on the cigarette. His expression was a tapestry of confusion and sorrow, and I feared he might recognize me. I shifted the cigarette aside, but Randy seemed lost in a realm of his own, oblivious to my presence.

In that moment, a theory crystallized in my mind: Randy, the alleged murderer, was perhaps ensnared in a web of schizophrenia. His apparent delusion, mistaking me for Bruce, opened a door. I could masquerade as Bruce's ghost, hoping to haunt him into confession.

With deliberate calm, I spoke, my voice a spectral whisper. "Randy, you betrayed our bond. No matter what promises were made, you are the murderer! Do you not feel the weight of guilt? You killed your friend!"

I anticipated a dramatic response—tears, perhaps, a plea for forgiveness. Yet, Randy's reaction was not what I had expected. He shouted, aggrieved, "What are you saying? Kill? kill?"

His repetition of the word "kill" was tinged with confusion, as if it were a foreign concept. Then he continued, "Bruce, It was originally my turn to go, but I couldn't compete with you, so you went first. I truly don't understand your accusation!"

These phrases, "It was originally my turn to go," "I couldn't compete with you," echoed in my memory. I had heard Randy utter them when Bruce's lifeless body was discovered on the riverbank, but their meaning eluded me. Now, as they resurfaced, clarity still danced just out of reach.

I pointed emphatically at his chest, my voice sharp. "You stabbed me here!"

Randy's response was immediate, almost automatic. "Yes, the stab was precise. Your heart nearly ceased to beat instantly!"

In my lifetime, I had encountered an array of peculiar and ruthless individuals, yet none quite like Randy. There was a chilling complacence in his voice as he recounted his brutal actions, an appreciation I found both baffling and unnerving. At a loss for words, I resorted to an emphatic rebuke, my voice echoing with accusation: "You killed me! You are a murderer!"

The impact of my words was palpable. Randy recoiled as if struck, a sudden retreat that spurred me to seize his shirt, preventing any escape. He cried out, bewildered, "You are not Brace, who are you?" His breath came in ragged gasps, then his eyes flickered with desperate hope. "Did Bruce send you? What did I do wrong? Why do you insist I killed him?"

A profound sadness gripped me, a melancholy realization that Randy existed in a fractured reality. He had driven a knife into Bruce's heart yet seemed oblivious to the gravity of his actions.

With one hand gripping him firmly, I fished out a lighter with the other, igniting it to cast light upon his face. "Randy, do you recognize me?"

Randy stared at me. Despite the changes I'd undergone in the past twenty days, he recognized me almost instantly, proving his sanity. As soon as he realized who I was, he struggled, but I held him tightly, preventing his escape. Then, like a deflated balloon, he became dejected. "It's you," he muttered, "you don't understand, you don't understand!"

I rotated, pressing Randy against the wall, his back trapped by the unyielding stone. "Of course I don't understand," I conceded, "that's why I've gone to such lengths to find you. What eludes me is why you killed Brace!"

A bitter smile twisted his lips. "I told you, you don't understand. You truly don't! I killed Bruce? Why do you keep using that word 'kill'?"

His response, both vexing and sorrowful, stirred a mix of anger and amusement within me. "Alright," I challenged, "then enlighten me—when one plunges a knife into another's heart, what word should describe that act?"

Silence stretched between us as Randy blinked, his mind grappling with the question. I extinguished the lighter, plunging us into darkness. In that void, his voice came as a whisper, a mantra of confusion, "You don't understand, you don't understand!"

My anger surged as I confronted Randy, "Forget it, I don't understand. I don't need to understand. The police and the judge won't need to understand to convict you."

Randy struggled violently, reminiscent of the last time I mentioned dragging him to the authorities. But this time, I held firm, pushing him out of the ancient temple and into the open space where hundreds were gathered. Despite his resistance and loud protests, no one paid us any heed.

For nearly an hour, I moved him forward—pushing, pulling, and dragging. Eventually, Randy's energy waned, and he ceased struggling. Exhausted, he panted, "If I tell you everything from beginning to end, will you believe it?"

I replied, "That depends on what you say."

Randy lowered his head, silent for a moment, before beginning, "It all started when a Nepalese named Bain sold antiques to me and Bruce—"

I hadn't planned to listen to his full story, intent instead on delivering him to the police in Kathmandu and then focusing on the enigmatic connections between Bain, the king, and the mysterious seven-story underground structure. But Randy's mention of Bain caught me off guard. Until then, I'd seen Bain and the sculptures, the underground building, and the king's involvement as separate from Randy and Bruce. Yet, Randy's words suggested an unexpected link between them.

Randy looked at me, defeated. I nodded, urging him to continue.

He explained, "That afternoon, I was with Bruce, and a Nepalese named Bain was selling us antiques. Bruce suddenly became very interested and agreed without even asking what the antique was."

I interjected, "Bain didn't tell you what the antique was?"

Randy shook his head, "No, actually Bain himself didn't know what it was at the time. Later, Bruce and I discovered what it was."

Suppressing the urge to demand why Randy had killed Bruce, I instead asked, "What is it? A real antique?"

Randy drew a deep breath, his gaze distant as he spoke, " Yes, real antiques, as ancient as humanity itself, their origins lost in the mists of time. Can you even guess how long we've been walking this earth, generation after generation?"

Realizing Randy was veering into more nonsense, I shook him gently but firmly. He seemed to snap out of his reverie, "Where was I?"

I replied coldly, "You were talking about the dawn of human history. If you keep digressing, we'll never get to what happened between you and Bruce."

Randy nodded, "You don't understand, but maybe you'll understand once you see the antique."

My interest piqued. The "holy object" he referred to was the very artifact Bain had stolen. The old man, before his death at Bain's hands, had implored Bain to retrieve it, but Bain claimed it had been sold and was unrecoverable. Now, it turned out that Bruce and Randy were the buyers. This "holy object" seemed pivotal to the tragic events involving Bruce and Randy. Given Randy's erratic story, seeing the object might provide clarity.

"Okay, where is it?" I asked.

Randy hesitated, "I hid it under Bruce's body."

I felt a surge of frustration. Randy hadn't mentioned this crucial detail before! Sensing my ire, he added quickly, "It was a secret between Bruce and me. We promised not to tell anyone."

I retorted sarcastically, "Should I swear an oath before you show me?"

Randy's expression turned dour, "That's not funny, sir. Not funny at all."

I brushed off his mood. The realization that Bruce's murder and the mysterious artifact were connected was electrifying. "How long have you known the Nepalese who sold you the antique?"

Randy paused, "I didn't know him at all, and neither did Bruce. He just approached us to sell it—" I waved for him to stop; it mirrored my own initial encounter with Bain.

Keeping a close watch on Randy, we traveled several miles. Randy remained silent, lips pursed, as we walked. Eventually, I employed a hefty sum to convince a British couple to lend us their car, driving us swiftly to the riverbank where Bruce's body lay.

This journey felt like a pivotal moment. I hoped that uncovering the "holy object" would shed light on the tangled web of events and relationships surrounding Bain, Randy, and the king—a web that had thus far eluded comprehension.

As the sun set over the river beach, the ethereal glow on the snow-capped mountains was lost on me. My focus was solely on the task at hand. I quickly retrieved two makeshift digging tools from the suitcase and tossed one to Randy, urging him to dig.

Together, we unearthed Bruce's remains with relative ease, as I had only hastily buried the body before. In less than a month, decomposition and scavengers had reduced Bruce to bones, their pale surfaces stark against the encroaching darkness and the cold, eerie light of the snowy ridges.

I studied Randy, looking for any sign of remorse, but he seemed unperturbed by the sight of the skeleton. Instead, he helped me move the bones aside, revealing a square hole underneath. Within lay a black metal box.

I watched Randy closely as he nodded, affirming my unspoken question. With determination, I leaped into the pit, reaching for the enigmatic box. It was a hefty metal container, its weight resisting my grip until I mustered every ounce of strength to hoist it. As I strained, I caught sight of Randy's face, his features drawn with an intensity that bordered on obsession, his lips moving in a soundless incantation.

With the box in my grasp, I climbed out of the pit, and Randy quickly bent low to remove its lid. Unlike a conventional lid, this one detached from the side, showcasing an impressive craftsmanship that belied its age—a testament to skilled artisanship rather than crude handiwork.

The evening shadows deepened around us as Randy lifted the lid, revealing the contents within. Despite the dim light, I discerned the object nestled inside the box. For a moment, its nature eluded me, a mystery wrapped in layers of the unfamiliar.

At first, the object appeared to be a square mass composed of countless thin layers, its substantial weight reminiscent of a transformer. Yet, a second glance dispelled that notion. This was no ordinary transformer. Fine, hair-like filaments adorned its surface, an oddity that defied easy explanation. Imagine, if you will, a transformer cloaked in a shroud of hair—an image both peculiar and unsettling.

I glanced at Randy, whose gaze was fixed intently on the strange object. "Alright, what is this?" I asked, reaching out to touch the delicate "hairs." But the instant I did, Randy shrieked and roughly pushed my hand away, his reaction as sharp as it was protective. With careful reverence, he lifted the object and placed it on a flat stone.

Once the entire item was out, it measured about half a foot square. Randy gestured for me to come closer and began to fumble with the base. Without warning, there was a "snap," and the upper part, covered in those hair-like filaments, sprang open. The sensation was akin to witnessing a skull being split, a visceral reaction that sent a shiver down my spine.

Standing beside Randy, I peered inside, my eyes widening at the sight. Words failed to capture the complexity within—an intricate network of exceedingly small, luminescent crystals. These crystals pulsed with light, their hues shifting between blue, white, yellow, and red in a rapid, synchronized dance. It was mesmerizing and utterly bewildering.

This didn't look like an ancient relic; rather, it seemed like a marvel of advanced technology, resembling a miniature computer, and it was very much alive. Its sleek design and intricate circuits hinted at a sophistication far beyond anything I had ever seen. The device pulsed with a faint, eerie light, as if it held the secrets of countless generations.

This didn't look like an ancient relic; rather, it seemed like a marvel of advanced technology, resembling a miniature computer, and it was very much alive. Its sleek design and intricate circuits hinted at a sophistication far beyond anything I had ever seen. The device pulsed with a faint, eerie light, as if it held the secrets of countless generations.

I was filled with skepticism. "This is what Bain sold you? What kind of antique is this supposed to be?"

Randy nodded, taking a deep breath. "Yes, when Bruce and I opened the box, we thought we'd been duped by Bain. But we didn't pursue it. We just left the box near where we slept."

He continued, "A few days later, we used it as a pillow. That night, both of us had a dream."

I listened carefully, curiosity mingling with the chill of the night as I scrutinized the object. But comprehension eluded me. The darkness deepened, and the wind picked up, biting through my clothes. I suggested we continue the discussion in the car, but Randy, lost in his tale, seemed deaf to my words. Resigned, I pulled my collar up against the cold, turning slightly to shield myself from the icy gusts. The mystery remained, its secrets tantalizingly close, yet still out of reach.

"Dreaming is something everyone experiences. You have dreams too, right?" Randy asked earnestly.

Suppressing an urge to mock his obvious question, I replied seriously, "Of course I do."

Randy pressed on, "Have you ever had a dream so vivid that you remember it clearly after waking, as if you truly lived it?"

"Sometimes, yes," I admitted.

Randy smiled wryly, "But have you ever shared the exact same dream with someone else? So precisely that when you try to recount it, the other person can finish your sentences, knowing every detail?"

I shook my head, intrigued but doubtful. "No, I've never experienced that."

Randy sighed, brushing back his wind-tousled hair. "It happened to us. We thought it was an impossible coincidence, but we realized the common factor was using the box as a pillow."

I nodded, curious, "Did you try it again?"

"Yes, the second night was the same. We had identical dreams with identical content. It continued for seven or eight nights."

Randy met my eyes, "What would you do in such a situation?"

I pondered, "It sounds like hypnosis. If someone suggested actions in those dreams, your subconscious might drive you to follow through."

Randy listened intently, considering my words. I pressed on, "What did you dream about? Did someone urge you to kill each other?"

He seemed taken aback by the suggestion but quickly denied it. "No, nothing like that. Bruce wasn't in the dream. It was... something else. Very strange."

His tone was earnest, conveying an experience that defied easy explanation. Whatever the dreams were, they hinted at a deeper, perhaps supernatural, connection to the mysterious object. It seemed to hold the key to understanding the bizarre events surrounding them, and I realized I needed to know more about what those dreams entailed.

I was waiting for him to tell me about the dream he and Bruce had shared. But Randy suddenly stopped talking, his eyes locked onto mine, his voice dropping to a conspiratorial whisper. "It's no use," he said, pausing dramatically. "You haven't had the dream. If I were to tell you its contents, you wouldn't believe me. The best way is for you to experience it yourself." His eyes bore into mine, a challenge and an invitation wrapped in one.

Despite my curiosity about the dream that had somehow tied Bruce's death and Randy's inexplicable actions together, I found myself nodding in agreement. Experiencing the dream firsthand seemed the only way to unlock its mysteries.

I pondered for a moment, then asked, "So if I use this box as a pillow, I'll have the same dream?"

Randy nodded, his voice steady. "At least, that's what happened for Bruce and me. The whole thing is too bizarre, so we didn't dare involve anyone else."

I carefully sealed the box, its contents hidden beneath layers of metal, and clutched it tightly as I made my way to the car. Randy trailed behind, silent and watchful. We drove back to Kathmandu, the city looming in the distance as I wrestled with questions that begged for answers. "Why did you think I was Bruce's reincarnation when you first saw me?" I asked, eyes flicking to Randy.

His response was cryptic, yet chilling. "Because Bruce promised he'd find me again." He noted my confusion and added with a knowing smile, "You'll understand once you've had the dream."

I let his words hang in the air, focusing on the road ahead. My mind was a tempest of thoughts, each competing for attention, yet I forced myself to drive with precision and calm. Reaching Kathmandu felt like waking from a dream itself—surreal, yet real.

We parked at a hotel, and I gestured for Randy to keep the box close as we stepped into the lobby. I approached the counter to book a room, needing a place to process everything—and to contact the British couple who owned the car. As I handled the paperwork, a familiar voice pierced through the bustling lobby.

"We had a deal! No returns!"

I turned to see Bain, still clad in the regal attire I had last seen him in, though now it was soiled and creased. He was backing away, eyes wide, while Randy advanced, the iron box clutched firmly in his grip. Bain's voice rose, a mix of desperation and defiance. "I can't take it back. Even if I wanted to, I don't have the funds to refund you!"

In that moment of chaos, a realization crystallized in my mind. Bain's paranoid retreat and frantic cries of "No returns" painted a vivid picture of misunderstanding and fear. Randy must have approached Bain, perhaps with questions only Bain could answer. But seeing the iron box in Randy's hands, Bain had assumed the worst—that Randy had discovered his deception and wanted retribution.

Yet, it was clear to me that Randy had no intention of returning the box. Bain's reaction, however, revealed a crucial truth: he had no idea what the so-called antique truly was.

My predicament was clear. Bain was a key piece in the puzzle I was trying to solve, yet approaching him openly was risky, given my recent expulsion by the king. Bain would undoubtedly recognize me, and the situation could spiral out of control.

As I wrestled with my next move, the scene shifted dramatically. Bain's loud retreat attracted a growing crowd, and his panic intensified. Spotting security guards, Bain's desperation peaked, and instead of retreating, he charged forward.

His sudden rush caught the guards off guard, and in his frenzy, he collided with Randy. The impact sent Randy sprawling, and the box he held so dearly slipped from his grasp. The hotel lobby erupted into chaos as the iron box hit the floor and split open. Its contents—a mysterious object now exposed—crackled with energy, emitting sparks and a series of soft explosions. Crystals scattered across the floor, shimmering like a thousand tiny stars.

The sparks caught the attention of a nearby security guard, who shouted in alarm, drawing more eyes to the spectacle. It was a moment demanding quick action. I grabbed Randy's arm, urgency in my voice. "We have to go!" I urged, pulling him with me as we dashed through the pandemonium.

Outside, with the hotel behind us, we paused to catch our breath. Randy looked devastated, his voice a whisper of defeat. "It's over," he lamented. "No matter what I say, you won't believe me now."

I met his gaze, understanding the weight of his words. Yet, the mystery had only deepened, and despite the setbacks, I knew this was far from over. The dream, the box, Bain—each was a clue, and I was determined to piece them together.

As I watched the remnants of the mysterious object scatter across the ground, a cold realization settled over me. The chance to experience the dream that had so profoundly affected Randy and Bruce was gone. Yet, the conviction in Randy's eyes, the certainty with which he spoke of the dream, left no room for doubt in my mind. I could sense the weight of truth behind his words.

I placed a reassuring hand on Randy's shoulder, trying to lift the shadow of guilt from his demeanor. "It's alright," I said, my voice steady. "Just tell me everything, no matter how unbelievable it may seem. I'm ready to hear it."

Randy remained silent for a moment, his gaze fixed on the ground as he nudged a pebble with his foot. "It's my fault," he admitted, voice tinged with regret. "I approached Bain, hoping to get another item like the one we lost. But then he just... went mad."

I shook my head, offering a different perspective. "I doubt Bain even knows the true nature of what he sold. Forget about him for now. What matters is the dream you and Bruce shared."

Finally, Randy met my eyes, deliberating over his words. "I had hoped you'd experience the dream yourself, but now..." He trailed off, searching for the right way to convey something so ineffable. I waited, giving him space to find his voice. After a pause, he continued, "It's an experience words can barely capture, but I'll try my best to explain."

Encouraging him, I suggested, "Let's find a quiet spot to rest. You can tell me everything there."

With a nod, Randy and I continued down the street, his narrative unfolding as we walked.

As he spoke, the world around us seemed to blur, his words painting vivid, impossible scenes. Despite my skepticism, I resisted the urge to interrupt. When he finally concluded, I felt as if I had emerged from a dream myself. Distractedly, I realized we had wandered far, eventually accepting a local man's offer of shelter.

Seated on a rough felt mat in a modest room, Randy turned to me. "So, what do you think?"

My mind swirled with contradictions and possibilities. After a long silence, I admitted, "I need to hear it again, from start to finish."

Randy's brow furrowed. "Why? Do you doubt me?"

Taking a deep breath, I explained, "Randy, what you described defies everything we know. It's not that I doubt you— I just need to hear it again, to fully grasp it and integrate my thoughts."

Understanding, Randy nodded and offered me a marijuana cigarette. We smoked together, the calming effect helping to slow the whirlwind of thoughts and emotions. Under its influence, I could approach the extraordinary tale with a clarity that had eluded me before, ready to dive deeper into the enigma that had unfolded before us.

# CHAPTER 5

# THE FIRST UNCANNY DREAM

Randy began recounting his experience once more, and what follows is his narrative. To help you grasp his story, I've preserved his first-person account. The "I" within the quotation marks refers to Randy, while my reactions are in brackets.

Randy's recounting of the tale was mesmerizing, his voice carrying the weight of both fascination and unease.

"Bruce and I invested a significant sum in that artifact from Bain," he began, his eyes reflecting the memory. "Bain assured us it was an authentic antique, so ancient that its origins were beyond anyone's knowledge. Not even the palace had anything like it, he claimed. So we bought it. But as soon as we had it, Bain vanished, leaving us with a mystery we couldn't decipher. You've seen the item; its true nature eludes us all. Realizing we'd been duped was a bitter pill to swallow, but we had no recourse."

He paused, recalling Bruce's reclusive nature. "Bruce was a peculiar soul, with no companions but me. Though we lived in an ancient temple surrounded by others, we kept to ourselves, inhabiting a small, crumbling room."

Randy's narrative continued to weave a tapestry of intrigue and mystery. "Our lives were uneventful," he recounted, "and I can't quite recall how we ended up using the box as a pillow. After realizing we'd been deceived, we shoved it aside, letting it gather dust in the corner of our modest room. But that particular night, Bruce, perhaps on a whim, pulled it out. We lay down, each on one side of the box, using it as an impromptu pillow. You've seen the box; it's unremarkable, really. But it served as a bridge between us, facilitating our late-night conversations. As was our routine, the marijuana lulled us into slumber. Dreams were a rarity for us, but that night marked the beginning of something extraordinary."

Randy leaned forward, the weight of his words heavy with significance. "I must stress this: for ten consecutive nights, I had the same dream, each iteration a perfect replica of the last. It was as though the dream was not just a figment of subconscious imagery, but a continuation, a narrative unfolding each night and seamlessly connecting with my waking memory. It all started with my arrival at a place."

He paused, searching for words that could adequately capture the essence of an experience so surreal. "Describing this dream is nearly impossible. It's as if I was transported somewhere, yet I wasn't truly there. Imagine sitting in a theater, surrounded by screens showing scenes from some place. You feel immersed, as though you're there, but in reality, you're not."

(His analogy painted a vivid picture, and I found myself drawn into the enigmatic world Randy described. The dream was more than a dream; it was an experience that transcended the boundaries of the conscious mind. As Randy spoke, I could sense the profound impact it had on him, a journey into the unknown that defied explanation, challenging everything we understood about reality and perception.)

"I arrived at that place. I hesitate to define it as anything specific. It seemed like a room—a space filled with soft light. I couldn't see much, but I sensed people were there. Initially, I merely felt their presence without seeing them. Eventually, I vaguely discerned figures sitting.

"I could hear clearly. The language was unfamiliar, yet I comprehended it. Perhaps I shouldn't say I understood it; rather, as the sound entered my senses, its meaning became clear. Or maybe there was no sound, just an instant realization of someone else's thoughts entering my mind. Do you get it?

(I don't fully grasp it, but let's focus on what Randy "heard"!)

"I first 'heard' a voice asking: 'What is the final decision? Have you reached a conclusion?' There was a pause, then another voice responded—in fact, all the voices seemed the same, possibly without sound, just my perception.

(No need for such detail! What did the other voice say?)

"The other voice replied: 'The final decision has been made: expel those people. They can no longer stay here and live with us. Send them away, the farther the better!' Another voice questioned: 'Where should we send them?' The response was: 'Yes, the plan was delayed due to not finding a suitable place. Now we've found a location—not ideal, but they'll manage to survive there.'

(I don't understand, it really sounds like a dream, but I have to listen patiently. Randy's dream seems to delve into a surreal narrative involving an unknown council making decisions about displacing people. It's a perplexing story, filled with cryptic communication and an ethereal setting. The dream's implications are unclear, yet they seem to hold significant meaning for Randy, potentially influencing his actions and understanding of reality. As I listen, I remain open-minded, seeking to uncover the truth behind these enigmatic visions.)

"The conversation in the dream continued, and I tried to make sense of it the best I could. For clarity, I refer to the main voice as 'the host,' as it seemed to direct the discussion.

The host inquired, 'Where is it?' Another voice responded, 'It's a satellite of a 17th-magnitude luminous star. It has an atmosphere, but it's not thick enough, so it's significantly affected by the star itself. The temperature differences are extreme, with highs reaching 82% and lows at negative 104%.'

(I found the temperature descriptions perplexing. They didn't align with any known measurement system I was familiar with.)

"The host expressed concern, 'That won't work. Such temperatures would lead to mass fatalities.' Another voice suggested, 'Teach them adaptation. Let them learn from the planet's indigenous life. The creatures there have evolved thick fur to withstand the temperatures.' The host responded, 'We can't make them grow fur to withstand the winter's cold, but we can certainly instruct them on utilizing it for warmth. They might also endure high temperatures, but what about the atmospheric necessities?' Another voice replied, 'One-fifth, less than 50%, they'll survive but become lethargic and lack vitality. The relative humidity is only suitable briefly and in certain regions, leading to discomfort most of the time.'

(I couldn't comprehend where this place might be or what 'satellite of the 17th-level luminous star' referred to.)

"The host's voice echoed with a resigned finality, 'There's nothing else we can do. This is the most merciful approach. They cannot remain here. How's the situation with the food supply?' Another voice chimed in, "It suffices, though it hinges on their resourcefulness." The host's relief was palpable, a pause stretching before he ventured, "The pressing issue now is whether to retain their hair."

"I should clarify—I wasn't actually hearing voices. It was more of an impression, an imprint in my mind. These thoughts seemed to crystallize from the auditory sensations I perceived. Strangely, the term 'hair' was elusive, its significance slipping through my grasp. Bruce and I puzzled over it, sharing the same uncertainty. Yet, we were convinced the topic revolved around hair. You have to trust me on this."

(I trust him, yet it baffles me—why is hair so pivotal? From Randy's account, I sense a gathering, a deliberation about relocating a group deemed undesirable to some distant realm. But when and where was this meeting convened? Could it be the British deportations to Australia in the 18th century? Or perhaps Russia exiling convicts to Siberia in the 19th century?)

"Another voice interjected, 'Our genetic code dictates our appearance, an immutable fact. Their appearance must mirror ours, though subtle shifts might occur over time due to environmental factors, but fundamentally, they remain unchanged. They'll continue to grow hair. However, we can render the hair's functionality obsolete, that's within our capability.' The host concluded decisively, "Very well, let's proceed."

(The functionality of hair? What peculiar role does hair play? This is becoming increasingly perplexing!)

"Suddenly, I discerned figures—around seven—vague silhouettes akin to ordinary people, except with extraordinarily long hair."

"Simultaneously, within this defined space, I perceived an overwhelming throng, a multitude so vast it defied precise enumeration. Tens of thousands, perhaps, assembled in such a manner that conveyed an irresistible sense of sheer numbers.

(Large-scale deportation of criminals? When did that transpire? There appears to be no such record etched in the annals of history.)

"The host's voice resumed, 'Deprived of hair's function, their intelligence will dwindle to near idiocy.' Silence followed, until another voice cautiously added, 'This is likely, but genetic traits persist, mutating over generations. We can't predict the future, and the genetic memory cannot be fully erased.'

'Will they remember this place?' the host asked, surprised.

'Not remember,' the voice corrected, "but retain a vague impression.'

The host sighed, 'A daunting challenge. If they have even a trace of memory, they might strive to return, which we must prevent unless some among them adapts to our existence here.'

A voice reassured, 'No matter. The excessive radiation from the seventeenth-level luminous planet shortens life.

Their hair, devoid of function, cannot breach temporal or spatial barriers.'

(Again, the function of hair perplexes me. What is its purpose? Whether shaved or grown long, hair seems inconsequential to life itself.)

Then, a new voice emerged, 'So we simply send them away and disregard them?'

Silence stretched, heavy with unspoken implications, until the host inquired, 'What do you propose?'

The voice suggested, 'After a time, we should send someone to observe. If any among their descendants adapt to our way of life, we might consider their return.'

The place was cloaked in silence once more. The host's voice broke through, laden with gravity. 'This task is incredibly complex. Each of them has been meticulously examined and found to possess overwhelmingly strong sin factors. Who could possibly undertake such a mission?'

A voice replied with quiet determination, 'We might train a select few. I already have several candidates in mind who can handle this responsibility.'

The host's tone turned cautionary. 'This is no ordinary task. Are these individuals volunteers? Understand, sending them to live among those people is fraught with danger. According to our calculations, as their intelligence gradually resurfaces, their consciousness of sin is likely to eclipse their awareness of virtue.'

'How many will be there by then?' the host pressed. 'Isn't sending just a handful too perilous?'

'Undoubtedly, it's risky,' the voice conceded. 'But it's necessary to identify those worthy of return. I'm training four individuals, one of whom is my only son.'

Quiet enveloped the room again before the host's voice reemerged, resolute. 'Very well, your plan is approved. Exile is our last recourse. That place is inhospitable, yet I hold faith that, in time, some will prove themselves worthy of returning.' Footsteps resonated, and the host added, 'Let's observe these people.'"

Here, Randy paused.

Randy recounted his dream to me twice, and on both occasions, he halted at this juncture, his expression inscrutable.

The first time he stopped, I refrained from pressing him, needing a moment to digest his revelations. I transcribed his account meticulously, aware that his "dream" defied easy understanding.

What kind of dream was this? Before his pause, Randy hadn't witnessed anything concrete—only shadowy figures—yet he overheard a myriad of conversations (a meeting, it seemed). The discourse centered on deporting a cohort, presumably criminals, to a place barely fit for survival—a form of exile. It appeared these exiles would undergo procedures to blunt their intellect, rendering them akin to simpletons. The meeting's participants were divided, convinced that over generations, the exiles' intelligence might resurface, though never fully.

Among them, a figure of compassion emerged, arguing that in time, some descendants might transcend their tainted lineage, their inherited evil dissipating. This person advocated for their possible return, proposing to send emissaries to evaluate and retrieve those who showed promise. Remarkably, this individual volunteered four people for the task, including his only son.

Reflecting on Randy's vivid depiction, I found myself gripped by a peculiar notion. The meeting's dialogue, as relayed by Randy, resonated with an unsettling familiarity. The part about the sole son hit particularly close to home, though I couldn't pinpoint the source of this déjà vu. I pondered for a full ten minutes, during which Randy remained silent. Only when a faint idea emerged did I inquire, "Is the dream finished?"

Randy replied, "No."

I held my tongue, and after a brief pause, he resumed his tale.

"When the host expressed his desire to see the situation of those people, I, too, witnessed the spectacle. There were tens of thousands, marching out of a gleaming, spherical white building. This structure had seven doors, each one disgorging a steady flow of people. They moved with an unnerving precision, forming orderly lines as they advanced towards something peculiar—a massive object resembling an olive, magnified a hundred million times. One by one, they disappeared inside.

I observed them closely. What did they look like? They were like us—like you and me—tall and imposing. But it was their expressions that haunted me most. Almost uniformly, their eyes were wide, their faces devoid of emotion. Bruce and I later agreed it was the vacant look of imbeciles. And to see such a sea of vacant faces, tens of thousands marching in unison—it was truly terrifying.

(That was truly terrifying!)

Stranger still was the fact that these expressionless masses moved forward of their own accord. I saw no one guiding them, but in the vast open space, strange animals roamed. What kind of creatures were they? I couldn't say. Some seemed like hybrids—half cow, half horse; others a bizarre blend of dog and horse. It defied comprehension.

(It must have been beyond Randy's understanding, too strange to fully grasp.)

Then, the strangest event unfolded. Those gigantic olive-like structures, at least 500 meters long, erupted with a thunderous noise once everyone was aboard. They spewed brilliant flames, soared into the sky, and vanished!

As the cacophony and fiery spectacle faded, the host's voice returned. He seemed to confer with another, 'When will you execute your plan?' The reply came, 'In twelve cycles.'

The host queried, 'By then, how many generations will have passed?' A sigh followed, 'At least ten thousand generations. Time there flows differently, and they won't surmount the final barrier. By your decree, the function of their hair is gone forever!'

The host's voice carried a hint of resignation, 'It wasn't solely my decision; it was the will of the meeting. We've been benevolent enough.' Silence fell, suggesting disagreement, before the voice continued, 'The four volunteers will be reborn, as we are here.'

Mr. Morris, pay heed. This notion of 'rebirth' became crucial for Bruce and me. The host wished them success, 'Twenty cycles have passed since we conquered death's challenge! Yet, I still grapple with our scientists' findings on those people. After their death, is there truly nothing?' The response was somber, 'Not nothing. It's a state of void, akin to the time before we discovered the way to rebirth, devoid of life.'

The host simply grunted in acknowledgment, and the conversation ceased. At that moment, I awoke!"

Randy's account grew increasingly cryptic. I pondered his words, finding no direct connection to Bruce's demise.

In the dim light, I scrutinized him, my gaze laden with skepticism. Randy sighed, "Mr. Morris, I've dreamt this same dream for seven or eight consecutive nights, but Bruce's experience differed."

Annoyance crept in, "Didn't you claim Bruce's dream mirrored yours exactly?"

Randy took a deep breath, his gaze distant as if reliving the moment. "Yes, after we began having that dream, Bruce and I dissected its contents every morning. It was a bizarre, unsettling dream. Hearing it secondhand doesn't capture the visceral shock of experiencing it. After seven or eight nights of this, I went out to buy food one day, leaving Bruce alone with the ancient relic. We valued it immensely, so one of us always stayed behind to guard it."

He paused, and I leaned in, eager to hear more. "When I returned, I found Bruce clutching the artifact, a radiant, indescribable brilliance on his face. I'd never seen him so elated. As soon as he saw me, he exclaimed, 'Randy, I understand! I understand completely!' I was baffled. 'What do you understand?' I asked. Laughing, Bruce patted my head, 'Randy, I'm sorry. While you were gone, I gave myself a new dream.'"

I couldn't help but groan, "Randy, are you suggesting Bruce was unfaithful to you? He used the artifact to dream anew, and you don't know the dream's content."

Randy seemed unfazed by my insinuation, despite my conviction that he had a motive to harm Bruce. If Bruce's actions had angered him, it could be a reason.

But Randy shook his head, "I didn't blame him—not at the time. I simply asked, 'What new dreams have you had?' Bruce, eyes alight with excitement, asked me, 'Do you know who those expelled people were?' I shook my head, and he nearly shouted, 'They are our ancestors, and we are their descendants!' Then, gripping my shoulders, he implored, 'Randy, I want to go back! Help me!' Oddly, I felt a strong urge and said, 'Why don't we go back together?' But Bruce insisted, 'No, only one can go.' I repeatedly offered to go first, but it was futile. Bruce was adamant, and I eventually relented."

I furrowed my brow. Bruce's assertion, "We are their descendants," implied a broader lineage than just himself and Randy. Given the tens of thousands seen in Randy's dream, "we" clearly extended beyond the two of them. What, then, did "we" mean?

As I pondered, Randy continued, "Bruce was prepared. He produced a knife, pointing it at his heart, 'You've studied anatomy. Stab me here, the deeper, the better.' Mr. Morris, my reaction mirrored yours—I shouted, 'You want me to kill you?' But Bruce laughed, 'Randy, you don't understand? I won't die. I know how to go back. Once there, death is no longer a concern. Haven't you grasped the dream's message? Rebirth! Life perseveres; death is an obstacle overcome!' Though he forced the knife into my hand, I hesitated, unable to act."

Confusion clouded my thoughts, "But you ultimately did it!"

Randy nodded, "Yes, I did. Bruce was both anxious and exhilarated, 'Stab me, so I can leave my body swiftly. The body is merely a shell, like an old house. One must vacate the old to inhabit the new. You must act quickly, or the artifact loses its efficacy.' His urgency and sincerity were overwhelming."

I interrupted, "That's no justification. If he wanted to abandon—his body, why not simply commit suicide?"

Randy replied, "I asked him the same. Bruce explained, 'I could, but why choose a slow, cumbersome path when someone can help me swiftly discard the unnecessary? Randy, I promise to return and share everything, to take you back with me. We never contemplated the purpose of human hair—haha!' He laughed and urged me on. So I—"

"You finally stabbed him in the heart," I concluded, my voice heavy with the weight of what he'd done.

Randy gazed at the light, his voice a mere whisper. "Yes, I buried the object beneath Bruce's body, just as he required. I waited for his return, but he never came back. I—I—"

He turned to me, a deep sadness etched on his face. "To this day, I still don't know what human hair is truly for."

I believed my expression mirrored his sorrow, as Randy's question struck me as profoundly naive. It hinted at a disturbed mental state, suggesting that his account might be pure delusion.

In frustration, I exclaimed, "What is the use of hair? It protects the head! Even elementary school students know that!"

Randy suddenly laughed, a sound tinged with irony. "Elementary school students might accept that answer, but I doubt someone of your intellect would be satisfied with such simplicity. Do you know how thick the human skull is?"

I replied, still irked, "Nearly an inch, and it's incredibly hard and resilient!"

"Exactly," Randy continued. "Our thoughts, the essence of our being, reside in the brain—an organ critical to our existence. The thick, hard skull safeguards it. Not until the 18th century did we discover ways to penetrate it. So, with such a robust guardian, why do we need soft hair? Haven't you ever wondered about this?"

I couldn't answer. I had never questioned it before. The idea that hair protects the head was instilled in me from a young age. In truth, hair seemed superfluous beyond that. Whether one has hair or not seemed inconsequential.

While I remained silent, Randy pressed on, "Haven't you noticed the incongruity between hair's length and its purported 'protective' function? Human hair can grow up to 80 centimeters, nearly two-thirds of a person's height! Hanging loose, it could shield not just the head, but the back and buttocks, too—haha!"

Annoyed by his laughter, I demanded, "Then what do you think hair's use is?"

Randy shook his head, a shadow of regret crossing his face. "I don't know yet. Bruce might have, but he hasn't returned to enlighten me. In my dream, I heard them discuss hair and its functions repeatedly. They must be significant. As a medical student, I understand the human body is too intricate to harbor useless features. Yet hair, such long hair, seems pointless, so we're forced to assign it a purpose: protecting the head."

I fell silent, pondering his words. His reasoning was compelling. What is the purpose of hair? Why do we have such long hair on our heads? Most people don't consider hair reaching nearly a meter in length, as it's typically kept short. Yet, left uncut, it can grow astonishingly long.

My thoughts spiraled, tangled by Randy's musings. I shook my head, resolving to dismiss this trivial query. Just then, Randy leaned in, his demeanor conspiratorial, "You must have overlooked another strange phenomenon!"

The phrase "strange phenomenon" piqued my interest. I anticipated something remarkable, only for him to continue about hair! "How many species exist on Earth? Hundreds of thousands, if not millions, yet only humans have hair that can grow to such lengths. Its structure is remarkable—each strand hollow, with intricate organization. It must have once served an essential function, now ceased."

I blinked rapidly, trying to keep up with his fervor. Randy grew more animated, "Even though Bruce hasn't returned with details, I can predict one thing: the satellite of the seventeenth-magnitude luminous star is Earth!" His statement shocked me, though I couldn't fathom why. His tone drew me in, and I found myself asking, "The place you saw in your dream—"

Randy's expression turned enigmatic, his voice a hushed secret, "That's the place we all yearn to return to. I don't know its original name, but on Earth, across diverse languages, there's a common name: Heaven!"

My breath quickened, and Randy leaned back, "For centuries, people on Earth have longed to reach heaven, trying every conceivable method. Some even dreamt of building a tower to climb to heaven!"

His mention of "a tower to climb to heaven" struck a chord. Suddenly, I understood.

I understood why his narrative felt "familiar." It's a religious story!

I couldn't help but laugh, as words like "sin," "salvation," and "only son" floated through my mind.

In that moment, a wave of relief washed over me, settling my uneasy mind with the firm conviction that Randy was simply a troubled soul. Perhaps a hippie lost in the labyrinth of religious fervor, his mind tangled with mystical notions that birthed such bizarre dreams and a life steeped in chaotic illusions.

Reflecting later, I found it curious that I had so swiftly reached this conclusion. After all, Bain's so-called "antique" remained an enigma, unexplained and puzzling. But my decision then seemed justified—I had clung to the first rational explanation that presented itself, like a castaway grasping at a lifeline without questioning its origin. In the face of Randy's bewildering tale, I welcomed any semblance of reason, much like a ship appearing on the horizon for a marooned sailor, where the ship's flag mattered less than the hope it offered.

With this mindset, I set aside Randy's confounding words, resolved to move past the encounter. I gave his shoulder a reassuring pat and suggested, "Let's get some sleep."

Randy's eyes blinked, lingering in anticipation of further conversation, but I feigned fatigue, stretching and yawning as if sleep was all I desired.

He appeared crestfallen, murmuring, "It's a shame that thing broke. Otherwise, you'd have had the dream too. You're so curious—you'd surely find some meaning in it!" I offered a dismissive response, pretending exhaustion had overtaken me. As I lay down, Randy continued, his voice a low murmur, "I wonder if Bain has another one. I wanted to buy it, but perhaps he's afraid?"

I suppressed a chuckle. Why would Bain be afraid? The answer seemed simple: he had concocted a story around a trinket to deceive tourists. Naturally, a swindler would fear exposure when confronted by a duped buyer.

Randy continued muttering to himself, but I paid little attention. I remained awake, alert, wary of him attempting to flee.

The next morning, we left the Nepalese family. I told Randy, "Let's go see if Bain has more 'antiques.'"

Randy seemed pleased, sticking close as I wandered aimlessly. Eventually, I led him to a hotel lobby, where I asked him to wait. I found a staff member and requested a phone book, searching for the number of a mental hospital.

I had already decided against involving the police. It seemed more humane to get Randy professional help. Once hospitalized, he could provide his family's details for them to take him home.

I called the mental hospital, explaining the situation. After some deliberation and being passed through several people, I was connected to a doctor. I shared my concerns about Randy's mental state, omitting the stabbing incident but highlighting his dangerous delusions.

The doctor agreed to see Randy. After the call, I took Randy for a hearty meal, then led him to the mental hospital.

Poor Randy. Even as we approached the hospital doors, he remained blissfully unaware of my intentions.

# CHAPTER 6

# ANOMALOUS INCIDENT
# IN SOUTH AMERICA

Looking back, I realized the gravity of my actions—it was a despicable betrayal, deceiving someone who had placed unreserved trust in me.

The moment Randy and I stepped into the hospital, we were approached by a middle-aged doctor accompanied by two burly attendants. I stepped forward, inquiring about the doctor's name, and signaled to Randy. Instantly, the two attendants seized him.

Only then did Randy grasp the situation. The expression on his face, as he was dragged away, is etched into my memory—a mix of fury and betrayal. He struggled, his voice echoing through the halls, "Shameless, despicable! You embody the world's sin, a sin that binds us to this earth! You should not be saved; your salvation is undeserved!"

His voice faded as he was carried off, leaving behind an unsettling silence. The doctor turned to me, hands open in a helpless gesture. "Your friend's condition is far more severe than you described."

I forced a bitter smile. "He has moments of clarity. If you're short on resources, contact his family. They can take him back."

The doctor nodded, requesting my details for their records. I scribbled a fake name and departed.

Leaving the hospital, I dismissed Randy's words, feeling a sense of relief at having resolved one issue. Now, my focus shifted to finding Bain. I was convinced he remained in Kathmandu, likely continuing his trade with tourists. Frequenting tourist hotspots seemed the best way to locate him.

Tourists typically congregate around hotels, so I decided to visit the one where I initially stayed, hoping to find Bain or at least any messages from Flora. Her abrupt departure left me pondering what strange occurrences Professor Kim encountered in South America.

I visited several hotels without spotting Bain. By the time I reached my hotel, dusk had settled over the city.

Approaching the counter, the staff recognized me, their gaze curious. "Sir, you left with the Minister of State last time and requested checkout. You must know him well!"

Only then did I learn the middle-aged man was Nepal's Minister of State. I replied vaguely, "Do you have any messages or mail for me?"

The staff nodded eagerly. "Yes, yes! There's a recorded long-distance call from South America. Please wait."

In Nepal, patience is a necessity. The mention of a call from South America piqued my interest; it could only be significant. Yet "Please wait a minute" stretched into nearly an hour, leaving me fuming. Finally, the staff produced a tape. When I reached for it, they extended their hand for a fee comparable to buying a tape recorder.

Frustrated, I paid, then realized I needed a tape recorder to listen to it. I requested one, met again with, "Please wait a moment!"

This time, I could wait no longer. Frustration propelled me out of the hotel and into the bustling streets, where I quickly found another electronics store. There, I purchased a small tape recorder, inserted the tape with trembling fingers, and pressed play. Flora's voice crackled to life, filled with urgency.

She had sought me out, only to be informed by the hotel staff that I no longer resided there. Her voice was laced with anxiety, each word a testament to her distress. Flora had pleaded with the staff to leave a message for me, certain that I would return to retrieve it. But the staff, indifferent and unyielding, had denied such a service.

As the tape played on, my anger simmered. Flora's desperation grew more palpable, her pleas punctuated by the staff's rote insistence that her long-distance call was monopolizing the line: "Sorry, Miss, you have been talking for too long. Please don't interfere with other people's chance to talk!"

The recording climaxed with Flora's frantic cry: "Ash, come quickly! Come quickly!" And then, abruptly, silence.

I clutched the recorder, disbelief mingling with outrage. How could such incompetence be possible? Yet, in this place, I should have anticipated the limits of their efficiency.

Flora's message, distilled to a singular, urgent plea: "Come quickly! Come quickly!" suggested a matter of grave importance. She would not have reached out in such a manner if it were not so.

I was left in the dark about Professor Kim's circumstances, aware only that Flora's call had come days ago, when I had been in Darjeeling, adrift in a world of bohemian revelry with the hippies.

Despite not locating Bain, I realized I needed to leave Nepal immediately. An overt departure could attract unwanted attention and potential trouble. Traveling by land would cost precious days, and time was of the essence. It dawned on me that Flora, if faced with an urgent situation, would likely have contacted Wilson back home.

I chastised myself for not considering this sooner, pulling my hair—a reminder of one use it might have, I chuckled bitterly at the thought—and hurried back to the hotel to place a long-distance call. This time, the connection was swift. Wilson's voice erupted through the line, "I've been waiting for you for five days!"

"Cut to the chase," I urged. "What did Flora say?"

"It wasn't Flora directly," Wilson explained, "she sent a tape. I transcribed it. Listen!"

Within moments, Flora's voice filled my ear: "Ash, I can't call you myself, so I recorded this. Come quickly, use the fastest transportation. I can't explain everything now, but you don't need to look for Bruce anymore—Bruce is back!"

Her words floored me. "Bruce is back." How could this be? Bruce was dead; there was no way he could be in South America. Clearly, Flora was unaware of his death. Yet her message continued to baffle me: "It's very strange. I believe Bruce died in Nepal! Professor Kim is in a bad situation. Come quickly! Something is wrong here—"

Flora's voice grew increasingly frantic, underscored by a rhythmic "boom" in the background. I recognized it as the sound of Indian tribal drums, often signaling the gathering of a tribe for a major ceremonial event to honor deities. Such a significant ritual likely indicated something sudden and important had occurred.

I needed to act fast. Flora's call was a clear signal that events in South America were spiraling, and I had to get there immediately. The urgency in her voice, combined with the mysterious mention of Bruce, hinted at a situation far more complex and urgent than I had initially imagined.

In that moment, my focus wasn't on the drum sounds. I knew Professor Kim's lab was deep in the Amazon jungle, surrounded by isolated and fierce Indian tribes. Flora was likely in the lab when she recorded the message, so the drum sounds weren't surprising.

However, Flora's escalating panic was alarming. She wasn't someone who panicked easily, making her tone all the more concerning. Her voice trembled with urgency, "I'll do my best to handle things. Please come quickly. I'm not sure if I can finish this message, but the person I entrusted is reliable. He'll ensure this reaches you—wait, wait—"

The sudden interruption and Flora's cries of "wait" hinted at unforeseen trouble. I recognized Professor Kim's surprised outcry before the tape abruptly ended.

The situation was dire. The recording was likely made ten days ago, and I was continents away. If things had gone awry, I was powerless to change it.

As my anxiety peaked, Wilson's voice broke through. "The caller identified himself as Lieutenant Paul. He urged you to come as soon as possible."

I pressed for more information, "Did he mention Flora's condition?"

Wilson admitted, "No, he didn't. You—"

I cut him off, resolute, "I'm leaving immediately. I'll get there as fast as I can!" I hung up, my mind racing. I needed to act swiftly. To reach South America quickly, I'd need help from someone powerful. Despite the awkwardness, there was one person who could expedite my journey: the King of Nepal.

I arranged a car rental through the hotel and drove to the palace. The guards stopped me, and I requested an audience with the Minister of the Court. After a half-hour wait in the guard room, the minister—the same middle-aged man I had encountered before—approached me. I blurted out, "I need to see the king. It's imperative!"

His expression soured, "The king won't entertain a deceitful person!"

"I'm here to resolve a personal matter," I insisted. "It's crucial and has nothing to do with Bain!"

The minister's demeanor darkened further. "Bain? I don't know of such a person!"

I was certain of Bain's clandestine connection to the king. The minister's denial was a clear attempt to conceal this secretive link. Normally, I would have pursued this lead relentlessly, but my priorities were elsewhere.

"Fine," I conceded. "Forget Bain. I'm here for a favor."

The minister chuckled, "I manage the king's daily affairs. Ask me what you need."

I took a breath, "I need to get to South America urgently. Can you arrange for an Indian military plane? I can pilot it myself."

I knew my request was audacious, and the minister's incredulous look confirmed it. Before he could refuse, I pressed, "Help me with this, and I'll owe you. If your country ever needs my service, I'll repay this debt, no matter the challenge."

The minister studied me for a moment before announcing, "I'll discuss this with the king." After he left, I was accompanied by two officers. During the thirty minutes that followed, I was restless, pacing the room anxiously. When the phone finally rang, an officer answered and then turned to me with a salute, "Please proceed to the palace. The king is ready to see you."

Relief washed over me as the officers escorted me back to the opulent chamber where I had previously met the king and the minister. The king, wearing a half-smile, greeted me, "You are quite an interesting person."

I responded with a wry smile, "Thank you, Your Majesty. I have one difficulty that I am reluctant to mention."

To my surprise, the king sighed, "Like you, I have my own difficulties as well." He continued, "The minister has arranged for an Indian military jet. It will land at Kathmandu Airport. A pilot will accompany you so you don't need to pilot the jet back because I do not wish to see you again."

I was elated and bowed deeply, "I cannot express my gratitude enough, Your Majesty."

The king regarded me thoughtfully, "You should know the best way to express your gratitude."

Understanding his implication, I replied, "Of course, this is the first time we've met, Your Majesty." The king blinked, a mischievous twinkle in his eye, and laughed. His demeanor revealed him to be a gentleman with a sense of humor and approachability.

In that moment, I realized there was likely a complex issue underlying his relationship with Bain. Given his sincere assistance, I felt it only right to respect his situation and cease my investigations. I resolved then to let it go. Although circumstances would eventually compel me to revisit this matter, leading to further encounters with Bain, the king would later extend his forgiveness. But that was a matter for another time.

For now, my immediate problem was resolved. The Minister of the Court had secured diplomatic clearance for the flight path, allowing me to land at a military airport in northern

Brazil and proceed directly to Professor Kim's lab. This was undoubtedly the fastest route available.

While waiting for the plane, I had the opportunity to converse with the king for about half an hour. He inquired about the most peculiar events in my life, and I shared a few stories with him.

At one point, the king asked, "Do you firmly believe in the existence of advanced beings on other planets besides Earth?"

I replied confidently, "I do, and I am certain they exist."

The king's interest seemed genuine, and he posed several questions. I perceived this as mere curiosity, akin to that of any intrigued individual. However, his next question struck me as unusual.

He suddenly asked, "According to your beliefs, could some extraordinary individuals originate from other planets?"

I replied casually, "What kind of individual, for example?"

The king paused, weighing the gravity of his words before he finally spoke. "For instance, imagine someone like the Buddha."

His answer caught me off guard, a profound and challenging comparison. I replied, "That's difficult to encapsulate. Buddha is an extraordinary figure. The religion he founded offers a comprehensive theory on human existence, enduring for over two millennia. Yet, we remain unable to substantiate it through practice."

The king leaned in, his eyes gleaming with curiosity. "The ultimate goal of Buddha's teachings is liberation from the cycle of reincarnation, to journey back to Sukhavati. Do you understand what 'Sukhavati' signifies?"

His question hung in the air, laden with the weight of ancient wisdom and cosmic mystery. The mention of "Sukhavati" conjured images of an ethereal paradise, a realm of boundless peace and enlightenment, far removed from the mortal coil's endless cycle of birth and rebirth.

Surprised by the sudden depth of the conversation, I answered, "The 'Sukhavati' refers to the Western Paradise."

The king seemed lost in thought, almost speaking to himself. "In the Western Paradise, does one achieve immortality? Is there truly no death?"

I chuckled lightly, "To reach the Western Paradise is to transcend humanity, to become divine. And gods are, of course, are immortal."

He repeated, "Gods are, of course, immortal," as if unraveling a mystery in his mind. Something significant lingered in his thoughts, yet he hesitated to voice it.

I ventured, "It's peculiar how the ultimate aim of all religions converges."

The king nodded, "Indeed. They promise that after shedding the mortal coil, a part of us journeys to a sacred realm—whether it's Western Paradise or Heaven. Religions assure us of God's existence, emphasizing that the spirit or soul surpasses the body's importance."

I nodded, and suddenly, he asked, "Why?"

Why indeed? His question left me speechless, and he smiled, a wry, introspective smile. "Could it be that the founders of these religions hail from the same origin?"

His suggestion sent a shiver through me. "Jesus, Muhammad, Buddha, Laozi—did they know each other?"

The notion was absurd. Accepting the bizarre was one thing, but I shook my head, "Impossible. They lived centuries apart."

The king gazed out the window, lost in a temporal reverie. "Centuries to us, perhaps mere moments elsewhere."

The conversation grew increasingly surreal, as if tethered to some cosmic truth. The thought of these spiritual icons being contemporaries was astounding.

I sensed the king harbored deeper insights and was eager to hear more. Yet, at that moment, the minister entered, announcing, "The plane will land in ten minutes!"

I rose quickly, the king graciously escorting me to the door. His unspoken thoughts lingered in the air, a solitude shared by a man unable to find a confidant.

Pressed for time, my journey demanded I leave Nepal, meaning this might be our final encounter. The bittersweet reality of parting weighed on me as I departed.

The Royal Minister had arranged for a car to whisk me away to the airport, where a plane awaited. The pilot, a lieutenant colonel, greeted me with the reverence reserved for royal guests, unaware of my origins. I requested we fly at the precarious edge of safety, pushing speed to its limits, and he obliged.

Yet, despite the jet's impressive velocity, over 30 hours elapsed before I found myself navigating the dense jungles of northern Brazil by car. I had visited Professor Kim's laboratory once before, and the route was etched in my memory. Even under the cloak of night, I was confident I wouldn't lose my way.

The jungle at night presented its own set of perils, but I pressed on, heedless of the danger. The jeep's headlights cut through the darkness, illuminating the eerie green glow of wild animals' eyes, both unsettling and mesmerizing.

As I neared my destination, my anxiety mounted. By dawn, I arrived at a river—not wide, but fiercely turbulent. Professor Kim's laboratory lay just beyond a bend in the river, a mere ten minutes away.

The morning sun cast a golden glow over the riverbend, illuminating the path to Professor Kim's laboratory. My heart pounded in rhythm with the roar of the engine as I sped down the uneven road, each bump sending the car airborne, my grip tightening on the wheel with every jolt. The laboratory was close—just minutes away—and anticipation mixed with an inexplicable dread clawed at my insides.

As I rounded the final bend, a sight so shocking unfolded before me that instinct took over. My foot slammed on the brakes, tires screeching in protest. The world spun violently as the car skidded and flipped, coming to a rest with a shudder that reverberated through my bones. Ignoring the sting of pain, I clawed my way out from the wreckage, adrenaline propelling me to my feet.

Though my legs trembled beneath me, my eyes remained fixed on the scene of devastation. Where once stood Professor Kim's meticulously arranged six rows of huts, now lay nothing but charred remnants. The greenhouses, painstakingly assembled with glass and housing a botanical treasure trove decades in the making, had been reduced to ashen ruins.

In the stark light, shards of broken glass glistened among the debris like a field of fallen stars. I stumbled forward, the crunch of glass underfoot a haunting symphony of loss. There was no sign of life—no bustling assistants, no local workers, and most alarmingly, no trace of Flora.

The absence of answers hung heavy in the air. Where was Professor Kim? What catastrophe had befallen this place? And most pressing of all, where was Flora? The questions swirled in my mind, each more urgent than the last, as I stood amidst the remnants of shattered dreams and broken glass.

Despite racing here with all the urgency I could muster, a part of me knew it would be too late. Yet, nothing could have prepared me for the devastation that lay before me. What catastrophic event had turned this place into a wasteland?

Desperation gnawed at my insides as I ran back and forth over the charred remains of the six-row hut, my calls echoing into the void, unanswered and seemingly meaningless.

Flora had warned me of trouble, but with a confidence that suggested she could handle it. Unless things had spiraled into utter chaos, she would have left some sign, some clue, allowing me to piece together what had unfolded here.

But the ruins held their silence. I scoured every corner, every shadow, but found nothing but emptiness and echoes of what once was.

Exhausted, I sank to the ground, the sun now directly overhead, casting harsh light on the scene of destruction. Confusion weighed heavily on my mind, an unfamiliar paralysis of indecision. Never had I felt so lost, with no inkling of a next step.

Then, a distant rumble broke through the oppressive silence—the unmistakable sound of an approaching car. Hope surged through me, and I sprang to my feet, rushing toward the sound as though it were a beacon in the darkness, a lifeline to the answers I so desperately sought.

I sprinted just over a hundred meters when I spotted a military jeep approaching. Inside were three soldiers and an officer. The vehicle halted beside me, and the officer called out, "Mr. Ash Morris?"

Without questioning how he knew my name, I nodded. The officer continued, "I received a report of someone driving through the forest at night, arriving here. I figured it must be you."

Recalling Wilson's message, I quickly asked, "Are you Lieutenant Paul?"

The officer nodded, confirming my suspicion. "Yes, that's me."

Desperation crept into my voice. "What happened here?"

Lieutenant Paul sighed, stepping out of the jeep. I followed him to the smoldering ruins. "Things are quite unusual," he said, gesturing toward the east, where the mountains loomed. "The Black Army Tribe resides there."

The mere mention of the "Black Army Tribe" sent a shiver down my spine. "The Black Army Tribe! They keep to themselves, fierce but non-confrontational unless provoked."

Paul seemed taken aback that I was familiar with this secluded tribe, numbering under a thousand. He nodded, then added, "That's true, but—"

I interrupted, pointing at the devastation. "Was this the work of the Black Army Tribe?"

He grimaced, "I'm afraid I arrived too late. And you, even later."

A chill ran through me. "The Black Army Tribe—what about the professor and my wife? Are they—"

Paul shook his head. "I don't know their fate. I patrol regularly, and my last visit here was over a month ago. The situation was already peculiar then. The Black Army Tribe, usually isolated, had sent a wizard to summon Professor Kim into the mountains."

"Did the professor unknowingly trespass on their sacred ground while collecting specimens?" I asked.

"No, absolutely not," Paul assured. "The professor understood the tribe well and respected their boundaries. On my last visit, the day after the wizard's arrival, Professor Kim mentioned the encounter. He even joked, 'It's strange. The wizard claimed my son is with them and summoned me.'"

Paul looked at me quizzically. "Isn't that absurd?"

It was indeed absurd, yet an icy realization gripped me. "Bruce has returned." Flora had once said, "I believe Bruce died in Nepal." Her words echoed ominously in my mind.

Paul continued, "The wizard holds a high status within the tribe. His visit is significant. I asked if that guy was truly a wizard. Professor Kim replied, 'The feathers in his headdress are black and white. If not a wizard, then what?' These colors signify a chief priest, especially in major ceremonies. This was no trivial matter. When I left, the professor took my car, saying he needed to contact a friend in Asia."

I interjected, "That friend is me. I was in Nepal, searching for his son. My wife received his call."

Paul appeared bewildered, and I spared him further explanation. Professor Kim had only shared fragments of the truth, concealing much. A mere visit from a wizard claiming his son was with the Black Army Tribe wouldn't have warranted his urgent call to me, nor would it have prompted Flora's immediate journey.

Paul resumed, "Subsequently, nothing seemed amiss. I brought your wife here. On arrival, we heard the Black Army Tribe's drums summoning their people, signaling something significant. The drumming persisted for days. I visited every other day. On one visit, your wife gave me a tape for you, but you were still absent."

I nodded, "Yes, I heard the tape. She sounded dire. Didn't you notice?"

Paul, sensing my frustration, defended himself. "Of course, I noticed! Both she and the professor were visibly distressed, as if haunted by an unseen threat. But when I inquired, they refused to confide. Without their insight, I had to leave. When I returned later, I found this devastation."

I pressed, "What do you think happened here?"

Paul's expression hardened. "Of course it was the Black Army's attack," he said grimly.

I pressed on, "But where is everyone? Where have they gone?"

His silence spoke volumes, a gesture of helplessness. After a moment's thought, I declared, "Give me as much gasoline as you can spare from your vehicle."

Paul's face blanched, understanding my intent immediately. "No!" he exclaimed.

"It's not a matter of choice," I countered. "I have to go."

His horror was palpable, his breath a sharp intake of realization. "You're planning to enter the Black Army's forbidden zone! Do you not recall Sir Henry's expedition?"

Of course I remembered. Sir Henry, the intrepid British explorer, had attempted to breach the Black Army's isolation alongside seven volunteers. Defying Brazilian governmental warnings and even repelling a military deterrent, they ventured into the tribe's territory. At the time, British betting circles buzzed with wagers, placing the odds of their survival at a staggering 500 to one. Yet, fate's cruel hand dealt a blow that silenced even the most optimistic of gamblers. The odds did not favor them. Their bodies—Sir Henry among them—were discovered adrift on a solitary raft, floating along a tributary of the mighty Amazon. The eerie emblem of the Black Army marked the raft, a silent testament to the fate that had befallen them. All eight explorers lay lifeless, victims of an enigma that refused to reveal its secrets.

This event led the Brazilian government to establish a forbidden zone, restricting access within three miles of the tribe.

I said nothing further to Paul, simply reiterated my demand. His face was ashen, his voice a whisper. "This is suicide. I cannot give you gasoline."

I replied, "The outcome is the same. Even if I must proceed on foot, I will. Lieutenant, we found no bodies here. There's a chance they're alive in the Black Army's territory."

Paul blinked, disbelief etched on his face. The idea of outsiders surviving among the Black Army was ludicrous, yet for me, hope was all I had.

"Then at least wait," Paul implored. "Let me discuss this with the commander."

"I can't afford to wait, not even a minute," I insisted.

The air was thick with tension as Paul, with a resigned sigh, commanded his three soldiers. They hastily loaded six gasoline cans into my car, then strained to right the overturned vehicle. The moment it was set, I slipped behind the wheel, casting a quick salute to Paul before accelerating away. As I passed him, in a surprising gesture of camaraderie, he unholstered his pistol and tossed it to me.

With a swift hand, I caught the pistol, not daring to pause. My journey plunged me back into the jungle, a labyrinthine road of twisted foliage and gnarled tree stumps. The path was perilously narrow, challenging my every nerve. Despite my urgency, the car could barely crawl past five miles per hour.

Night enveloped the jungle, but my resolve was unwavering. My compass was set due north, the mountains looming deceptively close, yet a daunting seventy to eighty miles away. Darkness closed in, stretching the distance infinitely, and though I had not slept, adrenaline kept me wide awake and alert. Through the pitch-black, I navigated, until the break of dawn ushered me out of the jungle's clutches. Ahead lay a small plain at the mountain's base, a tranquil façade shattered by a massive wooden sign. Inscribed with cryptic symbols and primitive Indian pictograms, it was an ominous harbinger of the danger that lay ahead.

I eased the car to a halt beside the foreboding sign. Parched and hungry, I took a moment to sip water and nibble on some dry rations.

As I surveyed the scene, the plain stretched out peacefully, dotted with wildflowers swaying gently in the morning breeze. A group of deer grazed nearby, their eyes fixed on me with innocent curiosity. The mountain, now a mere five miles away, beckoned with the promise of revelation. Ten more minutes and I would reach its enigmatic shadow.

# CHAPTER 7

# THE SEQUEL TO UNCANNY VISIONS

I could never have anticipated what lay ahead as I pressed forward. But as I'd assured Paul, there was no turning back— I had to go.

After a brief respite of about half an hour, I resumed my journey, my foot heavy on the accelerator. The car surged toward the mountain's base. Upon arrival, the air was pierced by a rapid drumbeat. Suddenly, six Indians, their bodies adorned with dark red patterns, leapt into view with astonishing agility. Each bore a small bow, arrows poised for action.

Though these bows and arrows appeared diminutive, almost like children's playthings, I knew better. They were lethal, the arrowheads likely coated with one of the deadliest poisons known to man. I remained in the car, paralyzed by indecision. Familiar with several indigenous languages, I was clueless about the Black Army's dialect. Raising my hands in a universal gesture of peace seemed too risky, potentially misinterpreted as an act of aggression. So, I sat motionless, hoping for a sign.

The natives surrounded my vehicle, maintaining a cautious stance. The one with the most striking red facial markings spoke first. The words that followed were beyond my wildest imaginings: "Ash Morris?"

In an instant, the tension of the past days evaporated, replaced by a wave of relief. I couldn't help but laugh aloud. A native, isolated from the world, uttering my name? It could only mean one thing—Flora had taught them. There was no other explanation.

My laughter was contagious. The six natives joined in, their bows lowered as their expressions softened. Their curiosity about the car was evident. I gestured for them to enter, and once they were settled inside, I started driving. At first slowly, then picking up speed, we circled the plain. Their shouts of joy filled the air, a symphony of newfound delight.

After about half an hour of this impromptu joyride, I stopped the car and pointed to myself, saying, "Ash Morris." The natives nodded in unison, acknowledging my identity. The leader gestured for me to exit the car, leading me toward the mountain.

We traversed a canyon, its floor strewn with boulders, a testament to the mountain stream it became during the rainy season. As we made our way into the mountains, the ascent grew steeper. The path was non-existent, replaced by towering trees. The natives moved with ease, their familiarity with the terrain evident. I followed, determined not to lose sight of them.

Upon cresting the mountain and descending the other side, I noticed thick smoke rising from a hidden valley below, obscured by dense foliage. Concurrently, the rapid beat of drums filled the air.

Uncertain of the smoke and drums' significance, I turned to the natives, intending to inquire through gestures. But the scene that met my eyes left me stunned.

Initially, I hadn't noticed anything peculiar about the six natives. They had approached together, and I assumed they were a unified group. But now, they had split into two factions, each three, glaring at each other with palpable hostility. Each wielded a weapon—a sharp-ended bone, resembling a broad dagger. The air was thick with tension as they stared one another down.

Before I could fathom what had sparked this internal conflict, the drumbeats from the valley intensified, accompanied by the unmistakable cries of battle. The valley was a cauldron of chaos.

At that moment, the six natives erupted into shouts, each seemingly vying to be heard over the others. Their language was foreign to me; their words, unintelligible. All I could discern was their escalating aggression as they charged at each other, weapons clashing in a fierce skirmish.

The situation was beyond reason. Even if I spoke their tongue, quelling such fervor would be near impossible. As I stood, observing the melee, the tumult from the valley below rose in crescendo. The realization struck me—there were hundreds battling below, marking the valley as the Black Army's enclave. Flora and Professor Kim were undoubtedly amidst the turmoil. What was I doing lingering here?

Spurred into action, I abandoned the brawling natives and dashed down the mountain.

The descent was treacherous, the terrain dense with towering trees and exposed roots that threatened to trip me with every step. I stumbled, almost tumbling headlong, but managed to keep my footing.

As I neared the valley's base, the smoke thickened, a testament to the severity of the events unfolding below.

After traversing roughly 300 meters, I found myself on a stone platform. I paused to survey my surroundings, seeking a path downward, when suddenly, a group of about 20 natives emerged from below.

Their appearance was startling, and for a moment, they froze. Then, with painted faces of red-brown patterns and primitive weapons in hand, they charged toward me, shouting fiercely.

In my life, I had faced many dangers, but being besieged by over twenty natives, each brandishing rudimentary yet deadly weapons, was a rarity. The odds were overwhelming, but there was no time for fear—only action.

I dared not underestimate the primitive weapons wielded by the natives, knowing full well they might be tipped with toxins beyond the reach of modern medicine. As two attackers lunged toward me, I deftly sidestepped, delivering a swift kick that sent them sprawling. "Ash Morris! Ash Morris!" I shouted, hoping the mention of my name would halt their advance, as it had with the first group of natives I encountered.

Yet, despite my repeated cries, the relentless assault continued. Some of the natives fought with wild ferocity, forcing me to defend myself with increasing intensity.

Amidst the chaos, a sharp whistle pierced the air, catching me off guard. It was so distinct, so familiar, that I almost failed to dodge a bone weapon aimed at me. It was Flora's whistle—I'd recognize it anywhere!

Driven by newfound determination, I repelled my immediate attackers and sprinted toward the whistle's origin. As I neared, Flora emerged from behind a massive rock, a shotgun gripped firmly in her hands. "Come here!" she shouted, her voice a lifeline amidst the turmoil.

Seeing Flora filled me with an indescribable surge of relief and joy. In my excitement, I leapt into the air, flipping and landing behind a large rock just in time to avoid the advancing natives. Flora fired her shotgun, the loud blast scattering the attackers in retreat.

With a quick gesture, Flora signaled me to follow her. We dashed forward, diving over a large bush, and she pointed towards a narrow cave hidden behind dense foliage. We slipped inside, the darkness swallowing us whole.

The cave's entrance was well-concealed, and as we settled into the shadows, the tumult from the valley continued to echo around us—drums and shouts melding into a chaotic symphony.

I was filled with a torrent of questions for Flora, but the sheer number of them left me momentarily speechless. Sensing my turmoil, Flora spoke first, "Did you get my tape? What took you so long to get here?"

I exhaled heavily, unsure where to begin my explanations. Flora, sensing my hesitation, went on, "The Black Army tribe has splintered. The chief leads one faction and the wizard leads the other. They're embroiled in a civil war."

Her revelation was both bewildering and strangely amusing. The idea of a civil war within such a secluded tribe was astounding. "Why are they fighting?" I asked, almost rhetorically.

A voice, unexpected and calm, echoed from deeper within the cave: "For me."

Startled by the presence of another person, I turned sharply toward the voice. The cave's depths were engulfed in shadow, obscuring any figure within. Flora signaled for me to remain calm, indicating she was aware of the other presence.

"Who is that?" I asked, my curiosity piqued.

The voice answered before Flora could, "I am Bruce."

The sheer shock of this sentence was paralyzing. I leapt to my feet, only to bang my head against the cave's low ceiling. But the physical pain was nothing compared to the jolt of hearing that name. I dropped back down, peering into the darkness, struggling to comprehend.

The voice continued, as if understanding my disbelief, "Mr. Morris, things are indeed a little strange, but your wife said you can handle even the strangest things!"

I tried to steady my racing thoughts. How could this be? In Nepal, I had seen Bruce twice—once as a decaying body and then as mere bones. Yet here he was, speaking from the shadows. Flora had said, "Bruce is back." But how, and in what form?

Desperate to lighten the tension, I quipped, "I hope you don't look too scary!" fearing the apparition of a living skeleton emerging from the dark.

A chuckle resonated from within, "Not too scary, but not too pretty either!"

As the voice drew nearer, a figure emerged from the shadows. When he stepped into a shaft of light, I could see him clearly. He wasn't a skeleton, but a person—an Indian native from the Black Army tribe, with the familiar red and brown markings on his face, lending him an oddly whimsical appearance.

I turned to Flora, perplexed. "What a joke, this is a native!"

The "native" stepped forward, closer to me, and spoke with impeccable English. "Mr. Morris, when have you seen a native from the Black Army tribe speak such fluent English? I am Bruce!"

I had leapt up earlier, and now I found myself sinking to the ground in disbelief. The "native" squatted before me, his gaze intense. Despite his appearance, there was an undeniable air of familiarity. Yet, accepting him as Bruce seemed beyond belief.

We locked eyes, silence stretching between us. Flora broke it, "You can't imagine what happened—"

I gestured for her to pause, focusing on the figure before me. "Bruce, don't you want to go back? Why are you here?"

A shadow of sadness crossed the "native's" face. "Yes, I want to go back, but something is missing, or something went awry, so I ended up here."

I pressed on, "The dream you and Randy—"

His expression shifted to one of fervent excitement. "You've seen Randy! That's wonderful. Did he tell you about that dream? If you know, understanding the whole thing becomes much easier!"

Our conversation must have sounded cryptic to anyone unfamiliar with the backstory, Flora included. She exclaimed, "Oh my God, what are you talking about?"

Confusion and excitement warred within me. I was beginning to piece together the puzzle, ignoring Flora's question in my euphoria. I slapped my forehead, realization dawning.

"Oh my God, it turns out all this is true! But I sent Randy to a mental hospital, this—this is really terrible!"

The "native," unaware of the turmoil Randy felt when institutionalized, chuckled lightly. "Poor Randy!"

He leaned closer, eyes probing. "Is that thing still there?"

I understood immediately, though I sought clarification. "The antique Bain sold to you? It's been destroyed."

The "native" let out a deep sigh, his disappointment palpable. He stared blankly at the cave's ceiling, cradling his head in his hands. Flora tugged my sleeve, bringing me back to the present. "This really is Mr. Bruce, the person I sought in Nepal!"

Flora ventured, "I know now—the native's body houses Bruce's—soul?"

She hesitated over the word "soul," seeking my approval. I nodded, "Souls, ghosts, spirits—they're all variations of the same concept. The difference between the dead and the living. Calling it a soul is perfectly fine."

Flora continued, "Bruce's soul—after he died in Nepal, it came here? Entered a native! How does he possess such power?"

I replied, "It's due to a rather extraordinary thing."

In the cave's dim light, the mystery began to unravel. Bruce's soul inhabiting a native's body was an enigma born of remarkable circumstances—a testament to the inexplicable wonders and perils of the world we inhabited.

Upon hearing my words, Bruce—the native who housed Bruce's soul—cried out in despair once more. "How could that thing be destroyed? How could it be?"

His desperation was palpable as he grasped my arm, shaking me in his agitation. I steadied him, gripping his arm firmly to calm him down. "Don't get excited. I want to understand your story first."

Bruce's voice was a mix of pleading and frustration. "I want to go back! I want to go back! I don't want to stay here. I should be able to go back. What went wrong?"

I tried to soothe him. "Listen, if you don't calm down, we won't be able to figure out what went wrong."

Gradually, Bruce's breathing steadied, though his anxiety was still evident. "I'll tell you about my experiences in Nepal first, and then you can share your story," I offered.

Flora nodded in agreement, while Bruce appeared momentarily lost in thought. I gave him a gentle nudge. "Bruce, there are parts of my story where I'll need your input. You must listen carefully."

With a resigned smile, Bruce nodded. I began recounting my journey, sparing no detail. Flora listened intently, while Bruce seemed uneasy, his discomfort growing when I described the seven-story stone chamber and Bain's murder of the old man at its base.

I went on to relay the "dream" Randy had shared with me, keenly observing Bruce's reaction. He nodded throughout, confirming Randy's account.

Pausing, I asked, "Bruce, Randy mentioned you had a separate dream you never shared with him. It was this dream that led you to attempt such a bizarre experiment. What was it about?"

Bruce inhaled deeply, twisting his fingers as though grappling with how to articulate his thoughts. After a pause, he began, "That day, Randy was out buying supplies. I was alone with the instrument."

The word "instrument" caught me off guard. Bruce spoke of it with familiarity, suggesting an understanding beyond mere possession. Unable to resist, I interjected, "You refer to what Bain sold you as an 'instrument.' What kind of instrument is it?"

Bruce hesitated, meeting my gaze. I was momentarily reminded of his appearance—a native of the Black Army tribe, yet his eyes held a profound wisdom. It was a surreal juxtaposition, and I reminded myself: He is Bruce. He must be Bruce. Whatever circumstances led to his current form, his essence remained unchanged. Bodies and appearances could be altered—modern plastic surgery could transform a person completely—but the core of one's identity remained constant.

Bruce's presence, his struggle, and the mystery of the instrument all pointed to something extraordinary, something beyond conventional understanding. His story, I felt, would shed light on the enigma binding us all.

Framing Bruce's transformation as a result of comprehensive plastic surgery made everything feel less bizarre and more manageable. Although I knew that wasn't the case, this mental exercise allowed me to better grapple with the remarkable situation before me.

Bruce held my gaze, then said, "You've seen it too. If it's not some kind of instrument, then what is it?"

I nodded, acknowledging his perspective.

He continued, "It is indeed an instrument. I've at least discovered one of its primary functions."

Flora chimed in, "Yes, it can induce dreams."

Bruce's expression was grave, his features drawn tight, emphasizing the wrinkles etched into his face. "That's the simplest explanation. More precisely, when a person's head rests against it and they fall asleep, the instrument's recordings can be transmitted into their brain, allowing them to experience everything it has stored."

Flora and I exchanged glances, absorbing Bruce's explanation, which was both thorough and plausible.

Seeing our comprehension, Bruce elaborated, "Randy and I experienced the same dream for nearly ten consecutive nights. In other words, we accessed the same 'record' about ten times. We became intimately familiar with its content. I was convinced it wasn't just an ordinary dream. So, when I found myself alone, I wondered if this recording instrument held another set of recordings I could access."

Flora and I inhaled sharply, struck by the sheer audacity and incredibility of Bruce's hypothesis.

He pressed on, "I opened it—you've seen the device, so you know it can be opened and what ensues. I had no idea how to operate it. I used a wire to press every accessible point. When certain areas lit up, I knew I'd succeeded!"

Bruce's excitement was palpable, his hands animated as he recounted the tale.

He continued, "Once I was ready, I lay my head back on the pillow, trying to calm my mind and drift into sleep. Soon, I had a new dream—"

He paused for a deep breath before proceeding, "Much like the first dream, I heard someone speaking again. This voice was fervent and resolute. It said, 'My method is to make them believe me. I will explain my intentions and demonstrate my power through weapons to ensure their compliance! Those who obey me, and whom I deem worthy after scrutiny, I will bring back!' The speaker's assurance was striking. Since there were three more speakers to follow, let's refer to this one as A."

Bruce glanced at me, seeking my approval. I nodded, finding no reason to object. Using "A" to denote a person was no different from assigning them a name.

Bruce continued, "After A finished speaking, another voice, calm and serene, began. This person's tone was slow but persuasive. He said, 'They are our equals. They don't even understand why they suffer. Their greed, anger, and ignorance aren't entirely their fault. Once they recognize these flaws, I'll bring them back. And those who believe in me must know I am the most honorable. They must let go of everything. I'll ask them to remove all their hair, which is no longer useful—'"

Bruce paused, emphasizing, "This B mentioned hair again!"

I nodded, recalling the repeated mentions of hair in the first "dream," where mysterious figures discussed its significance.

Bruce resumed, "B hadn't finished. He added, 'Only by shedding the useless can they realize there are even more useless things, including the flesh they hold most dear!'"

I inhaled sharply at this, instinctively tightening my grip on Flora's hand.

Bruce, lost in thought, continued, "Then, the third speaker, whom I call C, said, 'They are truly pitiable! Genetic factors have pushed them closer to their ancestors, unbeknownst to them. Their home must be a city of sin. I want them to see their 'achievements' are hollow. I intend to demonstrate power, but power merely instills fear. Alas, I hope they believe in me! Believers can be saved!' His sincerity was striking."

Bruce paused, casting me an odd look.

I was bewildered, clutching Flora's hand tighter, sharing the uncertainty.

After a moment, Bruce spoke again, "The final speaker had the most relaxed tone: 'Of course, we must tell them the truth, but considering their understanding, the truth they receive won't be the complete truth. It depends on their comprehension. If they grasp their origins, they'll see their current life is an illusion. Once they realize this, they're eligible to return!'"

Bruce had recounted the four speakers, whom he labeled A, B, C, and D. He looked at Flora and me expectantly.

My mind was a whirlwind of confusion. I managed to say, "If that was all, it wouldn't be enough to make you ask Randy to stab your heart."

Bruce replied, "There's more. After these four spoke, I heard a familiar voice—the one who suggested sending volunteers in the first dream to test their eligibility to return. I realized one of these four was that person's only son."

I recalled their "first dream," identifying the person Bruce referenced.

Bruce continued, "This person said, 'Very well, you four have different personalities, and your methods vary, but the outcome is identical. Before you leave, reconsider. It's perilous. You can't imagine the suffering you'll endure! You lack their data for research, and we can't guarantee retrieval!' Silence followed, then B said, 'If not me, then who?' The others agreed unanimously."

Bruce's story painted a picture of a complex, high-stakes mission carried out by individuals with diverse approaches, united by a common goal. Their commitment to the task, despite the risks, underscored the gravity of their mission. The implications of their journey, and their willingness to embrace danger for potential enlightenment, hinted at profound truths waiting to be uncovered.

Bruce paused, closing his eyes as if to gather his thoughts, then resumed, "The man, presumably the leader of these four individuals, spoke again. 'The path you're about to take is set. You'll live among them, growing alongside them with no outward differences. Your knowledge remains intact. As you depart in separate directions, you'll experience varying degrees of time lag upon arrival. You may bring some practical items. Remember, initially, you'll have almost no abilities, but they will gradually return.' The four agreed in unison. The leader added, 'Success or failure, I will do my utmost to retrieve you.'

"D then asked, 'What if I can't return?' The leader replied, 'That's the worst-case scenario. In such an event, the three of you should seek each other out. Temporary challenges are inconsequential. Unlike them, we are immortal.' Mr. Morris, isn't that a profound temptation? Eternal life!"

My mind felt adrift, grasping at fragments of understanding yet unable to anchor them. I didn't respond to Bruce's comment on immortality.

Bruce pressed on, "The second dream ended there. Upon waking, I pondered deeply. When linked to the first dream, clarity emerged. Mr. Morris, I realized that humans on Earth aren't native creatures—they're from elsewhere. Our distant ancestors were a group of criminals, stripped of their intelligence and exiled to Earth to survive. Initially, their intelligence was akin to that of imbeciles—primitive beings!"

Flora and I exchanged glances, neither of us voicing our thoughts.

Bruce's enthusiasm grew, "I can't say how many primitive humans were sent to Earth. Initially, they were indistinguishable from the beasts here. Yet, they had once been incredibly intelligent, beyond what we can currently fathom! Through generations, as they reproduced, their inherited wisdom began to resurface. The pace of recovery was exponential. For millions of years, there was stagnation, but in the past few thousand years, progress has been rapid. Mr. Morris, this is the history of human evolution on Earth!"

I stood in silent contemplation, while Bruce gazed at me intently. I eventually said, "Such an assumption seems quite arbitrary."

Bruce laughed, "Don't you find it odd how ill-suited we are to Earth's environment? Even after all these years, humans struggle with Earth's climate. The air's moisture is problematic. Remember the dream? When humidity exceeds 80%, people feel uneasy; when it drops below 60%, discomfort returns. Is this typical of Earth-evolved creatures?"

I countered, "That alone doesn't prove humans are extraterrestrial."

Bruce fixed his gaze on me, "And consider how different humans are from other Earth creatures!"

Flora added, "Yes, humans have hair. They're the only Earth creatures with such long hair near the brain, its purpose unknown!"

This discourse on humanity's origins, while speculative, challenged conventional understanding and broadened our perspective on evolution and existence. The implications were vast, prompting reflection on our place in the universe and the mysteries yet to be uncovered.

Flora's long hair was a testament to her individuality, and as she spoke about it, I couldn't help but glance at her tied-up locks. She was often resolute and quick to form intuitive reactions, whether she truly believed in something or not. At this moment, it appeared she had wholeheartedly embraced

Bruce's theory. The astonishing fact that Bruce had become a native of the Black Army tribe seemed to underpin her acceptance of his ideas.

Bruce, noticing her apparent agreement, exclaimed with enthusiasm, "Yes, humans have hair. We can use tools. We can invent things seemingly from nothing. Consider this: refining metals from minerals is an incredibly complex process. Without a sudden surge in wisdom genes among a few individuals, what other creature could have conceived such an idea?"

I waved my hand, trying in vain to dispel the chaotic thoughts swirling in my mind. "Let's take this one step at a time. Tell me more about yourself."

Bruce obliged, "Alright! I realized that we originate from another place. That place is our true home. Humans on Earth can return there. Here, life is fleeting, a mere sigh filled with suffering and wrongdoing. But once back in our homeland, we can achieve eternal life. It is—heaven!"

He pronounced "heaven" with deliberate emphasis, stretching each syllable to underscore its significance.

The notion of another world being our true origin, a paradise offering immortality, was both tantalizing and overwhelming. Bruce's conviction was infectious, and his revelations invited reflection on the possibilities beyond our known existence. It posed profound questions about the nature of life and the destiny of humanity, challenging us to reconsider our understanding of where we truly belong.

# CHAPTER 8

# "The Illusion of Death and the Truth of Eternity

Bruce continued his narrative with a fervor that was almost contagious. "When I realized this, my only desire was to return! I analyzed the words of the four individuals and their leader, concluding that to return, I must relinquish what we consider most precious: our physical bodies!"

His excitement was palpable, his face flushed with a purplish hue. "Blood coursing through veins, cells in constant motion, air flowing, metabolism ticking away—these are not true life! How long do these last? On Earth, perhaps a century? In our true home, that's merely an instant! This is not life. Real life is eternal, unshackled from the flesh!"

He paused, gathering his thoughts. ""When Randy returned, I told him about the second dream. He wanted to go back before I did, but he couldn't compete with me. So he stabbed me in the heart. Haha, it's amusing—those sent to Earth as if they were fools, cherishing the heart they believed could last a hundred years, haha—"

His laughter was genuine, not forced, yet Flora and I couldn't join in. Flora asked, "What happened after the knife went in?"

Bruce replied, "It was extraordinary. The instrument was right beside me. I felt dizzy, and everything went dark. Then I experienced a very subtle sensation."

I interjected, "At that point, from a medical standpoint, you were dead, yet you still experienced feelings?"

With a hint of impatience, Bruce waved me off. "Don't talk to me about human medicine! I studied it and regret wasting years on it! Yes, I had feelings. Dead, but still feeling!"

Flora posed another question, "Are you suggesting that everyone's death is similar? After death, can feelings persist?"

Bruce pondered this, "I can't be sure. I only know what I felt then. What I am certain of is that my unique experience was entirely due to the presence of that instrument!"

He chuckled, "So, without that instrument, I wouldn't recommend trying it lightly!"

Flora seemed to have a thought but kept silent.

Bruce continued, "The sensation was peculiar. I felt a connection to the instrument. My life force was ebbing away through multiple channels—not just one—leaving my body.

During this, everything was dark, then a gentle light appeared, allowing me to see everything, including myself."

As he spoke, he gestured animatedly. "I could see, though I don't know how, it was just a sensation. I saw myself on the ground with a knife in my heart. I saw Randy looking at me strangely, muttering something I couldn't hear, and the instrument beside me. I asked Randy to place the instrument under me, and when I saw it, a button seemed familiar."

Bruce paused, searching for words. "I don't know how to explain it. Initially, I wanted to press the button. But without a body or fingers, what could I use? As I pondered this, suddenly, the button seemed to activate on its own."

I mused, "It's like a remote control activated by thought!"

Bruce tapped his fingers together, producing a "clapping" sound. "Exactly, it was controlled by my spirit. I don't know what went wrong. My deepest wish was to return—to return to my hometown! You understand what I mean by hometown. At that moment, I was enveloped in light, a series of lights, each shining brightly. It was a brief process. During this, I thought of my father and the South American jungle where I grew up. Perhaps the mistake was there, because when my vision went black and then cleared—I found myself here."

Bruce's expression turned into a bitter smile, revealing the irony of his situation. Even if he hadn't said it, I could deduce what had happened. When he regained consciousness, his spirit—his soul—had entered the body of a native from the Indian Black Army tribe.

He explained, "Those flashes of light were brief." But how brief? In that time, he had traveled from Nepal to South America—a journey of tens of thousands of miles. If it happened at the speed of radio waves, it would have taken mere fractions of a second!

Bruce continued with a rueful smile, "I opened my eyes and immediately sensed something was amiss. First, I realized I had a body again, but I didn't want one. Without a body, I could return. How did I end up with a body again? Then I noticed people dancing around me, and a native with black and white feathers sweeping my body with a feather broom. I screamed and sat up."

He grinned mischievously, "You can imagine the chaos that ensued when I sat up. My body belonged to someone who had just died and was suddenly resurrected! My astonishment was equal to that of the natives around me. I tried speaking, but no one understood. I calmed down and assessed my surroundings, confirming I was in an Indian tribe. I attempted various tribal languages I knew, but none of those around me understood. I deduced I was in the Black Army tribe. They were isolated from outsiders and wouldn't understand other tribal languages. I overheard their discussions. The one with multicolored feathers seemed to be the chief, and the priest with black and white feathers was arguing. I tried to explain my situation, but it was futile."

Bruce's predicament was clear. Even in a civilized society, such a scenario would be astonishing, let alone in a semi-civilized Indian tribe, where confusion reigned.

Bruce continued, "After some time, they brought an old native to me. He had been captured by the Black Army tribe over ten years ago and was spared. He spoke an Indian language I understood and knew the Black Army's language, so I communicated through him."

Bruce's subsequent experiences can be summarized briefly, as they were just a side note to the main story.

Once Bruce realized he was truly in the Black Army tribe, he remembered his father's laboratory was nearby and revealed his identity to the natives. Naturally, they were skeptical, but the was wizard more credulous. The wizard proclaimed that Bruce was a messenger sent by the gods and decided to hold a grand ceremony for him. It was only fitting, he believed, to have a divine messenger lead the tribe.

The original chief naturally opposed the wizard's proclamation, leading to a division within the Black Army tribe. Two factions emerged, engaged in prolonged debates. During this time, Bruce found himself both amused and bewildered by the situation. Desperate to find a way out of the mountains and reunite with his father, he convinced the wizard to seek out Professor Kim, taking the old native as a translator.

When Professor Kim heard from the wizard that his son had somehow transformed into a native of the Black Army tribe, he was understandably baffled. Faced with this bizarre and inexplicable situation, he instinctively thought of reaching out to me for assistance. Unfortunately, I was in Nepal at the time, so his call was answered by Flora.

Recognizing the urgency and peculiarity of the matter from Professor Kim's retelling, Flora decided to act immediately. She knew the professor needed help and promptly set off to assist, leaving a message for me to join her as soon as possible.

By the time Flora and Professor Kim met, tensions within the Black Army tribe had escalated. The debates had intensified, leading to small-scale conflicts. Bruce understood that to connect with the civilized world and resolve the situation, he needed the wizard's influence. Thus, he requested the wizard to arrange a meeting with his father, Professor Kim.

After the wizard agreed to facilitate the meeting, the chief took his own measures, sending people to confront Professor Kim. Luckily, the wizard's messengers reached the professor first, escorting him and Flora to the mountains. In the meantime, the chief's followers set fire to the professor's laboratory, reducing it to ashes. Once Flora and Professor Kim arrived at the tribe's valley, they reunited with Bruce. Tensions within the Black Army tribe escalated into fierce arguments.

Flora, ever resourceful, declared that another "messenger of God" named Ash Morris was on his way.

She spent several days training a group of natives to recognize and pronounce my name. Thus, when I eventually encountered the first six natives, they were Flora's "students," able to call out my name upon sight.

Just before I reached the valley, the chief, sensing his authority threatened by one "messenger of God," feared the arrival of another would worsen his situation. He initiated an attack, sparking a civil war. The intensity of conflict among these brave, powerful natives was unimaginable. As the situation deteriorated, Flora fled with the professor and Bruce, seeking refuge in the cave where we now were.

Once they finished recounting the events, I quickly asked, "Where is the professor?"

Flora sighed deeply, "While we were escaping into the mountains, a group of natives loyal to the chief attacked us. The professor was struck by a poisoned arrow and died instantly."

I inhaled sharply and glanced at Bruce, who showed no visible sorrow. His unique perspective on "death" was vastly different from that of most people.

After a moment of silence, I asked, "Bruce, in your view, when the professor died, did his spirit experience what you did? Did he see his own body?"

Bruce replied thoughtfully, "I've pondered that, but I'm uncertain. Our earthly life is fleeting; immortality is what truly matters. Imagine a creature with a lifespan of merely three seconds. If it dies after one second, we wouldn't mourn, as the difference is negligible. Whether it's a hundred years, fifty, or twenty-five, it's all the same in the grand scheme."

I paused, grappling with Bruce's distinct views on life, which were challenging to embrace fully. As I approached the cave entrance, the sounds of battle lingered, though the fighting seemed to have subsided. Flora joined me, expressing concern: "The chief's loyalists have won. We're the culprits in their eyes. We must escape!"

I turned to Bruce, "With him?"

Bruce asserted, "Of course with me! I want to go to Nepal, find the instrument again, and return—not to Earth. I harbor no evil thoughts and am fully qualified to go back!"

I regarded him thoughtfully, "But if you take a plane as you are now—"

Bruce interrupted, frustrated, "I don't need you. I can get to Nepal on my own!"

I responded naturally, "You claim to have no evil thoughts, yet anger is one of them."

Bruce was taken aback, his anger giving way to a profound realization, leaving him momentarily speechless. He appeared deeply saddened. His expression tugged at my conscience, and I reassured him, "Don't be disheartened. You've had an extraordinary experience. You might be the only person reborn on Earth. If anyone can return, you are certainly the most qualified."

Bruce sighed, "I just fear being trapped in an earthly body forever."

I attempted to lighten the mood, "At the very least, it's an interesting situation!"

Bruce, however, was unmoved by my attempt at humor. "Interesting? What's interesting about it? Imagine suddenly becoming a baby, spending a year learning to walk again. That wouldn't be interesting at all!"

Despite the gravity of his concerns, the situation was a testament to the complexities of identity and existence, challenging us to navigate the boundaries between worlds and confront the essence of what it means to belong.

As my mind raced through the implications of Bruce's second dream, a realization struck me. The four individuals had come to Earth with a mission, guided by their leader's words: "The way you go has been determined. You will live with them and grow up together—" Could it be that, like Bruce, they entered Earth as infants, their abilities returning as they matured? If so, they would indeed appear no different from ordinary Earthlings, save for their eventual supernatural powers.

The thought sent a shiver down my spine, and I glanced at Flora, who wore a similarly bewildered expression. She whispered, "Ash, among those four, the leader's only son—"

I nodded before she could finish, "It's the baby born in the stable!"

Flora continued, "The passionate and determined A—"

I turned to Bruce, who murmured, "Holding a sword in one hand and the truth he preached in the other!"

A lump formed in my throat as I added, "And B, who urged people to relinquish everything, starting with their hair, viewing earthly life as an illusion—"

Bruce and Flora both gestured emphatically. Flora remarked, "And D sighed, saying that the truths comprehended by Earthlings won't be the real truths—"

I exclaimed, "It's all so strange! The king once asked me a peculiar question. It seemed odd at the time, and it seems even stranger now!"

Flora and Bruce, familiar with my recounting of my experiences in Nepal, both looked intrigued. Bruce recalled, "Why would the king have such a notion? He asked, 'Did the four of them know each other before? Of course, they did. They're the four 'volunteers'!'"

I continued, "There's a bizarre connection between the king and Bain. Bain clearly committed murder, yet became the king's esteemed guest. The king mentioned having his own reasons, and Bain possesses the instrument! There must be a link!"

Flora pondered aloud, suddenly raising her voice, "These four possess abilities surpassing all Earthlings, undoubtedly. They've endured much but remained steadfast in their mission. Have they returned to their homeland? Why haven't they come back? Do they believe the people here aren't worth saving?"

Bruce added, "Absolutely! Didn't C endure great betrayal from someone he trusted? Fortunately, he's immortal, able to resurrect even after death!"

Flora glanced at me, "And D 'turned into a Indian', becoming someone else. Is his situation similar to Bruce's now?"

Their words resonated deeply, prompting me to exclaim, "Let's stop using the code names A, B, C, and D. We can call them by their Earth names! Are they truly from another planet, here to save Earthlings?"

Flora affirmed, "I believe it."

Bruce agreed, "I believe it too!"

The conversation left us pondering the profound possibility that these individuals, perhaps revered figures in history, were indeed extraterrestrial beings with a mission to uplift humanity.

I waved my hand, trying to steer the conversation back to something more tangible. "Alright! These four people each have distinct theories. Which one do you believe in?"

Bruce replied confidently, "They all lead to the same end. Despite their different personalities and methods, their shared goal is to help those who can return, do so."

Flora nodded in agreement with Bruce. "Bruce has shown that the human body is not the key; it's the spirit that matters. The spirit is immortal, and life is eternal!"

I couldn't argue against the evidence. Bruce's "spirit" had indeed journeyed from the Himalayan foothills in Nepal to the upper Amazon in South America, a testament to the power of the spirit.

"Still," I said, "Bruce's situation is unique. He had that instrument with him."

Flora immediately responded, "That's why we need to go to Nepal right away, find that instrument, and we can all return!"

Her words caught me off guard. The way she said "we can return" was so casual, as if returning meant just going back to our earthly home.

My voice rose a bit in surprise, "Do you realize what 'return' actually means?"

Flora smiled serenely, "Of course. My 'return' means death from an earthly perspective. They would think I'm dead, but in reality, I've gained eternal life."

I felt a swirl of emotions. I closed my eyes briefly to regain composure before asking, "If you can go back and I can't, would you go alone, leaving me and everything here behind?"

Flora's smile was warm, "Of course you'll come with me!"

I pressed on, "But if only you could go back, and I couldn't, what would you do? No changing the question, just answer honestly."

Flora hesitated, a look of conflict crossing her face. She was usually decisive, able to make tough calls with a single word. But this question clearly stirred a deep inner struggle. After a while, she sighed and gently placed her hand on mine.

Her silent gesture spoke volumes—she couldn't leave me behind.

I took a deep breath, realizing the truth. "Those who can't let go can't go back. One of the four has made that clear."

Flora nodded, "You're right. But Bruce has no such attachments, and we have a chance to go together. We must go to Nepal and continue this search."

To anyone reading, our conversation might have seemed like a simple exchange between a couple. But in reality, it had profound implications for everything that followed. It played a crucial role in why I'm able to recount this story from Earth today, as you'll come to understand.

That night, we waited in the cave until the sounds of conflict subsided. Under the cover of darkness, the three of us slipped away. I recalled the path the natives had taken me on, and we navigated our way out of the mountains. By early morning, we reached the remnants of Professor Kim's laboratory, ready to face whatever came next in our quest for understanding and resolution.

Upon arriving at Professor Kim's laboratory, we encountered an unexpected sight—Lieutenant Paul, standing by with unwavering loyalty. He had remained there since my departure, and his disbelief was evident as he repeatedly rubbed his eyes upon seeing us.

Before reaching the laboratory, we had agreed on a story to present regarding Bruce. The truth was too extraordinary, and we doubted anyone would accept it.

Despite knowing Lieutenant Paul's integrity, I fabricated a tale. I explained that we had an adventure in the Black Army Tribe, during which the professor tragically died. We had brought back a native who willingly shared insights about the tribe.

Paul accepted our account without suspicion. When he scrutinized Bruce, Bruce responded with a fierce expression, causing Paul to step back in fright.

We borrowed Paul's car, escaping the jungle to reach a nearby town. Thanks to the international document I possessed, bearing signatures from numerous police chiefs, arranging Bruce's exit from the country was straightforward.

Upon returning home, our butler Wilson was overjoyed, bustling around in excitement. Although Bruce's appearance was slightly unusual, once dressed in regular clothes, he blended in without attracting undue attention.

That evening, we meticulously planned our journey to Nepal. I felt a pang of guilt for returning, breaking my promise to the king once more.

Nevertheless, I was compelled to proceed—for Bruce, for myself, to unravel the mysteries, and for Randy, whom I had unwittingly consigned to a mental hospital.

After deliberation, we decided Flora would enter Nepal through official channels, while Bruce and I would retrace my previous route.

The following day, we took a flight to Darjeeling. Flora continued to Kathmandu, tasked with rescuing Randy. Bruce and I lingered in Darjeeling, utilizing my prior experience to navigate the hippy lifestyle—a milieu Bruce was already familiar with.

In the eyes of most, hippies appeared uniform, regardless of their ethnicity. Bruce, donning a felt hat and letting his hair grow, attracted no special attention.

We crossed into Nepal amid a group of hippies, rented a vehicle, and drove directly to Kathmandu. Arriving by evening, we proceeded to the hotel where we had arranged to meet Flora.

According to our plan, Flora and Randy were to meet us upon arrival. However, neither was present in the hotel lobby. Upon inquiry, the staff initially ignored me due to my attire.

Only after a generous tip did they become accommodating, but the news was unexpected. Flora, scheduled to arrive four days prior, had not checked into the hotel.

Though surprised, I remained calm, confident in Flora's adeptness at handling crises. She had navigated the perils of the Black Army tribe, surely no other challenges could deter her. My thoughts immediately turned to Randy.

Once in our hotel room, Bruce and I promptly contacted the mental hospital. After several attempts, we reached the doctor. "Doctor, it's Ash Morris. Do you remember me? I admitted a patient to your hospital."

The doctor immediately acknowledged, "Yes, I remember. About that patient—"

I interjected, "I apologize! He's not insane; he's extraordinarily normal!"

The doctor's shocked response echoed through the phone, "What?"

I was overwhelmed with shock and regret upon hearing the doctor's words. "This is a terrible misunderstanding. I'll come to get him immediately. It's all my fault!" I insisted, desperate to rectify the situation.

The doctor's response was measured but grim, "I'm afraid it's too late."

Stunned, I asked, "Late? What do you mean? Did you act so quickly to send him back to his hometown?"

The doctor explained, "No, after you left, we placed him in the ward for dangerous patients. The next morning, the administrator found he had committed suicide."

The news hit me like a physical blow, and the shock was so intense that I dropped the phone. Regret flooded over me, thinking of Randy's angry expression and words as he was taken away.

My hands clenched into fists, my heart aching with remorse. The phone lay on the ground, emitting a faint "Hello," but my mind was a whirlwind of confusion.

Bruce looked at me with concern, "What happened to Randy?"

I had never felt such profound regret and sorrow in my whole life, knowing I had hurt Randy. I could only imagine the bitterness he must have felt in his final moments.

While I stood there, paralyzed by shock, Bruce retrieved the phone, speaking softly into the receiver. He then handed it back to me, and I heard the doctor continue, "It's peculiar. After Randy was admitted, he seemed very calm, even smiling occasionally. The staff didn't consider him a risk. Before his death, he left four words on the wall. It's truly strange."

With a strained voice, I asked, "What were those words?"

The doctor replied, "He wrote, 'I am going back.'"

I inhaled deeply and exchanged a look with Bruce, who nodded solemnly, "He went back."

I placed the receiver down, questioning, "How could he have gone back without the instrument?"

Bruce shook his head, "I don't know. There are many things we don't understand. If Randy gave up his body so calmly and confidently, perhaps he truly did go back."

Despite the bitterness of the situation, Bruce's words offered a glimmer of hope. "You're trying to comfort me, but you've reminded me of my duty. Wherever Randy has gone, I must do my best to help him truly go back."

Bruce's hand rested heavily on my shoulder, his face a mask of indifference. His lack of emotion was unsurprising; here was a man who had survived a knife to the heart and emerged unscathed in spirit. Expecting him to mourn a friend's misfortune was like asking the wind to weep.

In stark contrast, sorrow weighed heavily on me. I was running on the fumes of a restless night, sleep having eluded me entirely. As dawn ushered in a new day, we plunged into the winding streets and hidden alleys, determined to find Bain.

Yet, Bain, the notorious purveyor of counterfeit antiques, had vanished as if swallowed by the earth itself. Our inquiries were met with the same refrain: Bain had been seen four days prior, but since then, not a soul had crossed his path.

It wasn't until dusk that we encountered an elderly man. When we inquired about Bain, I began to describe his features and mannerisms. Before I could finish, the old man exclaimed, "I know Bain! I saw him four days ago—"

Another echo of the same frustrating timeline. Disappointment gnawed at me, until the old man continued, "He was with a very beautiful woman. She seemed to be Japanese."

My heart quickened. "Can you describe her?" I pressed.

As he painted a verbal portrait of the mystery woman, Bruce and I exchanged knowing glances. It was Flora. She must have reached Kathmandu four days ago and encountered Bain immediately. But where had they vanished to?

Bruce dismissed the old man, his mind working quickly. "The so-called ancient artifacts Bain peddled likely originated from the seven-story stone chamber you explored. We should head to Bain's village and see if he returned there."

I nodded, though my mind raced with unspoken thoughts. Flora had found Bain, and something unforeseen had unfolded. She wouldn't deviate from our plan without a crucial reason. We had to uncover the truth, and quickly.

We rented another jeep and set off, passing the ancient temple where Bruce and Randy had stayed. We continued until we neared the location of the seven stone chambers from my memories. I halted the jeep, convinced we were close. "It should be around here," I said.

Bruce stood up, scanning the area. It was late, and the moonlight was dim, casting long shadows. Despite the snow-capped mountains reflecting some light, visibility was limited.

"I can't see any buildings!" he called out after searching the horizon.

I joined him, looking toward where I remembered the stone house to be. My recollections painted a vivid picture—the peculiar stone house should have been about 100 meters to the left. Yet, all I saw was flat land.

Bruce eyed me with skepticism. "Are you sure this is the right place?"

Ignoring his doubt, I jumped out of the jeep and moved forward, with Bruce following. I retraced my steps, trying to match them with the memory of that day. The stone house should have stood before me, but only emptiness awaited my gaze.

I surveyed the ground. In Nepal, "flat land" often means a level area on a mountain slope, strewn with rocks. The landscape felt barren and desolate. I walked slowly, circling the area, pondering if the stone house had been dismantled for some reason. An above-ground structure might be removed, but what about the seven underground levels? Even if demolished, there should be some indication—yet I found none.

As I mused over the possibility of demolition, a certainty in my memory told me the stone house should be there. Its absence suggested deliberate removal. But who would remove such a structure, and why? These questions lingered as we continued our search, the mystery deepening with each step.

# CHAPTER 9

# MIDNIGHT DISCOVERY

# OF THE KING'S SECRET

The absence of any trace of the stone house left me increasingly suspicious, suspecting Bain and perhaps some villagers had dismantled it. My thoughts were interrupted by Bruce's sudden shout, "Someone is coming!"

I looked up to see a car speeding toward us, its headlights glaringly bright, forcing me to shield my eyes. The vehicle approached swiftly, and as it neared, my instincts from past adventures kicked in. Being illuminated while the other party remained in shadow was a disadvantage, so I instinctively retreated into the darkness, out of the headlights' range.

From the shadows, I observed the scene unfold. Bruce, lacking my experience, remained in the light, shielding his eyes but holding his ground. "Hey, what are you doing?" he called out.

The vehicle was a luxurious RV, bearing the emblem of the King of Nepal on its door. Whether the king himself was present or not, being discovered by his entourage was not ideal, prompting me to step further back.

The car door opened, and two officers emerged, followed by a familiar figure—the minister who had first summoned me to meet the king. My heart raced. Returning to Nepal was already complicated, and now this encounter added another layer of difficulty.

As I pondered how to handle the situation, I overheard the minister's brusque inquiry to Bruce, "Who are you? What are you doing here?"

Bruce, slightly irritated, retorted, "Who are you again?"

The officers beside the minister barked, "The Minister asked you a question. You must answer. Put your hands down!"

Momentarily taken aback, Bruce complied, lowering his hands and letting the light reveal his face. As a native of the Black Army tribe, his appearance was distinctive, especially as he squinted against the harsh light. His adaptability impressed me, likely informed by my stories about the minister. With a casual demeanor, he replied, "I'm a tourist and lost my way. How can I get back to the hotel?"

The minister scrutinized Bruce before glancing in my direction. Given the distance and darkness, I doubted he could recognize me, so I remained still, hoping my nonchalance would avoid raising suspicion.

Bruce's quick thinking and calm demeanor seemed to pacify the situation, at least momentarily. I watched, ready to intervene if necessary, as the minister considered Bruce's words. The connection between our presence and the mysterious disappearances surrounding the stone house might yet remain concealed, but I knew we needed to tread carefully to avoid further entanglement with the king's men.

Just as the Minister of the Court's gaze settled on me, Bruce quickly intervened, calling out, "Henry, don't worry! These officers can surely guide us back!"

I mumbled in agreement. The Minister had taken a step toward me but then reconsidered, turning back to Bruce. "This area is a military restricted zone. You need to leave immediately!"

The mention of a restricted area piqued my interest. Bruce, continuing his act, questioned, "Military restricted area? There were no signs when we arrived."

The Minister's patience was visibly thinning. "I'm telling you now. Leave at once!"

Bruce grumbled his dissatisfaction but started heading toward our car. I joined him, catching up quickly. "You've got quite the talent," I whispered. "If the Minister recognized me, we'd be in a mess!"

Bruce nodded, "Did you notice there was more than one person in that car?"

I replied, "I saw someone—"

"He was sitting on the left side of the back seat," Bruce interrupted. "That's typically the owner's seat. Whoever it is, they're of higher status than the Minister. Who do you think it is?"

Keeping my voice low, I speculated, "The King?"

Bruce remained silent as we reached the jeep, climbed in, and drove off. The headlights from the other vehicle followed us until we were out of range.

As we drove, Bruce turned to me, "I'm certain the stone house with the statues was exactly where we were standing."

Surprised, I asked, "Why are you so sure?"

"Didn't you hear the Minister? He declared it a military restricted area because of the stone house. They don't want anyone near it," Bruce explained.

I chuckled, "But there's no stone house any longer. Why worry about people approaching?"

Bruce shook his head, "I don't know, but if the King was in that car, there's likely a secret involving him and Bain. There's a connection between the King and the stone house."

Although my thoughts were muddled, Bruce's reasoning resonated. I nodded in agreement. Bruce suggested, "We should split up. I'll continue searching for Bain and Flora in Kathmandu. And you—"

I immediately understood his implication and quickly interjected, "No, I won't go!"

Bruce sighed, acknowledging my decision. "Fine, if you won't go, then I must. I have to try. I feel like I can uncover something important there."

I observed Bruce, noting his keen intuition and ability to read people's thoughts—traits that seemed enhanced since his transformation. His confidence was almost unsettling, as if he believed his words were commands that couldn't be refused.

I had no reason to believe Bruce had been this way before. Typically, hippies like him and Randy were known for their laid-back, often aimless demeanor. Had Bruce's new form bestowed him with heightened intelligence and capability? Or was it something deeper within him, now unleashed?

Before I could ponder further, Bruce pressed me, "Isn't that right? Don't you agree?"

I considered his plan, then cautioned him, "Bruce, you understand that sneaking into the palace is no small feat. If you're caught, the consequences could be severe."

Bruce was unfazed, "If I'm caught, I'll request an audience with the king. I believe he harbors secrets. Knowing this, the worst he can do is expel me from the country."

I offered a wry smile, "The king is known to be a gentleman. But your approach—"

Bruce's words sliced through the air with a sudden vehemence. "I don't care. I want to go back! I'll do whatever it takes to return. I must go back!" His voice was a jagged edge, his clenched teeth and the bulging veins on his forehead testifying to an intensity that caught me off guard.

What startled me even more was the rapid transformation that followed. Realizing his outburst, Bruce swiftly masked his ferocity, adopting a disarmingly calm demeanor. His tone softened, almost pleading. "I really want to go back, you know, more than anything."

This sudden shift was jarring, leaving me unsettled. Bruce hoped his gentler approach would erase the impression of his earlier brusqueness. Yet, the speed of his change was more alarming than reassuring. His words betrayed a willingness to cast aside all scruples for the sake of "going back."

This didn't align with any conditions of "going back" that I understood. His yearning for eternal life, perhaps, drove his desperation. But the way he masked his ruthlessness hinted at something darker.

I quickly gathered my thoughts and offered a casual response, "I understand—" I paused, choosing my next words carefully. "In that case, perhaps I should go. I've been there twice and know the place well."

Bruce's eyes lit up with relief. "You're perfect for this. Go tonight! As soon as you have news, contact me at the hotel!"

As I prepared for the night's mission, I couldn't shake the feeling that Bruce's transformation was more than physical. His motivations, his sudden shifts in temperament, suggested a complexity I needed to understand. But first, there was the palace and the secrets it held, waiting to be uncovered.

I remained silent as the car continued its journey into the city. At a street corner, Bruce halted and gave me a meaningful look. I had to admit, my curiosity about the palace was growing. The sudden disappearance of the stone house, the designation of the area as a military restricted zone, the presence of the minister and potentially the king—it all hinted at a deeper mystery connecting the king to the ancient house.

Feeling a shared purpose rather than any coercion from Bruce, I stepped out of the car. "If all goes well, I'll be back before dawn," I assured him.

"Good luck," Bruce replied, waving as he drove off. Alone, I leaned against the corner, lighting a cigarette to calm my thoughts. Yet, despite the smoke, I couldn't shake the nagging feeling that something was amiss with Bruce.

After finishing my cigarette, I set off under the cover of darkness. An hour's walk brought me within sight of the palace's grand silhouette. Knowing a direct approach was impractical, I circled to find a less conspicuous entry point along the palace wall.

The high stone wall was intimidating but climbable, the uneven stones offering a makeshift ladder. Reaching the top, I surveyed the area. The palace grounds seemed surprisingly unguarded—perhaps due to Nepal's peaceful recent history, no one anticipated an intruder.

Moving through the shadows of the expansive palace buildings, I encountered no one. My goal was the king's study, a place I had visited twice before. Yet, navigating the vast network of corridors proved challenging. After wandering for half an hour, I paused in a particularly long, dimly lit corridor, attempting to orient myself.

Suddenly, I heard footsteps approaching. Instinctively, I pressed against a large pillar, its shadow enveloping me completely. I dared not peek out, acutely aware of the potential consequences if caught. The thought of ancient punishments—perhaps even beheading or amputation—crossed my mind, amplifying my caution.

Hidden behind the pillar, I listened intently, heart pounding. The footsteps grew louder, then paused nearby. Whoever it was seemed to hesitate, as if sensing something amiss. I held my breath, hoping the darkness would keep me concealed and that they would move on without noticing my presence.

I remained hidden behind the pillar, holding my breath as the footsteps drew nearer. Two individuals approached, their conversation gradually becoming audible. To my surprise, it was the king and the minister.

This corridor seemed remote, an unlikely place for such a significant meeting. I listened intently, ensuring my concealment. The king sighed, "Do you know who I most wish to see now?"

The minister replied, "I don't know, Your Majesty. If you wish to see someone, you can summon them."

The king sighed again, "This person—I want to see him, yet I fear it. Speaking with him is enjoyable, but his relentless pursuit of truth is unsettling to me. I don't know where he is now."

My heart skipped a beat. Was he talking about me?

The minister paused before speaking, "Your Majesty, are you referring to Ash Morris?"

The king's voice carried a hint of bitterness, "Yes, that's him."

Silence followed as they walked past me, their backs visible in the dim light. A strong urge to reveal myself surged within me, to step out and declare, "I'm here!"

Yet, I resisted. The king's tone suggested he harbored a significant secret. Those with secrets often yearn to share them, and perhaps he enjoyed our conversations because they danced around this secret. However, he seemed unwilling to fully disclose it. Meeting him now might only repeat past encounters, yielding little. It was wiser to observe and investigate from the shadows.

As they continued walking, the king remarked, "This item has been moved to the palace. Is he satisfied?"

Puzzled by this cryptic comment, I listened closely. The minister's response was scornful, "Humph, he's forgotten his ancestors' teachings. Money and wine are his only concerns now. He even sold ancestral antiques! I bet if someone offered 1,000 rupees, he'd sell the whole thing."

My heart raced as I connected the dots—the "person" they mentioned was Bain! But what was the "item" moved to the palace? My curiosity was piqued, and I knew I had to find out.

As I crouched behind the cold, marble pillar, my heart pounded like a ceremonial drum. Ahead, the king and his minister vanished around a shadowy corner. Seizing the moment, I slipped from my hiding spot, keeping close to the stone wall, footsteps echoing softly in the silent corridor. Reaching the corner, I peered around to see them paused before an imposing door. The minister, with a flourish, produced a key of considerable size, its metal glinting ominously in the dim light. He unlocked the door, ushering the king inside before following and sealing the entrance with a decisive click.

I stood before the door, the air thick with anticipation and the faint echoes of rhythmic footsteps resonating from the corridor's far end—guards, patrolling with metronomic precision. Pressing my ear against the door's ancient wood, I strained to catch any whisper of their conversation, but the barrier was resolute, betraying nothing.

The minutes ticked by, each one stretching longer than the last. Suddenly, the door handle turned with a metallic groan, and I melted into the shadows. The king emerged, a cloud of perplexity shadowing his regal features, while the minister locked the door with exaggerated solemnity. I stifled a laugh, knowing I could breach that lock in mere seconds with the simplest of tools.

The king's voice, tinged with frustration, sliced through the silence, "I truly don't understand. I am tempted to venture into the seven stone chambers and bring light to the deepest one to see what will happen."

His words struck me like a bolt of lightning. My suspicions were confirmed—the king was indeed aware of the enigmatic chambers' secrets. His decision to declare the area a military zone was no mere chance!

Yet, my astonishment paled in comparison to the minister's. His face blanched, hands trembling as he implored, "Your Majesty, you mustn't do that!"

The king's smile was rueful. "Do you know what happens if the bottom chamber is lit?"

"I don't know," the minister admitted, panic in his voice. "But such a prohibition must exist for a reason. Something extraordinary could occur. Your Majesty, forget this ever happened. No one knows about this. The patriarch is dead, and Bain is a fool. If neither of us speaks, the secret dies with us."

The king fixed the minister with a steady gaze. "You're wrong. There's another who knows—Ash Morris."

I couldn't help but smile bitterly at his error. Not only I but also Bruce and Flora were aware of the secret, having shared it with them.

The minister's panic was palpable, but the king simply walked on, the minister trailing behind. With their departure, I took a moment to steady myself. The conversation had revealed much. The old man Bain had killed in the mysterious stone chamber's depths was a patriarch, and Bain was the last of his line.

This revelation added urgency to my mission. With the king's interest in the chambers and the minister's fear, there was more at stake than I had imagined. I needed to uncover the truth behind the king's secret and the role Bain played in this unfolding mystery.

As I pondered the mysteries of the tribe, its relationship with the king, and why the king would protect Bain despite his actions, I deftly used a wire to pick the lock. Within moments, the door clicked open, and I stepped inside.

What I saw left me momentarily speechless. In the palace, of all places, stood the enigmatic object I'd first encountered in the mysterious stone house, revered like a sacred idol. The entire setup—the stone altar, incense, and candles—had been transplanted here. It was as if the stone house itself had been deconstructed and reassembled within these walls.

The cryptic conversation between the king and minister now made sense. "This item" referred to the mysterious object, and "he" was clearly Bain. The king had relocated the object to the palace, presumably to appease Bain or for reasons yet unknown. This explained the absence of the stone house; it had been dismantled by royal decree, leaving no trace.

The thoroughness of the demolition—leaving no sign above ground—was beyond the capabilities of ordinary villagers. Yet, the king's comments about the seven underground chambers suggested they remained intact, still shrouded in their ancient secrets.

I lingered beside the object, absorbing its presence for about thirty minutes. The first time I saw it, its nature eluded me. But now, with the insights gained from Bruce's dreams and other revelations, I began to understand.

Though revered as a "god statue," the object resembled a component of an intricate machine. Perhaps it was part of a vehicle—a car, a spaceship, or something else entirely. It appeared heavily damaged, as if struck by a tremendous force.

I examined a metal sphere on the object, which seemed to rotate freely, akin to a spherical wheel. Could this be a piece of a spaceship? Was this "spaceship" related to the "recording instrument" Bruce mentioned Bain had sold him? Could it have originated from a distant, unknown planet, possibly the ancestral home of humanity? Were our forebears exiled to Earth, stripped of immortality as punishment for a crime?

These questions swirled in my mind, tantalizing yet unanswered. The connections were tantalizing but elusive, leaving me with a mix of excitement and frustration. The truth lay tantalizingly close, yet just out of reach, waiting to be uncovered through further exploration and understanding.

As I stood in the room, grappling with the dilemma of what to do next, the weight of my discovery pressed heavily on my mind. Should I inform Bruce about the mysterious object? If I did, I was certain he would insist on returning to the original site of the stone house to explore the seven-story underground chamber without delay.

There was a strange certainty in my prediction, fueled by Bruce's recent behavior. He had become increasingly assertive, almost single-minded, in his desire to "go back." His actions seemed driven by this singular purpose, regardless of the consequences. I couldn't help but feel uneasy about his newfound determination, wondering if he would stop at nothing to achieve his goal.

Bruce's attitude troubled me, and I feared that following his lead might inadvertently harm the king. The king, burdened with his own secrets and struggles, was entitled to keep them. By pursuing our investigation, Bruce and I risked violating that right to privacy.

Unsure of the best course of action, I lingered in the room, contemplating my options. Ultimately, I resolved to leave the palace and seek out Flora. Together, we could discuss the situation and decide on the next steps.

As I prepared to depart, I glanced one last time at the enigmatic object. The king's words echoed in my mind: "I really don't know what happened!" His uncertainty mirrored my own, and for a moment, I felt a kinship with him in our shared confusion.

Quietly, I retraced my steps, leaving the room and the palace behind. My thoughts were a whirlwind of questions and possibilities, and I hoped that with Flora's guidance, we could unravel the mysteries that had brought us to this juncture.

I carefully locked the door behind me, retracing my steps through the palace corridors. Navigating the familiar path, I climbed the wall again, making my escape without detection. As I put distance between myself and the palace, a sense of relief washed over me. But my reprieve was short-lived, interrupted by a chilling cry piercing the night.

The cry, echoing through the stillness, sounded eerily like Bain. I turned toward the source, my heart pounding with uncertainty. Listening intently, I hoped for more clues to explain the situation, but only silence followed. Driven by urgency, I ran toward the cry, rounding corners until I heard the sound of labored breathing.

Cautiously, I approached the source, and there stood Bain. He was visibly terrified, clutching his bleeding shoulder. His fear, however, was not from the injury but from the knife poised at his throat, its blade gleaming ominously in the darkness.

The sight was shocking enough, but the identity of the knife's wielder stunned me further—it was Bruce.

Bruce's expression was unrecognizable, a mask of ferocity and menace, a stark contrast to the person I thought I knew. In Nepal, there was no mistaking the man with red and black tattoos on his face. But what had driven him to this point? Why was he threatening Bain?

I clenched my fists, ready to intervene, when Bruce's harsh voice cut through the air. "You don't recognize me? I want another antique you sold before. You must find it for me!"

Bain's voice was a quivering whisper, "I—I can't find it. That place is sealed. I've sold everything—all of it!"

Bruce's grip on the knife tightened, his voice laced with venom. "No, I must have it. If you don't give it to me, I'll kill you!"

Desperation colored Bain's reply, "You can't kill me! I'm protected by the king!"

Bruce's laughter was chilling. "I don't care about the king! If I can't achieve my goal, I'll kill him too!"

The scene before me was surreal. Bruce's transformation was complete—he was the embodiment of malice, more malevolent than anyone I'd encountered before. I had sensed something off about Bruce, but never imagined it would escalate to this.

The shock of Bruce's actions mirrored Bain's terror. This was a side of Bruce I hadn't foreseen, and the full extent of his obsession with "going back" was laid bare. I needed to act, to stop Bruce before he did something irrevocable, but I also had to understand—what had driven him to this breaking point?

Just as I was processing the unsettling scene with Bruce and Bain, I heard footsteps and a familiar voice calling, "Bruce!" It was Flora. Her sudden presence added another layer of complexity to the situation. My mind raced, debating whether it was safe for her to encounter Bruce in his current state.

To my astonishment, Bruce reacted with swift efficiency. He struck Bain's head with the handle of the knife, rendering him unconscious, then swiftly dragged Bain into a nearby alley, concealing him from view. By the time he emerged, he had transformed his demeanor entirely, tucking away the knife and adopting an innocuous expression.

The change was startling. Moments ago, Bruce exuded pure malice, but now he appeared as his usual self—honest and approachable. It was as if the malevolent figure I'd just witnessed was a mere illusion. His ability to mask his intentions so effectively was both impressive and deeply unsettling.

I've long believed that the greatest threat is not overt evil, but evil that conceals itself beneath a facade of goodness. When malevolence is hidden behind a guise of loyalty, it becomes truly dangerous, striking when least expected. At that moment, Bruce embodied this chilling concept of hidden evil.

As Flora approached Bruce, my concern mounted. I feared for her safety, worried that Bruce might harm her as he had Bain. Without thinking, I called out, "Bruce!" and hurried towards them.

My shout caused Bruce to spin around, his surprise evident before he quickly regained composure. Flora ran to me, smiling, and I took her hand protectively. Bruce, with a seemingly innocent demeanor, asked, "You—how long have you been here?"

Feigning ignorance of the earlier confrontation, I replied, "I just arrived. How did you find Flora?"

Bruce explained, "She was already at the hotel when I returned."

Turning to Flora, I questioned her delay in joining us, "Why did it take you four days to meet us? Do you have a reasonable explanation?"

Flora chuckled, "Of course, but it's a long story!"

Bruce, maintaining his facade, appeared eager for news, asking, "Did you find anything when you went to the palace?"

I hesitated, unsure how much to reveal. The encounter with Bruce had rattled me, and I needed time to think through my next steps. However, for now, I decided to keep my discoveries close, uncertain of Bruce's true intentions and wary of his potential for duplicity.

# CHAPTER 10

# HE THAT IS WITHOUT

# SIN AMONG YOU —

I was caught in a web of deception, trying to navigate the intricate dynamics between Bruce, Flora, and Bain. My initial impulse was to share my findings from the palace, but I quickly decided against it. Instead, I feigned anger, "Why don't you ask about my harrowing escape from guards and wolfhounds in the palace?"

Bruce seemed taken aback, momentarily silent, while Flora suggested, "Let's discuss it back at the hotel. Bruce, did you find Bain?"

Bruce, without glancing at the alley, replied, "No, you two head back. I need to continue searching for him."

Having witnessed Bruce deftly incapacitate Bain and discreetly drag him into the alley, I marveled at the elegance of his deception. I suspected that Bruce had plans to extract further information from Bain once we were safely away. With this in mind, I swiftly crafted a plan of my own, masking my intentions with feigned enthusiasm. "Do you know where Bain is? Let me help you find him!" I offered, injecting urgency into my voice.

Bruce dismissed my offer, "No need, I'll find him easily enough at midnight. I'll bring him to the hotel."

Smiling as if nothing was amiss, I quipped, "Be careful, you look quite intimidating as an Red Indian!"

Bruce shrugged, feigning helplessness, "It's fine. Bain's never seen an Red Indian before."

Flora seemed ready to protest, but I gently pulled her away, leading her in the direction she came from. We turned a corner, and Flora's questioning glance met mine. I gestured for silence, leading her to another corner where I whispered, "I want to show you something."

Though still puzzled, Flora followed without protest. We approached the opposite end of the alley where Bruce had taken Bain. I whispered again, "Be quiet and careful," pointing to the alley.

In the dim light, we saw Bruce pressing Bain against the wall. Bain's voice, filled with confusion and fear, echoed softly, "Why do you want to kill me? I don't even know you!"

Bruce's reply was chilling, "I am Bruce! The one with Randy! Remember the antique you sold us?"

Bain's exclamation was abruptly cut off, likely by Bruce's intervention. Bain then gasped, bewildered, "Why have you—changed?"

Bruce's voice was as unyielding as before, "Your antique caused this. I want another. How many do you have? Where are they? Tell me, or I'll kill you!"

Even under threat, Bain muttered incoherently, his words mostly lost to the distance. But I caught fragments: "That's true! That's true!" His voice then rose in a mix of disbelief and horror, "Are you—already dead?"

The situation was spiraling, with Bruce's desperation driving him to extremes, and Bain's cryptic response hinting at deeper mysteries. I had to tread carefully, balancing between intervening and uncovering the truth hidden within this tangled web.

Bruce's temper flared, and Bain's choking sound echoed in the alley as Bruce's grip tightened around his neck. At that moment, Flora impulsively stepped forward. Alarmed, I quickly pulled her back, retreating to avoid detection. Our slight commotion caught Bruce's attention, and he shouted, "Who? Who's there?"

I swiftly guided Flora behind a protruding stone pillar, holding my breath as Bruce emerged, knife in hand, scanning the area with a menacing glare. His demeanor was terrifying, a stark contrast to the friend we thought we knew.

After a tense moment of searching, Bruce, unable to spot us, returned to the alley. Flora, bewildered, whispered, "Oh my god, who was that just now?"

I replied gravely, "It was Bruce—the same Bruce we're familiar with."

Flora, eyes wide with disbelief, asked, "Did you know he was like this?"

I shook my head, "I only realized it recently, just like you."

Her concern deepened, "He might kill Bain!"

I sighed, "Let's head back to the hotel. I doubt he'll kill Bain right away. He needs information, and Bain holds those secrets. Without them, Bruce won't eliminate him. Let's return and discuss this in a safer environment."

Flora questioned my urgency, "Why the rush to the hotel?"

With a bitter smile, I admitted, "I'm overwhelmed. I need to clear my head, and we need a place to talk without interruptions."

We made our way out, staying silent until we were a safe distance away. Then, I revealed, "Randy committed suicide in the mental hospital."

Flora's reaction was immediate, her eyes wide with shock. I continued, "It's devastating. I feel responsible. But the doctors said he seemed calm, smiling even, and left four words on the wall that they couldn't understand. But we know what Randy meant. He wrote: 'I am going back.'"

Flora gasped, looking skyward as if searching for answers in the stars. The weight of Randy's final message hung heavily between us, hinting at a deeper, more unsettling truth. It seemed that both Randy and Bruce were caught in the grip of something beyond our current understanding, compelling us to uncover the full scope of this mysterious connection.

As Flora and I gazed up at the vast, star-filled sky, I understood her silent query: which of those distant stars might Randy now inhabit? The thought was both comforting and bewildering.

After a quiet moment, Flora voiced her thoughts, "Did Randy really go back?"

"I'd like to think so," I replied, spreading my hands.

"How did he manage it?" Flora wondered aloud. "Did he use some kind of instrument? What method allowed him to return?"

I shook my head, unsure. "I don't know, but I doubt he used the same means as Bruce."

We continued walking in silence, burdened by the weight of our thoughts. Back at the hotel, after two glasses of wine, Flora spoke again, suggesting we discuss Bruce first.

"Alright,"I nodded, gauging her reaction. "You've just seen it. What impression did Bruce leave on you?"

Flora pondered for a moment, her eyes narrowing as if recalling a long-buried memory. "It feels like the essence of evil itself," she finally declared. Her words hung heavy in the air, and she paused, letting the weight of her statement settle. A bitter smile tugged at her lips. "If the malevolence displayed by Bruce is indeed a legacy from our ancestors, then perhaps it's no mystery why they were exiled to Earth."

I opened my mouth to respond, but Flora was quicker, her voice slicing through the silence. "In truth, we have no right to condemn Bruce—" Her laughter, a string of sorrowful notes, echoed with a harsh truth. "He that is without sin among you, let him first cast a stone at her," she quoted, the weight of her words hanging heavily in the air.

As her gaze met mine, a reluctant smile mirrored her own. The 'dream' of Randy and Bruce was one I struggled to embrace. Yet, if I dared to delve deeper, the truth was inescapable: Earth's evils were the handiwork of humankind, distinct from any other creature that roamed its surface. Acceptance was inevitable; the legacy of those 'dreams' was ours to bear. Earthlings, heirs to ancient wickedness, carried within them the seeds of malevolence, ever sprouting, ever spreading. Evil, it seemed, was the cornerstone of our nature, the architect of our actions.

I tapped my forehead thoughtfully. "Do you think Bruce was always like this, or did something change him?"

Flora sighed, "I believe we all have this potential. Our ancestors were like this, and it's passed down, worsening over time."

I challenged, "Does that mean education is pointless?"

Flora chuckled, a hint of rebellion in her voice. "Why do you think education exists? Since humans developed writing, we've promoted morality. Why?"

Before I could answer, she continued, "Because we lack it inherently. We must constantly reinforce it."

I felt the debate was futile and shifted focus. "Let's set this aside. What have you been doing these past four days?"

Flora paced, sipped her wine, and sat again. "I intended to come straight to the hotel from the airport, and I did. But as soon as I entered the lobby and before I could check in, I ran into Bain."

I was curious about Flora's encounter with Bain, especially since she had never met him before. "Oh, you haven't seen him before; how did you recognize him so quickly?" I asked.

Flora smiled, a hint of mischief in her eyes, and explained, "It was simple. As soon as I entered, Bain approached me, saying, 'Miss, welcome to Nepal. Are you interested in buying a unique Nepalese antique? It's a once-in-a-lifetime opportunity!'"

I responded with surprise, "So Bain really had that—thing?"

Flora continued, "When a Nepalese man said that to me, and considering your description, I was certain it was Bain. I didn't reveal I knew his trick, though. Instead, I played along, pretending to be interested in antiques while wary of being duped. Bain swore to his sincerity, and I seized the opportunity, asking him to show me the antiques."

I eagerly inquired, "So you obtained another—one like Bruce's?"

Flora lifted her eyebrows, "It's slightly different, but essentially the same, and I believe it functions identically."

I jumped up, agitation rising within me, "Does Bruce know?"

Flora shook her head, "No, I haven't told him."

I sank into my chair, Flora's words echoing hauntingly in my mind: "He that is without sin among you, let him first cast a stone at her." It was a reminder as old as time, yet as piercing as a freshly sharpened blade. Flora, ever resourceful, had procured a "recorder," but she wielded it with the precision of a seasoned tactician, her ploy hidden in plain sight, shielded from Bruce's unsuspecting gaze. The layers of deception were as intricate as a masterfully woven tapestry, each thread a testament to her cunning.

"Where is it?" I asked, curiosity piqued.

Flora discreetly glanced at the door, then opened a suitcase, lifting a layer of clothes to reveal the "recorder." Though it differed slightly in appearance from the one we'd seen with Randy, its structure was identical.

I took a deep breath, trying to steady the whirlwind of thoughts swirling in my mind. "So, if you rest your head on this device and drift off, you can experience a 'dream'?" I asked, the curiosity in my voice undeniable.

Flora nodded, her expression thoughtful. "It should work that way."

"Why do you say 'should'? You've had it for days now, haven't you tried it?" I pressed, intrigued by the mystery of it all.

She shook her head, surprising me. "No, I just got it today. You didn't hear the story of how it came into my possession. Plus, I want to share this 'dream' with you. I didn't want to experience it alone."

Her words lingered in the air, and I paused to consider them. "Alright, let's decide when to use it later. For now, keep it hidden." My voice trailed off, a pang of guilt gnawing at my conscience. Here we were, Flora, Bruce, and I, all in pursuit of this elusive object. Now that it was in our grasp, the instinct to conceal it from Bruce was overpowering.

Though I rationalized it—Bruce had transformed into something inscrutable, the very image of malevolence—I couldn't shake the self-doubt that whispered insidiously: Had Bruce remained unchanged, would I still have chosen secrecy?

Flora seemed to read my thoughts, her agreement swift and certain. "Yes, let's not let Bruce know," she said, her voice a quiet echo of my own resolve.

Our decision was driven by caution and self-preservation, but it also highlighted the complexities of trust and morality in our quest. As the night deepened, the weight of our secrets loomed large, and the potential of the "recorder" promised both revelations and challenges ahead.

As Flora and I exchanged glances, a silent understanding passed between us. The shame of our decision lingered in our eyes, yet it wasn't enough to sway us from our course of action. Flora quickly returned the "recorder" to its hiding place, eager to shift the conversation and dispel the awkwardness. She launched into a recounting of her encounter with Bain, detailing her experiences over the past four days, though she focused on the most pertinent details to our investigation.

Flora and Bain had exchanged only a few words before Bain eagerly offered to carry her suitcase, insisting, "Let's go see it now. If we wait, you'll miss your chance! But first, we need a car."

Flora reassured him, "No problem. I rented a car at the airport, and it's still parked outside."

Bain's excitement was palpable, as if he'd just secured a windfall. They exited the hotel and climbed into the car, with Flora at the wheel and Bain directing the route.

As Flora described the journey, I realized she was taken to the location of the enigmatic stone house, which the king had since demolished. They traveled through the afternoon, arriving at their destination under the cover of darkness. The stone house was gone, but large stones were neatly stacked, ready for transport, and a substantial object, meticulously wrapped, was being loaded onto a truck—the same mysterious object I later saw in the palace.

The area was heavily guarded by soldiers, preventing civilian access. However, Bain confidently approached them, proclaiming, "It's me! Look closely, it's me!" To Flora's bewilderment, his words worked. An officer approached, assessed Bain, and allowed them through.

Bain, brimming with pride, declared, "See, Miss? This ancient building is being taken down. It was the oldest and most mysterious structure in Nepal!"

Flora observed the precision with which the granite was dismantled, marveling at the craftsmanship. She pondered whether such intricate work could have been achieved by ancient Nepalese artisans. Yet, despite her curiosity, she refrained from questioning Bain further, suspecting she might know more about the stone house than he did.

Casually, she remarked, "Such an ancient building must hold genuine antiques."

Bain's laughter was buoyant, "Of course! So, naturally, the price might be steep. With the house gone, these antiques won't surface again!"

Flora reassured him, "Don't worry about the cost. Here's a thousand dollars as a start."

She handed Bain the money, watching as he danced with joy on the car seat, his excitement overflowing. Bain became even more talkative, fueled by his elation. "This house, small as it was, belonged to me. It was passed down from my tribe, but I'm the last of them, so it's mine alone! I hold the only key to the basement."

As Bain spoke, he pulled out a greasy, worn rope from around his neck, revealing a round iron plate at the end. The plate was about an inch in diameter and half an inch thick, inscribed with shallow interlaced stripes. When Flora saw it, her heart skipped a beat. If this was indeed the "key" Bain claimed it to be, it was no ordinary key. Flora immediately recognized it as a high-end magnetic lock key.

(Later, when Flora recounted this story to me, she showed me the key she'd bought from Bain, and I shared her assessment of its significance.)

The car skidded to a halt in front of the former site of the enigmatic stone house just as Bain revealed the "key" to Flora. The ground, once home to the mysterious structure, was now sealed off, with only a narrow, two-foot square opening remaining, through which a worker was busy pouring cement. Bain leapt from the vehicle, his voice cutting through the air with urgency, "Wait a minute! Wait a minute!"

A senior officer approached, his demeanor a mix of impatience and begrudging respect for Bain. "What's the matter?" he asked, trying to mask his irritation.

Gasping for breath, Bain gestured emphatically toward the square hole. "I need to go back down. There's something I need to retrieve!"

The officer hesitated, "I haven't received any instructions like that. My orders were—"

Before he could finish, Bain had placed a firm hand on his shoulder, leaning in to whisper something. The officer's resistance melted away, and he nodded, allowing Bain's hand to linger as they stepped aside for a private conversation.

They retreated a dozen paces, their exchange cloaked in secrecy, before Bain discreetly handed the officer something—perhaps an artifact or a token of persuasion. Whatever it was, it had the desired effect, and they returned together.

Bain turned to Flora with a determined look. "Wait here. I'll be back shortly. You'll see me bring the antique up with your own eyes, but you must promise not to reveal how you acquired it!"

Flora, her curiosity piqued, insisted, "I want to go down with you!"

Bain's resolve was unyielding. "No. Outsiders are strictly forbidden in this sanctuary."

Fora's lips curved into a sly smile. "No outsider has ever entered?"

His expression turned grave. "Since the Buddha and the seven venerable ones graced this temple, none but our clan have crossed its threshold."

She had been ready to mock this claim, aware of my prior visit and Bain's knowledge of it. But his words struck a chord. "What did you say? Buddha?"

Bain hesitated under her piercing gaze, visibly uneasy. "Legend speaks of Buddha and his seven disciples visiting this temple, entrusting it to our forebears with a decree that no outsider shall enter."

Flora, her mind a whirl of questions, reluctantly relented. Bain exhaled in relief, disappearing into the depths of the hole. Meanwhile, the senior officer rallied his men, cautioning them to keep Flora and Bain's presence a secret.

In mere minutes, Bain emerged, clutching an iron box tightly under his arm. He placed it carefully beside Flora, who immediately attempted to open it, her fingers searching for a latch that wouldn't budge. Bain joined her, his frustration mounting as they struggled in vain. "The antiquities must be inside. They must be. Look at how heavy this iron box is!"

Flora teased, "Or it could just be a massive stone inside."

Deflated but undeterred, Bain sighed, "I'll go back and try to find another one."

Flora cautiously asked Bain, "Is there more?"

Bain hesitated, "I'm not sure, but there should be more!"

However, when Bain turned back to the site, he realized the hole had already been sealed with cement. Despite his earnest discussions with the senior officer, the officer remained resolute, merely shaking his head. Bain returned to the car, visibly disheartened.

Flora proposed a solution, "Let's do this: I'll try to open the box. If it truly contains antiques, I'll give you another thousand dollars. If not, or if the box can't be opened, you keep the money, and I'll buy the iron box and key from you."

Bain, relieved at the prospect of not having to return the money, agreed eagerly. He handed the key to Flora, who then drove away, making a mental note of the stone house location.

As they departed, Flora noticed soldiers completing the stone house's concealment. They spread sand and soil over the site and placed stones atop it, ensuring the stone house's erasure from the landscape.

(This explained why I later found no trace of the stone house—it was a deliberate effort by the army to erase its existence.)

While driving, Flora queried Bain, "Your tribe seems connected to the king. Is the king part of your tribe?"

Bain, without questioning how Flora knew, puffed up with pride, "Yes! Our tribe is noble. When Buddha entrusted my ancestors with the temple's care, he promised that the King of Nepal would always protect us. Each new king is told of this promise by the previous king, and they all honor it."

Flora made a grave mistake by commenting, "So that's why, even though you killed an elder in your tribe, the king protected you from punishment!"

Bain reacted violently, screaming in shock. His mistake was underestimating Flora, thinking he could easily overpower her. In his panic, he swung a punch at her head.

Flora, maintaining control of the steering wheel with her right hand, deftly caught Bain's fist with her left, squeezing hard. Bain's fingers audibly creaked under the pressure, and he howled in agony.

Glaring at him, Flora asked icily, "What are you trying to do?"

Bain, terrified, pleaded, "Let me go—I won't try anything again!"

Flora pressed further, "Answer my questions properly."

Bain, desperate, replied, "Of course, just let me go first!"

Flora released his hand, and Bain cradled it painfully, nearly stuffing it into his mouth in an attempt to soothe the ache.

Flora was thrilled by the potential wealth of information Bain represented. He was clearly at the center of the mysterious events unfolding around them, and she felt confident she could extract more insights from him.

Bain, however, was visibly uncomfortable, his fear apparent as Flora began her interrogation, "Okay, now I ask, and you answer!"

He turned, his discomfort growing. Flora asked, "The place you descended into, it has seven levels, right?"

Bain visibly flinched, startled by her knowledge. Flora smirked, "I know a lot, even about the clansman you killed in the bottom stone chamber!"

Bain trembled, his body betraying his anxiety. Flora, unaware of any ulterior motives he might have, pressed on, "What is in each of these seven layers of stone chambers? And why in the last chamber—"

Before she could finish, Bain shouted, grabbed something, flung open the car door, and rolled out onto the road. Flora stopped the car and leaped out, but Bain was already sprinting, swiftly gaining distance. Despite her best efforts, Bain, familiar with the terrain, disappeared into the bushes, leaving Flora behind, frustrated and alone.

Desperate, Flora called out, promising Bain she wouldn't ask any more questions if he returned. But her pleas went unanswered. Resigned, she returned to the car and drove to a nearby village. There, the hospitable locals offered her hot tea, and she spent the night in her vehicle.

Over the next four days, Flora searched tirelessly for Bain, scouring villages for any sign of him. Though she found no trace of Bain, she uncovered details about him and his tribe. Known as the "Nigedila Tribe," meaning "unique tribe," they were said to have little interest in marriage or children, making their numbers few and their customs mysterious.

An elderly villager recounted tales of the tribe's past. In his youth, the tribe had over a hundred members, but a large group—eighty or ninety—once ventured to the perilous "Tianmu Peak" and never returned. The peak, known for its treacherous climbs, had claimed them, and their journey was seen as a doomed expedition.

With their numbers dwindling, only two tribe members remained, and now, according to the villager, none. Bain's prolonged stay in Kathmandu, avoiding the countryside, seemed to mark the end of their lineage. The tribe's unique traits and enigmatic history remained largely unexplained, even by the oldest locals.

Flora's journey had brought more questions than answers, but the information she gathered painted a vivid picture of a tribe shrouded in mystery—a puzzle awaiting further exploration.

# CHAPTER 11

# THE THIRD STRANGE DREAM

The villagers knew of the stone house and its mysterious seven-story stone chamber underneath, but a strange aura kept them at bay. Legends spoke of a bizarre statue within, once a blazing fireball, but Flora dismissed such tales. After four fruitless days searching for Bain, she returned to Kathmandu.

Upon reaching the hotel, she learned of my and Bruce's arrival but had no idea where we were. After resting, she wandered the streets, where she stumbled upon a group of tourists captivated by someone loudly promoting a "real antique." Recognizing Bain immediately, Flora approached him, seizing his arm, and declared, "As far as I know, you sold this antique to me a long time ago!"

Bain, caught off guard, turned with a look that made Flora laugh in recollection. Though she didn't detail his expression, it was clear it was priceless.

Bain relented, handing over the "antique" and the key to Flora. Meanwhile, Bruce and I had separated earlier, with Bruce returning to the hotel first. There, he encountered Flora, who chose not to reveal her acquisition of the antique. Instead, she mentioned seeing Bain on the street.

Intent on finding Bain, Bruce rushed out, with Flora trailing behind. However, Bruce vanished into the bustling streets. Flora was unsure how he tracked down Bain, but she persistently searched for them. Eventually, she heard voices, leading her to Bruce, where I soon joined them.

Even after Flora recounted her tale, Bruce was still missing. We waited for nearly an hour, yet he didn't return. Concerned, Flora speculated, "Where do you think Bruce went? Did he kill Bain and flee?"

I shook my head, "No, he needs Bain for secrets. He wouldn't kill him, especially not knowing we have the 'antique.'" I paused, pondering aloud, "Strangely, why didn't Bain mention the 'antique' being in your possession to him?"

Flora smiled, "Bain doesn't know my identity or our connection. He likely thought he sold it to an odd tourist. If he mentioned it, Bruce might press him to find me, which he couldn't. Better to stay silent."

Her reasoning made sense. I stood, a realization dawning, "I know where he is! He must have forced Bain to the stone house!"

Flora was taken aback, "It's possible! But—Bain's key is here. Without it, entry is impossible, according to him."

I pondered, "Not even one floor?"

Flora expressed concern about the potential danger Bruce and Bain might face if they attempted to access the stone house. "I don't know the details," she began, "but with the buildings demolished and the entrance sealed with reinforced concrete, it won't be easy to break through. Plus, it's a military restricted area. If they go there, they could be in serious trouble."

There was a subtle undertone to her words that made me wonder if she was a bit pleased at the thought of Bruce facing difficulty. Despite this, I couldn't help but feel a sense of loyalty towards him. "I really don't want Bruce to get into trouble," I admitted. "After all, we're companions. And he wants so desperately to return..."

Flora interrupted with a skeptical laugh. "Given Bruce's current state, do you think that place would welcome him back?"

Her point hit me hard. If Earth's ancestors were indeed exiled here due to their sins, Bruce's present condition suggested he might never be able to return, regardless of his efforts.

Taking a deep breath, I proposed, "Waiting here doesn't seem wise. We should either go find him or stop waiting altogether. I'm eager to experience the dream that Bruce and Randy had."

Flora agreed, nodding with a shared sense of urgency. With palpable tension in the air, she opened the box and placed the "recorder" on the ground. We exchanged a glance, then I lifted the lid to reveal two concave dents resembling comfortable headrests.

Without speaking, we lay down, mimicking the positions Bruce and Randy had used, with our heads nestled against the dents—my feet pointing east, Flora's pointing west.

We closed our eyes, eagerly anticipating the dream's onset. Yet, nothing happened. Neither of us felt sleepy, and after half an hour, we opened our eyes, disappointment evident.

"Did you dream about anything?" Flora's voice broke the silence.

I responded with a bitter smile. "Nothing. What about you?"

She shook her head, her expression mirroring my disappointment. "Perhaps we're not actually asleep," I mused aloud. "Maybe the recorder requires us to be in a true sleep state to interact with our brain cells."

"Maybe," Flora sighed, her brow furrowing as she contemplated the enigmatic nature of sleep. "It's strange, isn't it? Almost everyone dreams, yet scientists still can't fully explain what dreams are. Even the most mundane dreams remain a mystery."

The puzzle of sleep and dreams hung between us, a tantalizing enigma wrapped in the fabric of science and the unknown.

I sighed deeply, my interest in any other topic completely eclipsed. My mind was singularly focused on the impending arrival of the "dream."

I attempted self-hypnosis, weaving tendrils of calm through my thoughts, suspecting Flora was doing the same. Despite my exhaustion, a peculiar sense of purpose thrummed within me, keeping my nerves taut like a bowstring. I lay there for half an hour, but sleep remained stubbornly out of reach.

The mystery of what lay ahead only deepened the suspense, each passing minute a puzzle piece in the grand design of our quest.

Gradually, as my tension ebbed away, the veil of consciousness lifted, and I drifted into a "dream". I use quotation marks for "dream" because what I encountered was far from ordinary. Had I not been forewarned about the nature of this strange dream, I might have dismissed it as just another nocturnal reverie—unless, of course, it recurred frequently.

But knowing what I did, I entered the dream with a heightened awareness, feeling almost awake within it. It's difficult to describe, but the vividness of the dream was such that I remembered every detail, every word spoken, with absolute clarity. Later, I could verify each part with Flora, without a single discrepancy. In this "dream," I was a conscious observer.

I didn't participate in the dream's events; rather, I observed and listened, akin to watching a television program. I could perceive everything, yet I couldn't interact or communicate with the scenes unfolding before me.

Experiencing this dream firsthand revealed the extraordinary and indescribable nature of it. It also affirmed Bruce's assertion that the "antique" was indeed a kind of recorder, capturing not just audio or visual elements, but an immersive experience that engaged the mind at a deeper level. It allowed one to feel as though they were present at the recorded events.

Despite my attempts to articulate the essence of this dream, words fall short. Let me recount what transpired in my dream.

As I entered the dream, I found myself in a room bathed in soft, gentle light. I recognized it as the same room Bruce and Randy had mentioned, though what I witnessed differed significantly from their accounts.

The room was filled with people, their images indistinct, yet each wore a white robe and had long, dark hair. The contrast between their hair and robes, coupled with the ethereal lighting, etched a lasting impression in my mind.

The door opened, and several individuals entered. Instantly, someone exclaimed, "Welcome! Welcome, you are finally back!"

It appeared four people had entered, and the existing occupants eagerly approached to greet them. The newcomers silently took their seats.

I must note that the first words I heard imparted a curious sensation. It was as though I "felt" the words rather than heard them in the traditional sense. Later, Flora and I pondered whether the sounds truly reached our ears or if they resonated within our minds.

This dream, with its surreal clarity and immersive quality, defied conventional understanding, leaving me both bewildered and intrigued by the mysteries it hinted at.

As the four individuals settled into their seats, the initial voice offered reassurance: "Don't be sad, failure is expected."

One of the newcomers questioned softly, "Failure to this extent?"

Silence enveloped the room briefly before the first voice spoke again: "It can't be said to be a complete failure. At least you have helped them understand why they are there and what they must do to return."

Upon hearing this exchange, it struck me that the first speaker might be the leader from Bruce and Randy's dream. The four newcomers seemed to be the "volunteers." Had they returned safely? Yet, their discussion of failure was puzzling.

The room grew quiet once more until one of the four shared their experience, "Before going, I couldn't have imagined the situation would be like that. They look just like us, yet—I couldn't believe they were our kin. I was overwhelmed by the burden, Father. I even begged not to bear such a weight on my shoulders!"

Another voice interjected with empathy: "I heard your plea through the communication device, yet you volunteered wholeheartedly! Didn't your remarkable skills impress them?"

One of the four replied with a bitter smile, "I'm not certain. I confess I don't grasp their thoughts. Once they learned the origin, their sole wish was to return. It's as if they are driven by genetic factors, much like small creatures they call insects. Their existence seems dictated by these genetic impulses!"

The leader chuckled, "At least they learned to communicate with us!"

Another from the quartet joined in with a laugh, "Yes, they mimicked the form of communication. They observed me speaking with you, unaware of the intercom I used, and emulated the gesture: closing their eyes and raising their hands. Of course, their voices couldn't reach us!"

The leader inquired further, "What about the time ratio?"

One of the four, whom I suspected was C, responded: "I observed it to be approximately one to fifty thousand."

A group discussion ensued, and someone remarked, "One to fifty thousand!"

Another voice, likely D, confirmed, "Yes, their lives are fleeting. I tried to convey this to them, though it's uncertain how many grasped it. One to fifty thousand—their entire lifespan equates to just a day here!"

The leader sighed, "Thankfully it's so, otherwise, given their malevolence, a longer lifespan would be catastrophic."

A, among the four, voiced his anger. "But actually, it makes no difference. Each generation there, spanning forty to sixty years, grows more wicked. I can't fathom where it will lead!"

Silence fell once more. B, among the four, released a long sigh and reflected: "They fail to

that brief span, they endure pain, experiment with methods, resort to evil, and struggle—or as they say, fight. Few willingly abandon everything to swiftly traverse the sea of suffering to reach the shore of happiness."

The leader remarked, "Regardless, each of you has brought back at least a few individuals with unquestionable potential. This is a significant achievement, not a failure."

A responded with a smile, "Are you comforting us?"

The leader asserted with conviction, "Absolutely not, this is the truth!" After a brief pause, he posed a question, "Are you willing to go again?"

The four seemed to exchange silent glances and gestures. C shook his head, expressing a dire warning, "I told them if they continue this path, I'll return with destructive power to eradicate all evil."

B sighed, countering, "That opposes our original mission—we set out to save them."

A's voice, rough and resolute, declared, "Save those worth saving; destroy those who aren't."

D spread his hands, offering a different perspective. "Leave them to their own devices and let them find their own way. I trust the impact we've left is significant. It's up to them to awaken."

His words carried a sense of resignation and hope, a belief that the seeds of change had been sown, and it was now up to them to grow. The balance of intervention and autonomy hung delicately in the air, a timeless struggle for every society.

A quiet lull settled over the room, filled with low murmurs as attendees exchanged thoughts. Then, the leader spoke once more, "Given the vast time disparity, we should wait. For now, we must record your experiences. Someone must return and come back quickly."

B volunteered, rising to the occasion, "I'll go. I'll choose a secluded spot to leave the items I've brought. Perhaps, in time, the truth we've shared might become distorted. I hope these items will help someone uncover the truth."

A sneered, skeptical of the notion of truth, "Truth? During my time there, I found nothing but deception. The people don't seek truth at all!"

B remained steadfast, "Regardless, we must fulfill our duty!" As he stood and paced, I sensed his tall stature beneath a loose robe.

As B walked, he proposed, "I can arrange for someone from there to return here. Whoever they are, let them come so we can observe closely. Do you agree?"

After some deliberation, the leader approved, "That's feasible. Arrange it at your discretion."

With a sense of camaraderie, B raised his hands, prompting the others to approach, embracing him gently and patting his back—an apparent gesture of their customs.

Suddenly, I found myself no longer in the room but on a vast, verdant plain. The greenery was mesmerizing—a fine, soft grass, unlike anything I'd seen before. Its vibrant hue and expansive spread were breathtakingly beautiful, invoking a profound sense of tranquility and awe.

In the midst of the vast expanse of green, a high round platform stood with a massive olive-shaped object atop it. This object, a silver-gray hue, was surrounded by people, some of whom were entering it.

Suddenly, a captivating orange-red fire ignited, its beauty almost mesmerizing. With a powerful rumble, the scene unfolded like a fireball exploding, and the olive-shaped object began its ascent. Its speed was astonishing, and as it rose, two more fiery bursts accompanied its climb. In no time, it vanished completely from sight amid the brilliant display.

As I watched the mesmerizing ascent, I noticed the sky—a breathtakingly beautiful light blue, reminiscent of an enormous crystal. Scattered across this sky were silvery-white stars, each as large as a fist or a bowl, gleaming brightly.

Then, abruptly, the "dream" ended.

Upon waking, I sat up immediately, as did Flora, almost in unison. We sat back to back, unable to see each other's faces. My mind was reeling from the vivid dream, and I could feel the muscles in my face twitching with the intensity of it. I stayed silent, processing the dream's events.

I was certain Flora was doing the same. We turned to face each other at the same moment. Flora broke the silence first, exclaiming, "I have never seen such a large and beautiful grassland!"

Her words confirmed that we had shared the exact same dream. I replied, "Yes, and the sky was equally magnificent!"

Flora continued, "B came again, with the stone chamber and this recorder. He brought them all back—" She paused, a strange expression crossing her face.

Sensing her realization, I took a deep breath and reached for her hand. Flora hesitated, her lips moving before she finally spoke, "Ash, there's a special device in the seven-story stone chamber that can make people—"

Understanding what she was recalling, I squeezed her hand. Flora had indeed remembered B's final words from the "dream." She paused, her eyes wide with realization, "We can go back! Think about it, we can go back!"

Her excitement was palpable, her cheeks flushed with anticipation, her voice filled with breathless enthusiasm. "Such a beautiful environment," she continued, "I believe the air there is perfect for us, and think about it, eternal life!"

The prospect of eternal life and returning to such a paradise was undeniably tempting. It was akin to the promise of "going to heaven" or "reaching the Western Paradise," an allure almost impossible to resist. I couldn't fault Flora for her excitement, as I felt it too. The dream had revealed a glimpse of something extraordinary, stirring a deep longing within us both.

Despite the excitement from the dream, I managed to remain a bit calmer than Flora. I tightened my grip on her hand and asked, "Did you hear B mention only one person could go back?"

Flora paused, processing my question. "Yes, B did say that. But if he can send one person back, surely he can send two. The secret lies in the seven-story stone chamber. It was constructed by B, and the recorder was left by him. The key to going back is there."

I drew in a sharp breath and locked eyes with Flora. She leaned closer, her voice a whisper steeped in bewilderment. "I'm very confused," she confessed. But before I could formulate a response, the room reverberated with a sudden, violent "bang" at the door.

Both Flora and I were known for our quick thinking and sharp reflexes, but waking from that peculiar "dream" had left us in a fog of confusion, more profound than the mere life-or-death dilemmas faced by ordinary folks. Our minds were preoccupied with complexities far beyond the mundane, rendering our reactions sluggish.

As the room echoed with a second thunderous "bang," the door swung open with force, revealing Bruce. His entrance was akin to that of a fierce Indian headhunter warrior, eyes ablaze with fury, fixating on the recorder with an intensity that suggested it might burst into flames under his gaze.

With a swift, decisive motion, Bruce slammed the door shut behind him and stormed forward. Only then did Flora and I rise to our feet. His breaths came in rapid, ragged gasps as he advanced towards Flora, prompting her to instinctively retreat a step. Bruce's fists were clenched tight, his voice a harsh growl as he spat, "You two despicable pigs!"

I met his glare with a steady calm, asking, "Why do you hurl such accusations at us?"

He jabbed a finger towards the recorder, seething with accusation. "You've found what we're all seeking, yet you kept it from me! I thought we were allies in this quest!"

I replied, "Indeed, we discovered it first. But just as you knocked Bain unconscious and dragged him into the alley upon seeing Flora, we each harbored our secrets, didn't we?"

Bruce's fists tightened, the knuckles cracking ominously. It was clear that if he didn't know of our martial arts skills, he might have attacked us outright.

I kept my voice steady, "Bruce, there's no need for this. Everything on the recorder—"

Before I could finish, Bruce erupted, "You know? You already know? You have no right! This is mine. The chance to go back is mine. Who are you? You—"

His expression twisted with rage, and I quickly interjected, "Bruce, listen. You can go back, you can—"

But Bruce, consumed by anger, drew a sharp Nepalese machete. I had no idea when he acquired such a weapon, perhaps after his personality shifted to violence and darkness. Brandishing the knife, he charged at me, aiming a deadly blow at my head.

In that instant, shock and anger coursed through me. As the blade descended, I swiftly grabbed his wrist, stopping the strike. Simultaneously, I drove my knee into his lower abdomen, trying to subdue him before the situation escalated further.

The impact was forceful—I didn't hold back. Given that Bruce was intent on harming me, defending myself was my only option. As I struck him, he let out a strange cry and stumbled backward. I seized the opportunity to snatch the knife from his grasp.

Bruce staggered back a couple of steps, then steadied himself by clutching the armrest of a sofa, his anger evident as his fingers dug into the fabric. I discarded the knife, saying, "Bruce, it seems you've forgotten how people on Earth can go back!"

His voice was hoarse, and before I could finish, he unleashed a torrent of vicious curses, his voice sharp and piercing. For three minutes, he spewed insults, showcasing the rich vocabulary of human language when wielded for such purposes. Understanding his frustration, I let him vent. When he finally paused, I said, "Bruce, I have no intention of competing with you to go back."

I gestured to the recorder, "You can take this. It will show you how disillusioned the four messengers were with the world. You're a learned man; surely you know what B said before he left?"

Bruce, breathing heavily, glared at me in silence.

I continued, "Before B left, his final words were: 'All things are impermanent. Samsara is extremely terrible; you should work hard to escape the cycle of birth and death.'"

Bruce's face twitched with raw emotion. "Beyond the cycle of birth and death! Do you understand what that means? I do! I've already experienced death. Now, I need to go back. I want to go back!"

His words reverberated with a desperate urgency, the weight of his past experiences driving him toward an unquenchable desire. The cycle of existence, life and death intertwined, presented a puzzle far more intricate than any physical or historical challenge. It was the ultimate quest for truth and transcendence.

His desperation was palpable as he shouted, "I want to go back!" with all his might.

His plight evoked both sympathy and disdain. I tried to remain calm, saying, "I've told you, you can go back, though your actions don't merit it—"

Bruce interrupted with a scream, "What gives you the right to judge?"

I replied with a bitter smile, "Your heart is consumed with malice to achieve your goals, much like those who commit all manner of evil."

Bruce roared, "I don't need your preaching!"

I sighed, "Fine, I won't say more. Take the recorder and go. I wish you happiness."

Bruce lunged for the recorder, clutching it tightly. In his haste, he couldn't stand, rolling toward the door, then leaping up and rushing out. Flora quickly closed the door and leaned against it, looking at me.

I spread my hands, apologizing to Flora, "I'm sorry, I gave your things to Bruce."

Flora offered a bitter smile and spread her hands as well. After a moment, she said, "Actually, we can get ahead of Bruce."

I was taken aback, but I understood her implication. We knew the recorder's contents and the existence of a device in the seven-story stone chamber capable of sending us back. Bruce would need time to discover this. If we set out now, we could easily reach the chamber before him, seizing the opportunity to return.

I stood there, transfixed, my mind racing through the labyrinth of recent events. Flora, unwavering, fixed her gaze on me, silently demanding a decision. A heavy sigh escaped my lips, breaking the silence. "Let's just pretend none of this ever happened," I murmured, the gravity of my words hanging in the air like an unsolved riddle.

Flora's response was a mere whisper of resignation, leaving behind an unspoken understanding. A bitter smile crept onto my face. "Professor Lucas Kim sent me here to Nepal with a singular mission: to find his son. Who could have foreseen the tangled web of intrigue that awaited us? Yet, despite the chaos, we managed not to let Professor Lucas Kim down. We aided Bruce."

Flora's eyes darkened. "Bruce isn't worth our help," she retorted, her words sharp as a scholar's quill.

Her sentiment lingered in the air, and I found myself echoing Bruce's own musings. "As he reminded us, we are in no position to judge the sins of others unless we ourselves are free from genetic factors of sin."

Drawing a deep breath, I continued, "It's a notion as ancient as time itself, captured in C's enduring words: 'Let he who is without sin cast the first stone.' A challenge to ponder, no less."

A smile danced across Flora's lips, a fleeting glimpse of her own acceptance. "Very well, if you can see it as a mere dream, then so shall I. Though the enigma remains, perhaps it's best left unresolved."

I chuckled softly, a rare moment of levity amidst the chaos. "Of all the mysteries we've unraveled, which one do you think haunts me the most?"

Flora shook her head, a playful glint in her eyes. "I've pondered it countless times myself—what on earth is the use of hair?"

A shared sigh filled the space between us, a whimsical acknowledgment of the question that defied our understanding. "Indeed," I conceded. "The conundrum of hair eludes even the most astute minds."

Our conversation drifted into a comfortable silence until a thought jolted me. "The key, Flora. The one Bain entrusted to you!"

Flora flashed a sly grin, her eyes twinkling with mischief. "This key," she mused, "could be considered a little keepsake from our extraordinary journey.."

"But Bain insisted," I countered, "that without this key, accessing the stone chamber on the bottom floor is impossible!"

Flora turned away, pondering. "Do you expect me to chase him down and offer it to Bruce?"

I offered a wry smile. "That seems to be the sensible course of action."

She shook her head, the memory of Bruce's earlier demeanor still fresh. "Did you see the fire in his eyes? If I approach him again, he might not hesitate to kill me on the spot!"

Recalling Bruce's fiery gaze, I couldn't suppress a sigh. "If he ventures inside without the key... he might never reach the stone chamber below. And then he—he—"

Flora interrupted, her voice firm. "He can't return. If someone like him could return, deportation wouldn't have been necessary in the first place."

Her words echoed the unresolved tension within me, leaving me stranded in a sea of ambiguity. How could I decipher the enigma of Bruce's actions, or the shadows cast by Flora's insights? She interrupted my musings, her voice a lifeline. "We've done what we could. The rest is his to unravel."

Reluctantly, I conceded. My intuition suggested that once Bruce unraveled the secrets contained within the second recorder, he'd naturally gravitate towards the stone chamber. He could attempt entry, strive to return. Our task here in

Nepal was done, and it was time to leave. I proposed an immediate departure, and Flora nodded in agreement.

Yet, our paths diverged in the details of our exodus. I proposed that Flora take a flight out of the country, while I would traverse the land. We would rendezvous in India, and from there, make our journey home.

# CHAPTER 12

# IN-DEPTH

# DIALOGUE WITH THE KING

Fate is a peculiar architect, weaving destinies with threads of seemingly trivial choices.

Flora, defying my initial suggestion, chose to accompany me on the land route to India. Had she opted for the aerial escape, our tale might have drawn to a close, the pages devoid of further intrigue. Yet, by her side, the journey stretched on, inviting both new wonders and unforeseen perils.

Traveling alone, I would have hastened toward the Indian border, slipping through Nepal's threshold unchallenged. But together, Flora and I meandered, ensnared by the breathtaking vistas that lay before us. We wandered off beaten paths, pausing to marvel at the snow-capped peaks and azure skies, each moment a stolen treasure. Thus, on the third day, Nepal still cradled us within its mountainous embrace.

That morning, our conversation drifted to the idea of purchasing camping gear and indulging in the serenity of the landscape for a few more days. Our jeep ambled along the rugged road when two military trucks loomed in our rearview mirror, their presence growing ever ominous.

Initially, I thought little of the trucks, maneuvering our vehicle aside to grant them passage on the narrow mountain trail. Yet, as we halted, the trucks did too, disgorging a cadre of soldiers whose machine guns were trained upon us with alarming precision. Flora and I exchanged bewildered glances, our minds reeling as two officers and a middle-aged man approached.

Recognition sparked like flint in my mind. "Oh no, the Imperial Minister," I murmured to Flora, my voice tinged with resignation.

Her gaze darted toward me, but before words could form, the Minister and his entourage reached our vehicle. His gaze was icy, his demeanor colder still. "You're here again," he stated flatly, a verbal gauntlet thrown at my feet.

Shame weighed heavily upon me, my promises shattered like fragile glass. I stammered, "I was just leaving! If you let me go, I promise never to return."

The Minister's laugh was devoid of mirth. "Promises are cheap. What worth do they hold?"

Caught in this web, I forced a bitter smile. "How did you know I was still here?"

"Bruce," the Minister replied curtly.

The revelation struck like a thunderbolt. "Bruce? But he shouldn't be—how did he—?"

Flora's expression mirrored my shock at the betrayal, our plans exposed by the very person we had aided.

Ignoring my protests, the Minister barked, "Get out of the car. You're coming with us."

My hands rose in surrender. "I've done nothing wrong this time. I swear, I've caused no harm!"

The Minister cut me off with a dismissive wave. "Relax. We're not here to execute you. His Majesty the King wishes to meet."

Relief washed over me like a balm. Seeing the king again was certainly more nerve-wracking than meeting the ministers, but the King was a man of honor, unlikely to subject me to humiliation. Eagerly, I responded, "Why didn't you tell me this earlier? I'm more than happy to meet him!"

The tension eased, replaced by a cautious optimism. The King's summons hinted at new possibilities, a twist in the puzzle that promised to lead us further down the path of discovery and revelation.

The Minister's sneer returned. "Don't celebrate too soon. Serious charges await you."

As I climbed out of the jeep, his words echoed ominously. My heart sank, a silent plea to the heavens that I was innocent of any wrongdoing. "There's been a mistake," I insisted, my voice barely above a whisper amidst the mountain winds.

The minister's gaze was unwavering, his eyes boring into mine with an intensity that made my skin crawl. "That Bruce," he declared, "he's your accomplice!"

I couldn't help but let out a small, incredulous laugh. "Accomplice is a strong word. He's the son of an old friend, albeit a peculiar one. If he's done something wrong—"

The minister cut me off with a sharp gesture. "He committed murder. The victim was under the king's protection, someone of significant importance."

Flora and I exclaimed in unison, the realization crashing over us like a tidal wave. "Bain. Bruce killed Bain!"

The minister's face contorted with anger. "Yes, and the manner of the murder was barbaric, beyond what any sane person could conceive."

Flora and I exchanged a glance, the weight of the revelation settling heavily upon us. Bain's death at the hands of Bruce was a shadow that had loomed over us ever since that fateful night on the street. I had seen Bruce's viciousness then but had hoped it was merely a means to extract information from Bain, not a prelude to murder.

I couldn't shake the feeling that Bruce's frenzied return to the hotel that day was spurred by a crucial revelation. He had finally coerced Bain into divulging the location of the recorder. Although Bain hadn't identified Flora, Bruce pieced together from Bain's description that the transaction had been made with her. Bain must have kept the existence of the key a secret, or Bruce would have undoubtedly interrogated us about it.

The question that haunted me was when Bain's life had been snuffed out. Had Bruce decided, once Bain had shared all he knew about us, that Bain was of no further use and ended his life without hesitation?

If that was indeed the case, then I bore some of the burden for Bain's untimely death. Had Bruce believed Bain still held secrets worth trading, his life might have been spared.

With a heavy heart, I murmured, "Poor Bain! Minister, surely you don't think of me as an accomplice?"

This thought stirred a deep worry within me. Bruce's irrationality was unpredictable. If he were apprehended, any implication of my complicity could mean a long battle to clear my name. The minister's response was icily noncommittal. "No one can definitively say whether you're an accomplice."

I pressed further, "And what of Bruce?"

The minister's eyes were hard. "Bruce breached a military restricted area, overpowered the guards, seized their weapons, and killed two soldiers. He was shot in the process—"

With each revelation, my fear mounted. The minister continued, "Even in his dying moments, he was talking nonsense—"

I was struck with shock. "Dead? Bruce is dead?" I echoed, the reality of it nearly knocking the breath from my lungs.

In that moment, the world shifted, the landscape of our journey irrevocably altered. The echoes of Bruce's actions reverberated through my mind, leaving me to grapple with the consequences of choices, both his and mine. The path ahead was uncertain, fraught with the shadows of past decisions and the looming presence of the king who awaited.

The minister's eyes bore into mine, his skepticism palpable. "There was an entire company guarding that restricted area. In the ensuing firefight, who do you think could have survived? Bruce was riddled with over twenty bullets, dead within moments of hitting the ground."

I squeezed my eyes shut, grappling with the finality of it. Bruce was gone.

At that moment, a whirlwind of confusion engulfed me, a bewilderment so profound it defied description. Bruce, driven by an insatiable curiosity, approached the enigmatic seven-story stone chamber hidden deep below the earth's surface. The chamber, shrouded in secrecy and whispers of ancient power, lay within the confines of a heavily fortified military zone. As Bruce breached the perimeter, tension crackled like electricity in the air. The confrontation was swift and brutal; the guards, ever vigilant, responded with lethal force. In an instant, Bruce's quest ended in tragedy, his lifeless body a stark testament to the perilous secrets buried within the depths of the chamber.

Yet this death carried a weight unlike any other. Bruce had never been an ordinary man, and his "death" had a history that defied comprehension. He had once died before, when Randy drove a blade into his heart. But that had not been an end; it was merely a transition. Bruce had somehow transcended that death, inhabiting a new body, that of an Indian Black Army tribe member.

Now, with his current body lying lifeless, I couldn't help but wonder if he'd find another. What form would he take next? Who—what—was Bruce truly?

These questions swirled in my mind, a tempest of confusion and intrigue. I opened my eyes, seeking clarity in Flora's gaze. She met my look with one of helpless understanding, mirroring my own turmoil.

The minister continued to scrutinize us, his tone icy and suspicious. "Why do you both seem so odd upon hearing of the murderer's death??"

I offered a bitter smile. "This entire affair is riddled with oddities. How else could we react?"

His eyes narrowed. "What's so odd about it?"

I sighed, the weight of the mystery pressing down on me. "The story is long and convoluted, impossible to unravel in this moment." I hesitated, then pressed on. "I need to know—what did Bruce say in those final moments?"

The minister hesitated, a flicker of frustration crossing his face. "I fail to comprehend why the King would—" He halted abruptly, realizing too late the impropriety of criticizing his sovereign. Embarrassment flickered across his features, but his unfinished thought lingered in the air.

I seized the moment. "Did His Majesty hear Bruce's last words, and is that why he sent you to find me?"

The minister nodded. "Indeed."

Flora leaned forward, her curiosity piqued. "What did he say?"

With a resigned gesture, the minister led us to his vehicle. He reached inside and retrieved a tape recorder, holding it aloft like an oracle. "This contains Bruce's final utterances. His Majesty believes that if you hear them, you'll have no choice but to accept his summons."

As I took the recorder from the minister's hand, a sense of foreboding settled in my chest. I pressed play, and the tape whirred to life, spilling forth Bruce's manic laughter, interspersed with his frantic shouts, "Get out of the way, get out of the way, I don't need you!"

The minister interjected, "He was pushing away the military doctor trying to attend to his wounds."

I nodded, absorbing the urgency in Bruce's voice as it crackled through the speaker. "Do you think I will die? I won't die, I won't die! Not only will I not die, but I will go back! None of you can go back, only I can! Where is Ash Morris? He comes with me, tell him! No matter what tricks he plays, I can definitely go back! I am luckier than anyone else, and I am superior to anyone else. I can go back, but you can't, hahahaha——"

Bruce's words were a haunting echo of his defiance, a proclamation of his indomitable will. I drew a deep breath, the weight of his conviction pressing on my mind. The minister turned to me, skepticism etched in his features. "Do you think he is talking nonsense?"

Flora was quick to respond, "No!"

But I countered, "Yes, he is talking nonsense, because he just thinks he can go back, but in fact, he can't go back!"

The minister's stare was one reserved for the unhinged, his curiosity tinged with disbelief. I shrugged off his incredulity, pressing on with my inquiries. "How did His Majesty the King come to hear this tape?"

"I am tasked with reporting all occurrences at the secret military base," the minister replied.

I pondered aloud, "So after hearing this tape, he realized I was involved again, and sent you to find me?"

"Yes," the minister confirmed. "His Majesty is quite eager to see you."

Sensing an opportunity, I probed further, "Does he hold it against me for entering the country once more?"

The minister let out a derisive snort. "I can't fathom why he wishes to see someone so untrustworthy."

I chuckled, patting him on the shoulder. "There are many things beyond your understanding, Your Excellency! Let's get moving—the king must be eager for our meeting."

With a mix of amusement and frustration, the minister led us to the vehicle. Flora and I settled in, the wheels spinning us toward our destiny. As dawn broke over a small town, the minister made arrangements, and we shared a makeshift meal beside the car. An hour later, a helicopter descended, whisking us to the palace courtyard.

Inside the ornate chamber, the king rose to greet me. Despite my usual composure, a pang of embarrassment flared as I shook his hand. "Your Majesty, the minister brands me a man of broken promises. I confess, my repeated failures to uphold my word are a source of shame."

The king, ever the gracious host, dispelled my concerns with a warm smile. "Nonsense. I admire your tenacity. Please, have a seat. Let us speak candidly."

I nodded, introducing Flora. "Your Majesty, Flora is privy to every detail of this intrigue."

I noticed a fleeting hesitation in the king's eyes—perhaps he had intended for a private conversation. But as I emphasized Flora's integral role, he acknowledged her presence. "Very well, please join us," he invited, his glance flitting to the minister.

The minister appeared discontent, a reluctant witness to this unorthodox meeting. "Your Majesty, are you sure—" he began, but the king silenced him with a wave.

"Rest easy. Mr. Morris poses no threat to me," the king assured, the weight of his confidence settling the room.

The minister's distrust was palpable as he cast one last glare my way. Yet, with the king's directive clear, he had no choice but to concede. After a formal bow, he retreated, leaving the door to close with a soft click behind him.

In the dimly lit study, an air of tension enveloped the three of us. We sat in silence, the weight of unspoken words hanging heavily in the room. The king, a figure of regal authority, appeared lost in contemplation, wrestling with thoughts that eluded articulation. Though curiosity burned within me, decorum held my tongue, and Flora, composed and enigmatic, mirrored my restraint. For a few endless moments, silence reigned supreme.

Finally, the king broke the stalemate with a weary sigh. "I really don't know what to do," he admitted, his voice laced with vulnerability.

Seizing the opportunity, I spoke with earnest resolve. "Whatever you ask me, I will tell you everything I know."

The king's eyes flickered with interest, his brow arching inquisitively. "Okay, then please start from the beginning."

With determination, I resolved to lay bare all that I knew, hoping for a reciprocal honesty from the king.

I embarked on my tale, beginning with the cryptic letter from Professor Kim—a missive that catapulted me into an unforeseen journey. From there, I recounted my encounter with Randy in the mystical landscapes of Nepal, relayed the clandestine secrets Randy shared, and described the ancient antiquities Bain had sold—artifacts that led Bruce and Randy to the elusive "dream."

The narrative unfolded with meticulous detail: the urgency of Professor Kim's summons, Flora's expedition to South America, and my subsequent pursuit. I spoke of our reunion with Bruce, the internal strife within the Black Army tribe, and the perilous odyssey that brought us to Nepal.

For four hours, my words painted a vivid tapestry of intrigue and danger. Throughout, the king listened with rapt attention, his silence punctuated only by the soft scratch of pen on paper as he noted his queries. Despite the labyrinthine twists of the story, he allowed me to speak uninterrupted, absorbing the full breadth of my experiences and revelations.

When I finally concluded, I gestured to Flora. "Her experiences in South America predate mine. She can provide insights, particularly regarding her encounters with Bain."

The king nodded, inviting Flora to fill in the gaps. Her account was concise, wrapping up in half an hour. Then, addressing the king, I said, "I recommend enhancing your security. I found it surprisingly easy to infiltrate last time."

The king chuckled softly, an acknowledgment of our shared reality. "We are but a small nation, striving to avoid entanglements with the world. Individuals like yourself are indeed rare."

I shrugged, accepting his gentle reproof. The king reviewed his notes, his gaze flicking over the pages. "According to your theory, it seems plausible that there was, indeed, an ancient mass deportation from some celestial body, sending criminals to Earth."

I nodded. "Not just my theory, but a deduction based on the convergence of many facts."

The king leaned back, his sigh heavy with contemplation. "Do you recall our last conversation, when I spoke of those four remarkable individuals?"

I responded quickly, "Of course I remember. Their names—A, B, C, and D—are etched in my memory. But what puzzled me was why Your Majesty asked me about them in the first place."

The king's gaze lingered on me, a silent acknowledgment of mysteries yet to be revealed. "Do you think you, Bruce, and Randy are the only ones who have experienced such dreams?"

His words were like a bolt from the blue, jolting both Flora and me. While Flora maintained her composure, merely blinking in surprise, I was unable to contain my reaction, springing to my feet in shock.

"You—" I began, but the king had already moved across the room, his silence a prelude to revelation. He approached an antique wooden cabinet, opened its door, and revealed a familiar object: a recorder, the third of its kind that I had encountered.

Flora let out a soft gasp, "Ah! Your Majesty, what is recorded in this device?"

The king's face clouded with a mix of confusion and introspection. He sighed heavily, avoiding a direct answer as he closed the cabinet door. "This device was given to me by the old man who Bain later murdered. Bain's family received special treatment from the crown. Over time, the reasons became lost, even to them. Their numbers dwindled, leaving only the old man and Bain.."

The king settled back into his chair, its wood creaking beneath his weight. "Every year, the old man brought me gifts. Once—though I can't quite place the year—he presented this item, claiming it came from a stone chamber beneath a mystical ancient temple. He believed it to be an antique and thought it worthy of my collection."so he passed it on to me."

I nodded thoughtfully. "Perhaps Bain learned of the old man's generosity and was inspired to sell the temple's relics as antiques."

The king gave a slight nod. "Perhaps."

He paused, the silence heavy with unsaid words. "When it first came into my possession, it piqued my curiosity. I couldn't discern its origin or purpose. My interest in the ancient temple grew. I knew little about it, which only deepened my intrigue. I pressed the old man for details and requested a visit to the temple. But he refused, warning that anyone outside his clan who entered would face dire consequences."

"I can attest to that," I replied. "I stumbled inside and suffered a blow to the back of my head. I nearly perished in the deepest chamber!"

The king chuckled, though his eyes remained serious. "His warnings deterred me. I kept the item close, studying it whenever time allowed. One day, I grew weary and fell asleep with my head resting on it. That's when the dream came."

Flora and I exchanged a glance. The king continued, "At first, I dismissed it as a vivid dream. But when I fell asleep again under the same circumstances and the dream replayed, I knew something was amiss. I confided in no one."

I leaned forward, intrigued. "What did you dream of—"

The king fell silent, his gaze distant. After a while, he sighed heavily, echoing his earlier reticence.

He finally spoke, "I summoned the old man, asking if his people experienced similar dreams. He denied it, explaining that his tribe had a fatalistic view of life. Many had taken their own lives or vanished into the mountains. Bain seemed the sole exception. I'd encountered him several times. Then you handed Bain over to the authorities—"

"Yes," I interjected, "because I'm certain he committed murder."

The king's smile was tinged with resignation. "Yet, despite everything, my duty compels me to protect him. It's a rule handed down through the generations."

"I understand," I replied. "But at that moment, I was genuinely taken aback by it."

The king gestured thoughtfully, recounting, "After our encounter, I questioned Bain about the ancient temple once more. Unlike the old man, he was less adamant, agreeing to escort me there. However, he refused to venture into the stone chamber with me, fearing the consequences if anything happened to me. Thus, I only glimpsed the enormous artifact within. Realizing Bain might eventually sell it to tourists, I proposed sealing the chamber entrance, demolishing the temple, and relocating the artifact to the palace."

Flora interjected with curiosity, "Your Majesty, why take such measures?"

The king's expression grew serious. "The implications of our knowledge are staggering. If the world were to learn unequivocally that we originate from a celestial realm where immortality reigns, the ensuing chaos would be unimaginable."

Flora spread her hands wide, her voice echoing through the ancient chamber. "At worst, people might foolishly attempt to construct a tower to return."

The King nodded solemnly, his face shadowed with concern. "Bruce's frenzied acts in his desperate bid to return only affirm my caution," he said, gravely. "Such knowledge must remain hidden."

I concurred, "Indeed, the fewer who know, the better."

The king seemed pleased with our alignment, then inquired, "What was that artifact?"

I suggested, "Flora should see it for herself, and then we can discuss its nature."

The king shook his head regretfully. "Unfortunately, I destroyed it after Bain's demise."

My surprise was evident, mirrored by Flora's disappointment. The king pressed on, "What do you believe it was?"

Having pondered the artifact, I ventured, "I believe it was part of a transportation mechanism."

The king leaned forward, intrigued. "Do you think they—those four individuals—arrived here using such means?"

I speculated, "I suspect it was used to transport equipment. The four themselves likely arrived by different means. The most detailed account is of C, whose arrival was marked by a strange celestial light witnessed by three shepherds."

The king waved his hand, signaling he needed a moment to absorb this information before continuing. His gesture was one of contemplation, as he grappled with the profound implications of our conversation.

I paused to gather my thoughts, then continued, "Remember the dream? They came just like us, lived among us, and their abilities only manifested at a certain age. This gradual revelation helped them understand life on Earth more profoundly."

The king nodded, murmuring in agreement. "Yes, yes—" He then raised his voice, "But how did they come?"

"I propose it wasn't their physical bodies that traversed dimensions," I ventured, my voice echoing softly. "But their souls—using the word 'soul' to represent the very essence of life. As long as this essence remains intact, life itself is eternal."

The King seemed to grasp the concept, breathing deeply. "I see. Is Bruce like this?"

Flora chimed in, her voice tinged with excitement. "I think everyone from their world might possess this ability, like Bruce. But on Earth, it's rare—an anomaly. Even in their world, the physical body might not be eternal. It's just that they can change their bodies at will to maintain the eternity of life!"

Her theory was speculative, yet it resonated with us. Later experiences would prove her insights remarkably close to reality.

The king pondered, "Everyone desires eternal life, but what do we lack that prevents us from achieving it?"

I reminded him, "Your Majesty, our ancestors were stripped of certain abilities when exiled to Earth."

"The function of hair?" the king queried slowly, each word deliberate.

Flora and I exchanged startled glances. If the king was certain that the lost ability related to hair, it must have been revealed in his dream. I pressed, "Your Majesty, did you learn this from your dream?"

He nodded, encouraging me to speak further.

I asked once more, "Can you describe this dream to us?"

For the third time, the king sighed deeply, evading my question. Frustration pricked at me; I had shared all my knowledge, yet he withheld his dream.

Sensing my impatience, the king explained, "It's not reluctance. The dream's contents are oppressive, painful to recount or even recall. But experiencing it yourself would be more enlightening than my retelling, wouldn't it?"

His offer thrilled me. "You mean, I can experience it myself?"

The king confirmed, "Yes, stay in the palace tonight. Use the recorder to enter the dream. Once you've experienced it, we can discuss further."

Excitedly, I agreed, "Yes, of course!"

The king summoned the minister via the intercom, instructing him to enter. Before the minister arrived, the king advised me, "Take the recorder to your room discreetly, without the minister noticing. Explaining it would be bothersome."

I nodded, wrapping the recorder in my shirt. As the minister entered, the king instructed him to ensure Flora and I were well accommodated and to prepare a room for us, promising further discussion the next day.

The minister complied respectfully, and we bowed before departing.

We enjoyed a sumptuous dinner, the day's events and travel having left us weary.

Upon reaching the lavish bedroom prepared for us, Flora and I settled down with the recorder, resting our heads upon it. Soon, we drifted into sleep, anticipation of the dream ahead weaving through our thoughts.

# CHAPTER 13

# THE THIRD STRANGE DREAM

Upon drifting into sleep, we found ourselves submerged in yet another "dream."

For context, let me clarify. There exist three recorders of this peculiar nature, each corresponding to a distinct "dream." The first recorder was in the possession of Bruce and Randy, granting them access to the first dream.

Only Randy and Bruce had experienced this first dream, and I learned of its contents through Randy's recounting.

I number these "dreams" for clarity in narration.

The recorder Bain sold to Flora facilitated what I refer to as the third dream. The dream we experienced in the palace turned out to be the second, as its events preceded those of the third dream.

Here is a description of the second dream:

The second dream commenced with a meeting, attended by six individuals. As I entered the dream, their identities became clear: A, B, C, D, the leader, and C's father.

I categorize this dream as No. 2 because it clearly depicts events following the return of A, B, C, and D. The six discussed initial occurrences before joining a larger assembly—depicted in Dream No. 3.

My account may seem disordered, yet it reflects the truth. Sorting the sequence is straightforward if you desire clarity.

In the "dream," a gentle light enveloped the scene. Six blurred figures gathered around a round table. Silence reigned initially, broken by the leader's voice: "Do you four share the same conclusion?"

C responded in a subdued tone: "Yes."

The leader sighed, "Is the situation truly dire?"

C replied with a bitter smile, "It's worse than our report suggests. Our understanding of sin is superficial; our report hasn't delved into the darkness within their hearts. Only they fully grasp their own depravity."

A's voice, tinged with anger, pointed at C: "He suffered the worst betrayal. He carefully selected twelve individuals, deeming them most trustworthy, yet one of them turned traitor!"

The leader and C's father sighed in unison, "What do you believe is the root of their sin?"

A moment of silence ensued among A, B, C, and D. B spoke first, his voice measured: "Their ignorance about their own lives is the root. The brevity of life dominates their thoughts."

A countered passionately, "No, the root lies in them being embodiments of sin! Their existence is marred by heinous acts—mass killings, valuing only their own lives while disregarding others'. This is the mortal flaw!"

D sighed heavily, "The biggest issue is their inability to truly communicate. No one can genuinely know what another is thinking. Language, which should bridge this gap, is instead a tool of deceit. Lies replace truth, and deceit runs rampant. They pursue inexplicable power, embrace tyranny, and are cruel to their own kind in ways no other creature is. Fairness and justice seem nonexistent there."

The leader nodded solemnly, "This is precisely why you four were sent there. If their ugliness wasn't so profound, your mission wouldn't have been necessary."

A agreed, "Yes, we went with the intent to change things, but our impact was minimal. I fear the situation will continue to deteriorate, and the sins will deepen until—"

C's father interjected with a grave tone, "Until we are forced to consider complete destruction?"

C murmured, resignation in his voice, "That day might indeed come. We must admit our failure."

A spoke passionately, "I've researched it. To obliterate that planet, we merely need to adjust the orbit of a 17th magnitude star. It would scarcely affect the nebula and leave us untouched."

Silence fell over the group, a heavy stillness. B finally broke it with a sigh, "Not everyone there is like this. Though selfish and destructive, some good people exist. They may be few, but obliterating them alongside the rest would be unjust."

A challenged, "Do you propose a better solution?"

B offered, "We could construct a large-scale receiving system at a distance. As their physical forms fail, we can scan their thought beams. Those deemed worthy could be brought back. This would serve as a final review."

The leader hesitated, "Their hair's function is entirely lost. What thought beams remain?"

B replied, "They are weak, but they persist. Occasionally, thought beams coalesce in emergencies. With precision, our device could retrieve those who meet the criteria."

The leader considered this, "Very well, I'll work to make this possible." He paused, then asked, "Will any of you return?"

A, B, C, and D exchanged glances, then collectively replied, "We have no plans to return."

D sighed, reflecting on their experiences, "Admitting failure is difficult. We were patient, offering forgiveness for past transgressions if they renounced them. Yet, their inner ugliness is entrenched, and few truly listened."

The leader waved his hand, summarizing their conclusions, "The root of their evil is their obsession with their brief lives. This breeds hypocrisy, deceit, greed, jealousy, violence, cruelty, selfishness, and brutality—"

As the leader listed these traits, his voice was stiff, as if foreign to such concepts. C's father interjected with a bitter smile, "No need to continue. These behaviors are distressing to hear about. It's baffling why they inflict such pain on each other throughout their lives."

The atmosphere in the dream was somber, the weight of their discussion heavy with implications. It was a poignant reflection on the darker aspects of human nature, and the efforts—or failures—of those who sought to guide them toward a higher path. This dream, a window into the struggles and decisions of these enigmatic beings, left me with a deeper understanding of the challenges they faced and the complexities of their mission on Earth.

The leader paused thoughtfully, his gaze distant. "The four individuals we sent have done their utmost to promote virtues as a counterbalance," he said, his voice heavy with responsibility. "The principles they espouse will undoubtedly be passed down through generations. Now, we must allow things to take their course and let them choose their paths. Establishing the receiving system is the best we can do. They must decide where they wish to go."

C's father nodded in agreement, "This is indeed the best course of action."

With that, A, B, C, and D rose from their seats, followed by the leader and C's father. The leader remarked, "Everyone is eager to hear your reports. It's time to address them."

A replied bitterly, "There isn't much good to report. We failed. That's the truth."

The six figures exited the room, their conversation trailing off as they departed.

Flora and I awoke abruptly, sitting back to back in silence. The dream had left us both speechless and drenched in sweat. The weight of its revelations hung heavily between us.

C's words echoed in my mind: "Only they themselves know how bad they are."

How deeply flawed are we? The leader had listed numerous faults in a stiff voice, yet those were merely a fraction of the transgressions Earthlings commit.

Flora and I understood why the king hesitated to share this dream. It was a harsh indictment of humanity—of us, Earthlings, being more malevolent than any other creature on this planet. And I, Flora, and the king were no exceptions to this harsh truth.

Turning to face each other, I saw Flora slowly pivoting as well. We locked eyes, and I wiped the sweat from my brow, my voice quivering slightly, "They've given up."

Flora's voice was hoarse with emotion, "No, they set up a guide, a receiving system at a suitable distance."

I offered a bitter smile, "Even with such a guide, how many on Earth are truly qualified to return?"

Flora murmured softly, "There will always be some—maybe 144,000?"

We leaned back again, supporting each other until dawn arrived. The minister came to escort us to breakfast, and after eating, we returned to the king's study.

The king greeted us with a probing question, "Do you think you two can pass the final review?"

Flora and I exchanged a rueful smile, words escaping us. The king sighed deeply, "In truth, everyone has the potential to pass the final review. The principles set forth by those four are clear, and all one needs to do is follow them. Yet, no one is willing to do so."

I replied with a wry smile, "Even among those who claim to champion the principles of the four, how many truly live by them?"

The king's expression was one of somber understanding, acknowledging the gulf between ideals and practice. It was a moment of shared reflection on the human condition, the persistent struggle to live up to our highest values, and the hope that some might yet rise to the challenge.

The king rubbed his hands together, deep in thought. "Indeed, it's troubling that no one can truly know another's mind. In such a world, evil thoughts remain hidden, truth is elusive, and deception prevails. I often wonder if anyone has truly been 'qualified' to return, despite the installation of a device to retrieve Earthling's thought beams."

I pondered this, while Flora spoke up with surprising certainty, "There is evidence that at least one person was taken back."

The king and I looked at her in surprise, curious about her conviction. Flora continued, "That person is the great inventor Edison. You must be familiar with the events surrounding his death, aren't you?"

The king and I exchanged a knowing look, our sighs mingling in the stillness of the room. We both nodded, acknowledging a mystery that had eluded explanation for decades. It was the tale of the great inventor, Thomas Edison—a story that, even now, sent shivers through those who heard it. As Edison lay on his deathbed, his breaths growing shallower, surrounded by doctors, family, and friends, he appeared to slip away. His heart ceased its beat, and just as the doctor prepared to declare him gone, Edison sat up with unexpected vigor. "I can't believe it's so beautiful over there!" he exclaimed, before falling back and passing on to whatever lay beyond this life.

Those around him were left stunned, left to ponder the meaning of his final words. What had Edison seen in those fleeting moments? What beauty had compelled him to rise and speak, even as his life ebbed away? The question lingered, locked away in official records and whispered in awe by those who recounted his last moments. It was a riddle unsolved, a glimpse into the unknown that defied interpretation.

The king, aware of this enigma, let out a hearty laugh alongside me after hearing Flora's words. To us, the once-inexplicable utterance of Edison seemed suddenly clear. For in his final seconds, Edison had "returned" to a place of indescribable beauty, a realm that had drawn from him a spontaneous cry of wonder.

Edison had indeed gone back—of that, we were certain.

The king, after a moment of contemplation, asked, "So it happens that quickly? Can someone return immediately upon dying?"

Taking a deep breath, I responded, "It appears so. Otherwise, Edison wouldn't have seen it so swiftly. As death approaches, most people's 'thought beams' start to leave their bodies. The body is temporary, lasting perhaps a century, but the 'thought beams' are eternal. Edison's brilliance, his groundbreaking inventions, might have been the result of a unique genetic mutation."

The king sighed, "Thoughts are not as tangible as physical form. Why can't we harness the power of thought beams? The recorders often mention the function of hair." He paused, rubbing his hands nervously, then continued, "Is it related to one of hair's functions?"

"I've considered that," I said. "It seems plausible that thought beams travel through the hair. Hair might serve as a conduit, which is why it grows so near the brain, with its peculiar structure and abundance. No other creature has hair quite like ours!"

The king nodded, reflecting on the possibility. Hair, as a conduit for thought beams, was an intriguing notion—one that could potentially explain the mysterious connection between the physical and the ethereal. It suggested a hidden complexity within our biology, a link to something greater beyond our immediate understanding. As we sat there, contemplating these profound ideas, a sense of wonder and possibility filled the room, reminding us of the mysteries still waiting to be unraveled.

The king's frown deepened, mirroring the myriad thoughts swirling in my own mind. I ventured, "I have another theory. Perhaps immortality is less about living forever and more about a transfer of life—much like Bruce transforming from a white man to an Indian. We might call it 'reincarnation' or 'rebirth,' where the mind stays the same but the body changes. And I suspect this transformation also involves the function of hair."

The king mulled over this idea. "For now, we can only speculate. There's no concrete proof."

I was about to add something when Flora interjected, "Actually, someone can prove it."

The king's surprise was palpable. "Ah!" he exclaimed, quickly piecing together the implication of Flora's words. He knew, as I had shared everything with him, about the device in the seven-story stone chamber capable of enabling a person to "go back."

A heavy silence fell over us, as if an invisible weight pressed upon our hearts. We were venturing into realms beyond the bounds of human understanding.

I completely understood the ambiguity around the term "return." Even if the legends were true, could we honestly claim we were "returning"? We were descendants of the original exiles, countless generations removed, continually grappling with the challenges of adapting to Earth's environment. Did we belong to Earth, or did our true roots lie in the unknown realms beyond?

The question hung in the air, a silent phantom that stole our voices.

In an attempt to dispel the tension clinging to us like a shroud, I spread my hands wide. "Your Majesty," I ventured cautiously, "if your duties permit, perhaps you could consider embarking on the journey to that distant realm."

My words were a whisper in the storm. Yet, they struck a chord deep within the king. He jolted, his eyes locking onto mine with a gaze that seemed to pierce through to the very marrow of my bones. After an eternity, he swallowed hard and asked, "Can I truly go there?"

"Why not?" I replied, my voice steady. "The records in the ancient manuscript indicate that it is possible for one to make the journey."

His breaths came quick and shallow, and he paced like a caged lion. "If I decide to go, how do I proceed?"

I shook my head, uncertainty clouding my thoughts. "I don't know, Your Majesty. But if we can reach the seven-story stone chamber, perhaps the answers will reveal themselves."

Flora interjected with a confident nod. "And Bain's key is in my possession. It will grant us passage directly to the chamber on the lowermost floor."

The king stood silent, his mind a tempest of thoughts. "But what if I venture there and find no way back? What then?"

Flora and I exchanged a glance, the weight of his question pressing heavily upon us. To venture there was to embrace the unknown, the final destination of humankind. Like Bruce before us, who yearned for the journey without contemplating the return. Yet now, the king gave voice to an unspoken fear—what if we couldn't return to Earth?

We stood mute, unable to provide solace. The king sighed, a sound imbued with the weight of his soul. "I fear I cannot abandon everything for this path," he murmured, the words more to himself than to us, yet they hit me like a thunderclap.

His resignation was palpable. He understood that if he couldn't leave everything behind, he couldn't reach the other side. The king would not—could not—undertake the journey. This realization etched itself across his features, a bitter acceptance shadowing his face.

"I cannot leave now," he confessed, his voice heavy with regret. "You both must understand—"

I inhaled deeply, locking eyes with Flora, who mirrored my uncertainty.

Finally, Flora broke the silence. "Your Majesty, whatever the outcome, we must at least explore the enigmatic stone chamber on the seventh floor."

The king's brow furrowed, then slowly smoothed, as though a burden had been lifted. He rubbed his hands together, resolution in his voice. "I will permit you both to descend into the depths of the stone chambers."

I blinked, startled by his decision. "You mean—"

He shook his head, a firm resolve in his eyes. "I won't be joining you. And no matter the outcome, you needn't report back to me. I intend to forget everything entirely."

Surprised, I gestured towards the recorder. "But how can you forget? With this relic as a constant reminder, how do you silence the echoes of its mysteries?"

The king chuckled, a sound both weary and amused. "That's quite simple. It would only take three minutes to destroy it."

I opened my mouth to protest, but Flora gently tugged at my sleeve, signaling me to hold back. "Your Majesty's decision is wise," she interjected. "He is unlike us; he has numerous responsibilities. He can't just abandon everything."

I raised my voice, fueled by frustration, "Responsibilities? From the perspective of the other side, his duties and everything he holds dear are ephemeral, illusions not worth clinging to!"

Flora countered swiftly, "But we are here, not there!"

I threw up my hands in exasperation, at a loss for words. The king, observing our exchange, stated firmly, "I've made my decision and won't waver. I'll grant you access to the military restricted area and instruct the minister and guards to provide any assistance you require." With that, he pressed the intercom button and summoned the minister.

Recognizing the futility of further argument, Flora and I acquiesced. The king wished to leave this mystery behind, and there was no sense in compelling him to dwell on it. Yet, our resolve to explore the seven-story stone chamber remained unwavering.

Once the minister arrived and received the king's directives, we took our leave from the palace.

Empowered by the king's orders, the minister's demeanor toward us was notably accommodating. He arranged transportation and accompanied us personally. By afternoon, we reached the "military restricted area."

Security at the restricted area was significantly tighter than during my previous visit, likely a response to Bruce's intrusion.

The minister spoke with two officers, who then guided us to a seemingly ordinary spot. Indicating the ground beneath our feet, they said, "The final seal is here."

The minister gestured toward me, "Proceed according to his instructions."

Once the minister had departed, leaving us with our thoughts and the task ahead, I felt a sense of solitude mixed with anticipation. The fewer people aware of what lay within the seven-story stone chamber, the better for our purposes.

I turned to the two officers standing by, their demeanor one of respect and readiness. "How many defenders are present here?" I inquired.

"Seven hundred and six," one officer replied promptly.

With determination, I instructed, "Have them all retreat thirty kilometers away. Leave no one behind."

The officers were momentarily taken aback by the unusual order, their eyes wide with uncertainty. Yet, my voice carried authority.

"All retreat!" I repeated emphatically. "Just leave the digging tools for us."

It took a moment for the officers to process the command, but once they did, they snapped to attention, saluted, and quickly set about the task. The sound of orders being relayed echoed around, followed by the rumble of trucks and the disciplined cadence of soldiers moving out. Two soldiers deposited a selection of tools at our feet before departing.

Within half an hour, the area was deserted, leaving Flora and me in profound silence. The only sound was our own breathing, a testament to the isolation of our endeavor.

Grabbing a mattock, I prepared myself for the task at hand, spitting into my palms for grip and rubbing them together. I began to dig, each stroke of the hoe breaking into the earth with purpose. Flora efficiently cleared away the debris, our teamwork seamless and focused.

In less than an hour, we had cleared the sand and soil, exposing the cement below. Flora started up the generator, its hum filling the night as I took hold of a pneumatic pick. The rhythmic "da da" of the jackhammer pierced the stillness, reverberating into the distance. The cement gave way under its assault, revealing reinforcing steel bars, which Flora expertly cut with a saw.

Together, we created the gateway—a two-foot square opening leading to the unknown depths below. As we peered into the darkness, it became clear: this was where the answers lay hidden, the greatest mystery of human history buried beneath the surface.

With careful preparation, ensuring both of us could descend, we paused to gather our resolve. Flora aimed a powerful flashlight downward, illuminating the entrance to the first stone chamber I'd encountered before. Its walls, constructed from meticulously arranged stones, stood bare, the chamber empty but for the weight of its secrets.

The moment felt charged with significance. We were about to step into a place where history, myth, and mystery converged, a place that held the potential to redefine everything we understood about our past and our place in the universe. The anticipation was palpable as we prepared to delve deeper, driven by the hope of uncovering truths long obscured by time and silence.

I was the first to jump down into the stone chamber, then helped Flora descend safely beside me. Together, we moved cautiously, finding the staircase that led to the lower levels and began our descent.

The second and third levels mirrored the first—completely empty, devoid of any distinguishing features or artifacts. Each level had a doorway at the base of the stairs, but these doors stood ajar, offering no resistance.

It wasn't until we reached the entrance to the fourth level that we encountered a closed door. I pushed against it, but it remained steadfastly shut. Scanning the door with my flashlight, I soon discovered a small round hole on the side, perfectly matching the size of the key Flora had obtained from Bain.

Since entering the depths of the stone chamber, Flora and I remained silent. The quiet was profound, bordering on oppressive, amplifying every sound. We could hear not only each other's breathing but even the subtle rhythm of our heartbeats. This intense hush exerted a peculiar pressure, one that discouraged any attempt at speech.

Upon finding the small hole, I gestured to Flora. She understood immediately, retrieving the key and inserting it into the slot. The moment the key slid into place, there was a distinct "click."

Though the sound was minimal, the surrounding silence magnified it, causing both of us to startle involuntarily.

With that "click," the door began to open inward, creaking slightly as it moved. Flora retrieved the key, and we stepped through the threshold, she leading and I following closely behind.

The fourth level awaited us, shrouded in darkness and mystery. As we crossed into the new chamber, I couldn't help but feel a mix of trepidation and excitement. We were delving deeper into the unknown, each step taking us closer to the heart of the secrets that lay hidden within these ancient stones. The anticipation was palpable as we ventured further, driven by the hope of uncovering truths long buried in silence and shadow.

# CHAPTER 14

# DESCENT INTO
# THE SEVEN-LAYER ENIGMA

Stepping into the fourth-layer stone chamber, Flora and I were immediately struck by the sheer artistry illuminated by the flashlight's beam. The reliefs carved into the walls were breathtakingly intricate, unlike anything we had ever encountered in our explorations of temple art.

Each wall was adorned with these exquisite reliefs, depicting scenes that seemed both ancient and profound. As we examined them closely, it became clear that these images were more than mere decoration; they told a story. Prominent figures, seven or eight in number, were depicted leading smaller figures in a procession toward an olive-shaped object. It was unmistakable: this was the scenario described in the "first dream," portraying the ancestors of modern Earthlings being sent to a satellite of the seventeenth-magnitude luminous star.

Beneath these scenes were symbols resembling text, composed of geometric shapes. Though their meaning eluded us, we surmised these were the writings of that distant place. We lingered in the chamber, absorbing the rich details before continuing down the stairs, using the key to unlock the next door.

The fifth-layer chamber revealed more astonishing reliefs. Each wall told a distinct story, centered around four individuals—A, B, C, and D. These reliefs chronicled their lives on Earth, capturing pivotal moments and experiences.

As we studied these narratives, Flora mused, "It's hard to believe Bain and his people have passed through here countless times without appreciating these reliefs."

I nodded, "It's not that they ignored them—they simply couldn't comprehend their significance. Without knowledge of the three dreams, we might dismiss these as just another example of temple art."

Flora pondered this before agreeing, "True, without context, they seem like ordinary religious art. Yet every temple holds stories like these."

We descended further, my thoughts consumed by the potential revelations awaiting us on the lower levels. As we moved to the sixth floor, the chamber surprised us with its starkness. Unlike the others, it lacked reliefs. Instead, a massive rectangular stone rested against the left wall, its size and shape reminiscent of a sarcophagus. This stone featured three grooves, perfectly sized for three recorders.

Our hopes of discovering additional recorders, and thereby gaining deeper insights into the mysteries of the other side, were dashed. The grooves suggested only three recorders existed, and none were here.

Determined, Flora and I spent ten minutes meticulously examining the chamber for hidden compartments or clues, but our search yielded nothing.

As we descended toward the seventh floor, the final layer of the stone chamber, our steps grew heavy with anticipation and an unspoken sense of dread. We both understood that the answers to the mysteries we sought likely lay within this deepest chamber. Despite our resolve, a part of us wished the stairs would stretch on indefinitely, delaying the moment of truth.

The staircase was short, merely a dozen steps, and even our slow pace could not prevent us from reaching the end.

We stood before the door, silent and pensive. As Flora inserted the key into the small round hole, I noticed her hands trembling slightly. Gently, I took her hand in mine, offering a steadying reassurance. She leaned closer, drawing comfort from my presence. "Don't worry," I whispered, my voice calm and soothing. "I've been here before. Everything will be fine."

Her voice was tense, "But remember what the old man told Bain before he died?"

"Yes," I replied, recalling the ominous warning. "He said there mustn't be any light in the seventh-floor stone chamber."

Flora looked at me, concern evident in her eyes. "So, what do we do?"

I considered our options. "Let's turn off the flashlight first. Once we're inside, we'll figure out our next steps."

She nodded, and we switched off the flashlight, plunging us into complete darkness. Flora, feeling her way, inserted the key. I gently pushed the door open.

Darkness enveloped us as we crossed the threshold, hand in hand. The door swung shut behind us, sealing us in silence so profound that even our breathing seemed loud. The inky blackness heightened our senses, and I could distinctly hear both our heartbeats, an eerie synchronization in the void.

After a time, Flora's whisper broke the stillness, "What should we do? Should we pray?"

Her suggestion almost brought a smile to my lips, an urge to laugh that I had to suppress. "Standing in the dark won't accomplish much," I replied. "Let's try to understand our surroundings."

Flora whispered, "Then we must make some light."

"Yes," I agreed, "without light, we can't see where we are or what's around us."

"Maybe we should go up and get an infrared observer," she suggested.

I grimaced, knowing how much time that would take. "Let's do this instead," I proposed. "You go up, and I'll stay here with the flashlight. If anything unexpected happens, it's just my business."

Flora's voice turned firm and slightly angry. "No, what are you talking about? If anything unexpected happens, we'll face it together."

I quickly conceded, "Okay, let's count to three and turn on the flashlights together."

"Let's do it," she agreed.

We took a deep breath, then called out in unison, "One! Two! Three!"

On "three," our flashlights blazed to life, illuminating the chamber in a bright, dual beam of light.

This was the seventh-floor stone chamber, the place where the old man had cautioned Bain against any light. Yet here we were, casting more than just "a little light"—the powerful beams of our flashlights pierced the darkness.

Anticipating something unusual, we were steeled for whatever might occur.

The beams revealed the upper sections of the stone walls, which were lined with devices resembling convex lenses. I recognized them instantly as photosensitive devices. At that very moment, a sound echoed through the chamber, and a secret door on the opposite wall began to open.

Flora and I exchanged glances, understanding why the old man's warning had been so adamant. It was simple, really. While the old man might not have known the full truth, his caution was a lesson inherited through generations. The photosensitive devices were undoubtedly extremely sensitive. The light from our two powerful flashlights was more than enough to activate them, but even the flicker of a match might have sufficed to trigger the mechanism and reveal the secret door.

This unexpected development filled us with a mix of apprehension and excitement. The opening door hinted at secrets long hidden—and now, we stood on the brink of uncovering them.

This highly sensitive photosensitive device was clearly beyond the capabilities of current Earth technology. Flora and I had braced ourselves for something spectacular the moment light touched it—perhaps a display worthy of the phrase "the power of the god is unpredictable." But the reality was surprisingly simple: the light merely triggered the opening of a secret door. We both chuckled, feeling a wave of unexpected relief.

I took the lead, stepping toward the secret door, which was low enough that I had to stoop to pass through.

As I reached the entrance and peered inside, I was momentarily paralyzed by the sight before me. I stood there, frozen, unable to proceed.

Behind me, Flora, unable to see past the doorway, asked anxiously, "What's going on?"

Her voice snapped me out of my stupor, and I exhaled deeply before stepping through. Flora followed, bending down to enter. Just like me, she was struck speechless by what lay beyond the door. I took her hand and pulled her in with me.

The room beyond was another stone chamber, surprisingly spacious and softly illuminated. Up until this point, the entire experience had felt surreal and ancient; everything we had encountered seemed steeped in history. Yet, within this chamber, everything appeared strikingly modern—though even "modern" felt inadequate, as it seemed ahead of our time. The devices in the room were like nothing I had seen before.

The metallic objects cast a gentle silver-gray glow. One side of the room housed what looked like a massive control console, adorned with an array of instruments and lights, their colors shifting and flickering as if in operation. On the opposite side, another secret door was slowly opening, revealing a metal box with the contours of a coffin, topped by a transparent cover.

The metal box stopped at the center of the room and began to rise, hovering about two feet off the ground before coming to a halt.

The instruments and lights on the console became even more animated. Flora and I stood there, overwhelmed. After a moment, Flora exclaimed, "Oh my God, was all this brought here by B when he returned to Earth?"

My own voice, tinged with astonishment, answered, "Of course, it was brought by B!"

As soon as I spoke, our voices echoed from a corner of the room, replaying our recent exchange. Flora and I turned toward the sound, searching for the source, but our eyes found only shadows and silence. No device was visible, nothing tangible to explain the voice that had sliced through the stillness. We exchanged a look, a silent agreement to investigate, when suddenly, the air was cleaved by an eerie voice—neither male nor female—intoning, "You are here!"

The strangeness of the voice sent a chill through us, yet understanding dawned quickly. The sound was peculiar because it was mimicking us, replaying the snippets of our own speech since entering the chamber. It was as if the unseen device was calibrating itself, seeking a language we could comprehend. The result was a voice that blended both male and female tones, reflecting our presence.

Once I grasped this, my heartbeat steadied, and the androgynous voice spoke again, weaving through the air with an unsettling calm: "Assuming that you already know everything, if you wish to proceed, please lie in the box. We will arrange everything."

Then silence fell, deep and resonant. Flora, urgency in her voice, called out, "We struggle to accept all this; can you offer further explanation?"

She repeated her plea thrice, but the chamber remained mute, as if the very air had swallowed her words. I turned to her, my voice low and thoughtful. "It seems we can't converse with them directly," I said, a realization dawning that communication here was a one-way street, an enigma wrapped in layers of silence and echo.

Flora agreed with my conclusion: "Then we should lie in the box."

Taking a deep breath, I held Flora's hand, and together we approached the mysterious box.

We hadn't discussed it further, yet we both felt an unspoken understanding: we intended to lie in the box together. However, as we reached the box, we were taken aback by what we saw.

Upon reaching the box, its transparent cover opened automatically. Previously, amidst the myriad of novel sights, we hadn't closely inspected the box's interior. Now, as the cover lifted, we saw a groove shaped like a human figure inside the box, with the rest of the space solid. At the head of the groove, there was an additional space of about two feet, the purpose of which eluded me. Crucially, the box could hold only one person, not both of us.

Standing beside the box, Flora and I exchanged glances, both of us hesitant yet resolute.

Flora asked, "Who's going?"

Without hesitation, I replied, "I'll go."

There was no doubt in our minds now: whoever lay in that box would be transported to the other side.

Flora, ever the pragmatic thinker, immediately weighed the complexities of our grim task. "I won't stand in your way," she conceded. "But we mustn't overlook the unpredictable forces at play."

"If you mean there might be danger," I countered, "then you should let me go."

Flora didn't contest further. She lowered her head, contemplating the gravity of our decision. After a pause, she asked softly, "If you go, will you come back?"

Her question reminded me of a similar moment in the cave where the Black Army lived in South America. Back then, Flora's answer had been confident. "Of course I will come back!" I assured her.

Flora looked at me intently, tears brimming in her eyes. Her vulnerability was startling; I had never seen her cry before. Her sudden tears left me flustered. "Then, you go!" I blurted out, my resolve wavering in the face of her emotions.

She shook her head gently, "Isn't it the same? Either way, we have to part."

Her words hung heavy in the air, the reality of our choices sinking in. We stood at a crossroads, faced with the prospect of separation, the unknown stretching out before us. The moment demanded courage and trust in the path we chose, knowing that the bonds we shared would endure regardless of distance or time.

In the dim, enigmatic chamber, where shadows danced like whispers, I felt a pang of bitter irony mingling with the gravity of the moment. Flora's reluctance to part from me was palpable, a silent acknowledgment that this farewell might stretch into eternity. Her tears, rare as a comet's tail, painted a portrait of her inner turmoil.

This realization weighed on me: it wasn't just about my departure; Flora couldn't bring herself to leave either. The gravity of our decision settled in like the finality of an ancient prophecy.

I lingered in contemplation, my thoughts a labyrinth of uncertainty. Finally, I sighed, the sound echoing in the stillness. "Alright, let's just forget about it. We won't go. Like the king, let's put this matter behind us."

Her eyes, sharp as a scholar's gaze, pierced through my resolve. "Others might let it fade into oblivion, but not you. These thoughts will haunt you, and you'll curse the moment I held you back."

I sighed again, "It's true that forgetting won't be easy, but I won't blame you. This is my decision."

As I spoke, I drew her into an embrace, a fragile peace settling around us like dust upon ancient relics. Her tears subsided, leaving us in a tranquil silence.

With the decision made to stay, a calmness settled over us, relieving the tension we felt upon entering. We took the opportunity to explore and appreciate the marvel of the place, knowing that once we left, the king would seal it permanently. This time, he might use a more permanent method, such as grouting, ensuring no one could return.

We wanted to absorb as much as possible, to engrave the wonder of this room in our minds. It felt like stepping into a scene from a science fiction movie, yet it was real. The soft, pervasive light had no discernible source, adding to the mystique.

We examined the various devices, clearly advanced and precise, yet their purposes were beyond our understanding. We hoped to find another recorder to gain more insights into the mysteries of "the other side," but none were visible.

After an hour, we found ourselves back at the box with the human-shaped groove. I intended just a final glance before leaving with Flora, but curiosity got the better of me.

Pointing to the space at the head of the groove, I mused, "Look at this space here. What's it for if someone's lying in the box?"

Flora considered it, "Maybe it's to adjust for height since they wouldn't know if the person is tall or short."

I disagreed, "That doesn't seem right. The groove is fixed to a typical human size, especially the head. If it were for height, there should be room at the feet. Feet can extend, but the head can't."

Flora chuckled, "How do you know the groove part isn't flexible? Maybe it is."

I replied quickly, "Well, let's see if it is."

With this newfound curiosity and determination, we decided to test the groove's flexibility, knowing that while our decision was to leave, the pull of discovery was strong. Every moment spent in this extraordinary place only deepened our awe and wonder at the unknown.

As I reached out to open the transparent cover of the box, I expected resistance, but it lifted effortlessly at my touch. I pressed down on the human-shaped groove inside. "Aha, look, it's hard, just like a plaster model!" I declared.

Flora, not interested in continuing the debate, shrugged. "It's hard, so what?"

"Then we still can't figure out the purpose of the space above the head," I mused.

With a laugh, Flora suggested, "Maybe it's for hair!"

I chuckled and leaned in for a closer look at the space. Tiny holes dotted one side, glinting metallically in the light. While their purpose was a mystery, I decided to join in on the jest. "Isn't it? Look at all these holes—perfect for strands of hair!"

Flora rolled her eyes. "Not funny. We may not know everything about hair, but it's not entirely without explanation."

I grinned, "So there's a book that explains the uses of hair?"

She glared at me playfully. "I didn't think your common sense was so lacking!"

While I could brush off other criticisms, being told I lacked common sense was a hit to my pride. "Give me an example!" I challenged.

With a confident smile, Flora began, "According to records, hair is the source of all power—"

Before she could finish, a light bulb went off in my head. "Samson!" I interrupted.

Flora nodded, "You remembered it too!"

We both laughed, the tension of our earlier dilemma dissipating in the shared humor. The biblical tale of Samson, whose strength was tied to his hair, seemed an oddly fitting reference in this room of mysteries. It was a reminder of how legends and science could sometimes intersect in the most unexpected ways.

Standing there, amidst the strange and advanced technology, it was clear that while we might not uncover every secret, the journey and the insights gained along the way were what truly mattered. Our shared laughter was a small victory against the enigma surrounding us.

I took a deep breath, reflecting on the notion that hair, indeed, could be a source of power. The story of Samson came vividly to mind—his strength was legendary, and it was all tied to his hair. If not for Delilah's betrayal, Samson might have remained undefeated.

"Yes," I agreed, "Samson's story is a unique example that highlights the significance of hair. It's well-documented."

Flora smiled knowingly, "There might be more such records that we just haven't come across yet."

I pondered aloud, "I still can't wrap my head around it. The voice instructed us to lie down in the box. Does that mean whoever does so disappears, or is transported to the other side?"

Flora frowned, considering the logistics, "It doesn't add up. This box can't possibly facilitate a space journey."

I shrugged, venturing a theory, "Maybe it has a function to decompose the body into atoms, then those atoms travel through space at high speed and reassemble on the other side."

Though I spoke earnestly, Flora burst into laughter, "Oh dear, what if they don't know how you look? They might reassemble you with a cross-eyed gaze and a crooked mouth! Perhaps you should send a photo ahead."

Her laughter was infectious, and I couldn't help but join in, albeit with a dry chuckle. "Very funny, isn't it?"

Playfully, I reached out to grab her, intending to enact my usual mock punishment for her witty remarks. I would pull her close and give a gentle tap on her head.

But this time, as I reached for her, Flora deftly blocked my hand with her arm and gave me a strong push.

Standing so close to the box with its open cover, I was caught off balance. The push sent me tumbling backward into the box.

As I fell, I heard Flora's laughter, light and unburdened. Yet, in that instant, a sense of unease gripped me. Something felt amiss, as if I had crossed an unseen threshold into the unknown, and the reality of the situation was about to shift dramatically.

# CHAPTER 15

# ARRIVAL AT
# THE UNFORESEEN REALM

As soon as I landed in the human-shaped groove, an immense force seemed to envelop me, pulling my entire body downward with a magnetic inevitability. Almost instantly, I was immobilized, lying perfectly in the groove.

Instinctively, I tried to rise, but the transparent cover swiftly closed over me. In less than a second, I heard Flora's startled cry, followed by the sight of her face, filled with panic, appearing above me on the cover.

Simultaneously, the box began to move backward at high speed—not my body, but the entire box itself. Having emerged from a secret door when we entered, it now retracted rapidly. I managed one last glimpse of Flora's anxious face before it disappeared from view, accompanied by her fading exclamation. I wanted to shout, to call out to her, but no sound escaped my lips. Instead, I felt a powerful suction at my head, pulling my hair taut.

In that surreal moment, an experiment came to mind—a scientist using static electricity to make hair stand on end. It seemed my hair was reacting similarly, under the influence of this mysterious force.

Just as my hair was pulled straight, everything went dark. My vision was obscured in an instant of profound blackness, lasting mere seconds before I slipped into a dreamlike state.

I found myself surrounded by concentric halos of light, advancing forward as if traveling through a luminous tunnel. The speed at which I traversed these radiant circles was indescribable, a sensation of moving beyond the constraints of the physical world. I couldn't see my body, only felt the relentless forward momentum.

Though the experience was both wondrous and mesmerizing, my mind remained acutely aware of the seriousness of my predicament. The dazzling display of lights held no allure; instead, my thoughts raced, piecing together the reality of the situation.

It was clear what had occurred—an outcome neither Flora nor I had anticipated or desired. Her unintended push had sent me into the box, setting me on a trajectory toward "the other side."

In that fleeting moment, my thoughts turned to Flora. Her cries, her look of alarm, and the knowledge that she was left behind filled me with a mix of regret and determination.

I had no idea what Flora saw at that moment or how she was feeling now. Under normal circumstances, I would have been consumed by anxiety. Yet, strangely, despite thinking about all this, I felt an unusual calmness.

I couldn't tell how long I had been enveloped by the halo of light. Just as I began to ponder the nature of this experience, my vision turned dark once more.

I felt as if I had passed through numerous dark passages, rapidly entering something unknown. This sensation was indescribably peculiar, as if my being was divided into countless parts, each entering a new realm.

The darkness was fleeting, and soon my surroundings brightened with a familiar soft light. I quickly surveyed the scene and noticed two figures in long white garments with long hair, observing me. I also caught sight of myself—dressed in a white robe and with hair at least a meter long, standing straight up, extending toward a metal plate adorned with innumerable small holes. Unlike the observers, whose hair hung down, mine reached skyward.

Realizing I had arrived at my destination, I felt a rush of disbelief. I reached out to push the transparent cover aside, but the sight of my hand stopped me cold. It was my hand, yet not my hand—larger and different. Shocked, I quickly retracted it and instinctively touched my face with these unfamiliar hands.

The two observers, witnessing my confusion, broke into joyful expressions. "Welcome! Welcome!" they exclaimed, and the transparent cover rose automatically.

In unfamiliar surroundings, it's natural to feel fear and hostility. But the friendliness in their faces and voices instantly dispelled my unease. I've heard "welcome" countless times in my life, yet this was different. I could feel the genuine warmth and sincerity in their words.

As the cover lifted and I stood, they approached me, one on each side, taking my hands warmly. The person on my left said, "We've known you for a long time, but this is our first meeting."

I was taken aback by the statement, unsure of its meaning, and could only stare in response.

Seeing my confusion, the man looked surprised. "You don't understand? Is something wrong with the translation? Or is it something you don't typically say?"

Quickly, I reassured him, "I understand! I understand!"

Despite the overwhelming strangeness of the situation, their genuine welcome and the realization that I was finally on "the other side" filled me with a mix of curiosity and cautious optimism. This was a new beginning, and I was eager to discover what this place held in store.

As I spoke, I took a deep breath and asked, "Where am I now?" My nerves made it difficult to get the words out smoothly, so I had to pause and gather myself.

The two people laughed, their smiles exuding a kindness and innocence akin to that of a baby. Seeing such warmth, I felt reassured, as if fear had no place here. "You are back! My friend, you are back!" they exclaimed with genuine joy.

I should mention that once the transparent cover lifted, my hair, which had been standing straight, fell naturally to hang long like theirs.

I swallowed and echoed their words in a whisper, "I'm back?"

"Yes, you are back," they confirmed. "Perhaps you don't fully understand, but we will explain everything to you—"

I interrupted, "No, I understand! I'm back! I understand!"

Their faces lit up with happiness. "You understand, that's great!" they said, clearly pleased.

Despite their reassurances, my heart raced with a new urgency. "I want to go back. How can I go back? I need to return!"

They exchanged a glance, their expressions shifting to something unreadable. Just as I prepared to plead further, a door opened, and another person entered. Upon seeing him, I involuntarily gasped, "Ah!"

This was someone I had seen before, in dreams that felt ethereal and distant. But now, standing before me in reality, he was undeniably present, tangible. It was D.

D walked in with a calm demeanor and addressed me directly, "Since you're here, why not stay for a while?"

His words sparked a moment of hope within me. "You mean, I can go back?" I asked eagerly, latching onto the possibility of returning to my world.

D's presence, familiar yet enigmatic, offered a comforting anchor in this unfamiliar realm. Here was a chance to understand more, to bridge the gap between dreams and reality, and possibly find a way back home.

Before D could respond, another figure entered the room. It was B. Seeing him, I instinctively placed my hand on my forehead in disbelief.

B addressed me directly: "Everyone on Earth dreams of coming here. Why, after arriving, would you choose to leave? The opportunity you've encountered is rare, something many people on Earth would never experience. Why abandon it so easily?"

My mind was a whirlwind of confusion. Overwhelmed, I retreated a few steps and collapsed into a chair, my gaze darting between D and B as I struggled to articulate my thoughts: "You—you—"

B smiled reassuringly, "You know us, don't you? In fact, everyone on Earth is familiar with us, though your understanding varies greatly."

Amidst my confusion, an absurd question escaped my lips, unbidden and almost regrettable: "Is Edison here?"

As if on cue, the door opened again, and A and C entered. C chuckled, "Indeed, Edison—a human whose genetic traits manifested remarkably. He returned here."

I took a moment to process this, glancing from A to B to C and finally to D. A spoke with a calming presence, "Relax, there's nothing to fear here. Initially, it was us who should have been apprehensive. But upon your arrival, we understood everything about you, so there's no need for fear. You may have some faults, but we believe you can become one of us. Don't worry."

Gradually, my anxiety subsided, replaced by a growing sense of clarity.

I realized one undeniable fact: I had returned. This place, wherever in the vast universe it resided, was the origin of Earth's ancestors. And now, I found myself here, far from my home planet.

With this understanding came a flood of questions, each vying for attention in my mind, leaving me uncertain where to begin.

In my distracted state, I hadn't noticed four chairs had materialized, and A, B, C, and D were now seated around a round table with me. It mirrored the scene from my second dream.

I mumbled, "Is this not a dream?"

D laughed lightly, "You could say it is, or it isn't."

C asked, "Is the situation on Earth still as dire?"

Momentarily taken aback, I responded, "It's even worse, you—"

B interjected, "Let's refrain from questioning him for now. He should first understand his circumstances."

A, C, and D nodded in agreement. B continued, "You're already familiar with everything documented by the three recorders. That simplifies my explanation."

Curiosity piqued, I asked, "How do you know what I know?"

B smiled and explained, "When you came here, it wasn't your physical self, but your thought beam. Do you understand? Your thought beam traveled here, while your—"

I interrupted, shocked, "My—my—body is still on Earth?"

B nodded, confirming my suspicion. I raised my hands, examining them, and B anticipated my question, "This isn't your original body. It's an extra one we keep for such replacements."

I swallowed hard, processing the information. "Can I—can I see what I look like?"

A, B, C, and D all laughed warmly, "Of course!"

A tilted his head slightly, and I witnessed something extraordinary. One of his long hairs rose, extending to touch a black spot on the wall behind him. As soon as it made contact, a screen appeared, displaying our reflection in the room.

I saw myself: a handsome man in my prime, dressed similarly to them. Yet, I had little time to admire my appearance. My mind was fixated on the realization—hair! They could use their hair to operate devices. With each hair potentially as versatile as a finger, the efficiency was astounding, far surpassing the use of mere ten fingers.

I stood there, mouth agape, stunned by the revelation.

D chuckled at A, "You've certainly surprised our friend!"

Turning to me, he explained, "Indeed, hair can activate special controls. This is just one of its uses. You can learn it too. It won't be any harder than learning to use your fingers when you were born on Earth!"

I replied, "I thought hair's function was merely as a conduit for thought beams."

B elaborated, "Yes, it's also a channel for thought beams. Your thought beam leaves your original body and enters this one. When not in use, it passes through an instrument, which allows us to understand you as well as you know yourself."

I nodded, processing B's explanation. One question answered, I ventured another: "Eternal life—is it achieved like this?"

B confirmed, "Yes! Here, that's how it is. Do you still wish to return?"

Taking a deep breath, I insisted, "I must go back! You don't understand—I'm from Earth! Born and raised there, with countless ties to it."

B chuckled, "But Earthlings originated here. The conditions on Earth are harsh, and Earthlings are less appealing. Since you're here—"

Before he could finish, a sudden impulse drove me to interject, "If Earth is so undesirable, why send so many of your people there?"

The question hung in the air, reflecting my deep connection to Earth and the complexities of our origins. It was a question that sought to understand the motivations behind the migration and the ties between our worlds, revealing the intertwined destinies of Earth and this place.

A responded, "They are full of sins and must be sent away!"

I was taken aback, "If everything here is so beautiful, why are there so many sinners?"

This question had lingered in my mind for some time, and finally voicing it brought a sense of relief. However, I didn't anticipate the reaction it would provoke. The four of them exchanged puzzled glances, seemingly at a loss for an answer.

After a moment, C suggested, "You might find the answer to your question from the leader."

Eager for clarity, I pressed, "Where is he? Take me to him so he can explain this to me!"

After a brief hesitation, D replied, "Since you've come here, you deserve to understand everything before deciding to return. We have no reason to keep anything from you." He paused before continuing, "Please come with us, and you can also see the environment here."

My emotions settled as I absorbed the reality of my situation. My "thought beam"—a concept previously unknown to me—had left my original body on Earth and traversed the vastness of space to reach this distant world, the birthplace of humanity.

Explaining it in such a manner might seem complex, but a simpler analogy might help: my soul (or thought beam) left my earthly body, traveled to "heaven," and entered a new body here.

In this "heaven," I encountered beings akin to immortal gods, possessing incredible abilities (technologically advanced) and eternal life. Ages ago, they had exiled a group of transgressors to Earth. Additionally, they had dispatched four individuals to Earth to guide the descendants of those exiles.

With my thoughts somewhat organized, I followed them out. We traversed a long corridor, empty of others, before emerging onto a vast lawn, alive with activity. I observed people moving about, along with unfamiliar buildings, animals, and plants.

I described everything as "unfamiliar" because nothing resembled what I had known. These sights were not only new but beyond anything I had ever imagined.

The grass beneath my feet was a green more vibrant than any I had seen, its softness offering a comfort beyond comparison. Flowers bloomed in vivid hues and designs that would surpass the creativity of Earth's top designers. The buildings, too, were architectural marvels, their forms both aesthetically pleasing and radiating a sense of safety.

As we walked, A, B, C, and D exchanged greetings with passersby, who nodded cordially at me. This place, with its harmonious blend of nature and innovation, felt like a utopia—a world far removed from the struggles of Earth.

The awe of this new world was tempered by the curiosity and anticipation of meeting the leader, who could hold the answers to the profound questions swirling in my mind.

In this completely unfamiliar environment, I felt a surprising sense of familiarity and belonging. It was as if I were a wanderer finally returning home after years of hardship, greeted by old friends and enveloped in warmth and intimacy.

As I walked with A, B, C, and D, I couldn't help but marvel, "This place is incredible! Even the air feels different from Earth's."

A knowing smile played on B's lips. "Of course. This place was once home to your ancestors. Over millennia, your genetic makeup has evolved to thrive here. This is your true homeland. On Earth, everyone is merely a guest."

Though I remained silent, I couldn't help but acknowledge the truth in B's words.

Humans had inhabited Earth for millions of years, yet it was clear we weren't originally from there. Earthlings struggled to adapt fully to Earth's climate; subtle changes in humidity could make us uncomfortable. Here, however, the sky was a pure, brilliant blue, and the air so pristine that the concept of "temperature" seemed irrelevant. I felt seamlessly integrated into the environment, perfectly at ease.

I glanced skyward, noting the light source. Unlike Earth's harsh, burning sun, the light here emanated from a vast, gentle halo. Its illumination was soft and soothing, inviting contemplation without discomfort.

We passed various landmarks, including a grand fountain. Observing others, I mimicked their actions, drinking from its waters. The liquid was refreshingly sweet, quenching my thirst and bringing a sense of calm.

After what felt like fifteen minutes—though I sensed time operated differently here—I entered another building. This notion of "fifteen minutes" was an Earthly perception, and I would need to explain this temporal discrepancy later.

Upon entering a particular room, a familiar jolt compelled me to exclaim, "Ah!"

The room was instantly recognizable—it was the one from my "dream." Without hesitation, I identified its occupants: the "leader" and C's father.

Their smiles were welcoming as they invited me to sit. "Please, have a seat! You've been remarkable for quite some time. We're delighted the device brought you here, rather than anyone else!"

Their words filled me with a mix of pride and curiosity. Sitting before these illustrious figures, I felt a sense of destiny unfolding, ready to embrace whatever revelations this encounter would bring.

C's father asked, "You've taken a brief look around. What do you think? Quite impressive, isn't it?"

I answered sincerely, "It's incredible! Beyond anything I could have imagined!"

C's father smiled, "Naturally, you belong here, as do all people of Earth."

I took a deep breath and sat down, joined by A, B, C, and D. Though the situation felt dreamlike, it was undeniably real, and I was an integral part of it.

Sensing that the leader and C's father anticipated my questions, I noticed a hint of hesitation in their gaze.

After a pause, C's father spoke, "You're curious about why a group of people appeared here years ago and why we had to send them to other planets, aren't you?"

I nodded, "Yes, I'm trying to understand why such individuals emerged. Is it like on Earth, where there's a struggle between good and evil, and good triumphs by banishing evil?"

A few soft sighs followed my question, their origin unclear, yet their expressions hinted at unspoken truths.

After a moment, C's father began, "Let's start from the beginning, if you have time—"

"Of course, I have time," I interjected. "Since I'm here, I need to understand everything before I leave."

C's father frowned slightly, and I suddenly remarked, "You know, on Earth, you have a name! It's called—"

Before I could finish, he waved his hand to interrupt, "I know, it's because of him," gesturing to C. "He made my name known on Earth. Here, everyone has a name, but you don't need to know them. I'll try to explain briefly to save time."

He repeatedly emphasized "saving time" and "do you have time?" At that moment, I didn't understand why he was so concerned with time, especially since everyone here appeared to live with the ease and freedom reminiscent of "immortal life" from ancient tales. Why the preoccupation with time?

This emphasis on time hinted at complexities I had yet to grasp, suggesting that, despite their eternal nature, there were intricacies in their existence that required attentiveness and perhaps urgency. As C's father prepared to unveil the history and reasons behind their actions, I braced myself for insights that would bridge the gap between the two worlds and illuminate the path forward.

Of course, as time went on, I understood why C's father emphasized time, and I came to appreciate his concern for me.

"Alright," I agreed, "please start from the beginning."

C's father began, "Our planet hosts a variety of creatures, and we are among them. Over time, we evolved to a stage where we could freely allow our thought beams to leave our bodies."

I nodded, "Yes, you have achieved the ability to live forever."

C's father continued, "Indeed, we accomplished eternal life, which is the pinnacle of evolution for any species. Once we mastered this, our lives transformed significantly. Originally, life perpetuated through cycles of death and rebirth, with no direct connection between the deceased and the new life, just varying degrees of influence."

He paused, gauging my understanding, and I assured him, "I understand. That's how life continues on Earth today."

"Exactly," C's father affirmed. "Back then, although we could control our thought beams, we couldn't prevent our bodies from aging and losing function. In other words, continual transformation of the body was necessary to achieve eternal life."

This revelation provided profound insight into their evolution. They had reached a stage where the mind's essence could transcend physical limitations, but the body still followed a natural cycle. Their journey hinted at an advanced understanding of life and consciousness, a journey that Earth, in its own way, was only beginning to explore.

As I absorbed this knowledge, I realized the gap between our worlds was not just physical or temporal but also philosophical. Their mastery over life and death was something that could reshape our understanding of existence itself.

# CHAPTER 16

# CRAFTING

# IMMORTALITY IN THE LAB

I took a deep breath, trying to grasp this method of immortality, which, in some ways, matched what I had imagined. But one persistent question gnawed at my mind: "How can you find so many bodies if you have to keep changing them?"

C's father responded, "Yes, that's an extremely challenging issue. After we discovered the secret of immortality, the greatest obstacle became the scarcity of suitable bodies. Naturally, new babies are born, but they have their own growth and mental development processes. We can't just take that away from them. To address this, some suggested the idea of self-continuation. The so-called self-continuation—"

He paused, closing his eyes briefly before continuing, "Self-continuation involves a couple keeping two of their children for their own life continuation. However, this approach has obvious drawbacks. First, it robs those children of their own life experiences. Secondly, once life becomes immortal, the continuation of the next generation loses significance. We can't support an ever-growing population without mortality."

I listened intently, agreeing, "Indeed, self-continuation doesn't seem like a viable solution."

C's father said, "So, we turned to a different approach."

I closed my eyes, struggling to conceive of any other feasible solution.

C's father explained, "Since our lives are eternal, new life isn't necessary. What we need is fresh bodies for continuous replacement. Our new solution was to create bodies."

I was taken aback, glancing around at everyone present.

B gave a wry smile, "Do you think we're robots? Of course not, we're flesh-and-blood beings!"

I stammered, "But you mentioned—creating bodies?"

C's father sighed, "Yes, it's a significant error in our evolution, or perhaps the only one. By 'creating bodies,' I mean we've shifted the development of flesh from the mother's womb to the laboratory."

I exclaimed, "In vitro fertilization!"

C's father paused, "Something along those lines. We cultivate bodies using human reproductive cells in the lab."

The concept was both astonishing and unsettling, yet I remained silent, absorbing what was said. This place continually exceeded my expectations and challenged my understanding of life and existence.

Despite the strangeness of it all, I realized they had ingeniously adapted to the challenges of immortality. Their solution, while controversial, reflected their commitment to sustaining life without infringing on the natural cycle of birth and growth. It was a testament to their advanced evolution, though not without its ethical complexities and implications.

C's father continued, "When we first implemented this method, it seemed like a breakthrough. The bodies developed in the laboratory could grow rapidly and be strengthened through special techniques. As the original body aged and lost function, anyone could choose a new body and begin anew."

The more I listened, the more bewildered I became, gesturing for clarity. C's father paused, sensing my confusion.

After a moment, I asked, "Hold on a minute! These lab-grown bodies—don't they have thoughts?"

The room filled with sighs, indicating the gravity of the issue. C's father didn't respond immediately but urged, "Just listen." He paused again, then explained, "Women no longer faced the pains of childbirth, which brought great relief.

Initially, we believed the problem was solved. But a significant issue lay hidden—the very one you mentioned!"

I asked, "These lab-grown beings—do they have their own thoughts?"

A profound silence followed. Then the leader spoke, "Yes, they do have thoughts, but these thoughts deviate from ours. They're extremely primitive, thoughts we abandoned long ago through evolution. Yet these beings, due to unknown factors, have remained disconnected from our evolutionary progress, becoming—"

"Sinners!" I interjected.

Silence settled again before C's father continued, "Yes. After a considerable turmoil, about a million of them clashed with us. It was a war unlike any seen in ages, resulting in this group's—"

I stood abruptly, raising my voice, "This large group was stripped of intelligence and sent to Earth by you!"

C's father confirmed, "Yes."

My emotions surged, and I couldn't help but exclaim, "So, these so-called sinners were your creation!"

My accusation hung in the air, leaving everyone speechless.

B sighed, "You could say that."

I gestured emphatically. Despite my chaotic thoughts, I spoke calmly, "That means these sinners aren't to blame. You bear the responsibility!"

The leader's expression was tinged with sorrow, "We have paid the price for this mistake."

I pressed on, "Price? What price? Sending four people to Earth to 'save' Earthlings? They just made a brief visit and returned. What did they truly accomplish? Your errors have led to untold suffering for countless sentient lives on Earth!"

The weight of my words settled heavily in the room. It was a stark confrontation with the consequences of their actions, a reminder of the profound impact of their decisions on Earth and its inhabitants. The leader's acknowledgment of their mistake was a step toward understanding, but it was clear that the repercussions were far-reaching and complex, requiring more than a simple resolution.

C's father protested, "It's unfair to say that! As for him—" he pointed at C, "do you know the suffering he endured on Earth?"

I found myself laughing, though I wasn't sure why. "I know," I replied, "according to what I've read, he was betrayed by someone he trusted and whipped with a two-section whip embedded with copper balls. His chest and abdomen were particularly brutalized, his hands and feet pierced by long nails, his face struck hard, and his skull pierced by a sharp weapon!"

C's father nodded solemnly, "Yes, his suffering on Earth was unparalleled! Why do you laugh?"

I explained, "He's different. Despite the pain, he had hope. He knew he'd be resurrected and return. What does temporary pain matter? He knew he'd be free of it someday. Even so, he found it unbearable and pleaded not to bear such a burden! But people on Earth are trapped in endless suffering without hope, living their lives in pain."

B quickly interjected, "No, no! We've already told Earthlings that if they truly wish to return, we will guide them back!"

I leaned forward, placing my hands on the table. "That's the problem. Without your presence, Earthlings are unaware there's another place for them. They must strive to improve their own world. But you've disrupted it and failed to see it through. Earthlings' suffering has only increased!"

A's frustration was evident. "Earthlings are so flawed; they deserve to suffer!"

I retorted, "Yes, but their flaws originated in your laboratory. Earthlings also have redeeming qualities. Many strive to better themselves despite their failures, which are even more dismal because you abandoned them. Your failure plunged the kind-hearted into despair. You created evil and then neglected to punish it. What is really happening?"

The room fell silent, the weight of my words hanging heavily in the air. After a long pause, A broke the silence, "I've always advocated for the ruthless elimination of all evils as the only way to correct our past mistakes!"

I took a deep breath and responded to A, "I agree with your idea. But it wasn't implemented when you came to Earth, nor is it now. And you—" I gestured towards B and C, "your methods are ineffective. It's a form of hypocrisy, leaving principles unacted upon. Your actions seek only to ease your conscience, ignoring their actual efficacy."

The silence that followed was thick with contemplation and unspoken regret. It was clear that the gravity of their past actions and inactions had far-reaching consequences. The responsibility they bore was not just to Earthlings, but to the ideals they once upheld and the future they still had the power to shape.

C's lips moved silently, as if struggling to find words. B offered a bitter smile, "The power of evil is deeply entrenched; you can't expect immediate change."

I sighed, "It's not about slow change; it's worsening! You left Earth thousands of years ago, and things have deteriorated. How many people have your devices actually brought back?"

C's voice was barely audible, "Not many."

I pressed, "Why not? Are there too few worthy individuals, or is your technology insufficient to retrieve the weakened thought beams of Earthlings?"

A fixed his gaze on me, "Your words contradict themselves. You acknowledge Earth's people's wickedness, yet criticize us for bringing too few back. Isn't that contradictory?"

I took a deep breath, "Not at all. Earthlings were inherently flawed, but when you visited, you shared truths and hoped for improvement. Those who grew better became victims of evil, isolated and vulnerable."

D shook his head slowly, "Are you saying our efforts were not only futile but exacerbated Earth's suffering?"

I replied, "Indeed!" Pointing at D, I continued, "You have taught that good and evil are relative; where good exists, evil persists. Do you understand? Without any good, people would wallow in evil unknowingly, like beasts. But you sowed the seeds of discernment between good and evil."

D questioned, "And what's wrong with that?"

I met his gaze, frustration simmering just beneath the surface. "I've said it time and again—it's not about what's wrong. The real issue is your absence. By leaving, by abandoning the mission to punish evil, you have relinquished the showcase of your power. The responsibility to rectify this is yours, and yours alone." I turned sharply, pointing an accusatory finger at B. "You harp on about cause and effect, about retribution, yet where on Earth is there any evidence of evil being punished? The chaos there is a direct consequence of your mistakes. You spared them from destruction, opting for exile instead. Now, that mercy demands accountability."

The leader exhaled, a deep sigh that seemed to echo in the stillness. "Are you suggesting we descend upon Earth, wielding our might to obliterate all that is evil, rather than entrusting the Earth's inhabitants to awaken to their conscience?"

"Yes!" I replied, my voice resolute, cutting through the tension like a blade.

"But," the leader hesitated, "such a course would mean the annihilation of countless lives."

"And yet," I countered swiftly, "it would also mean the eradication of evil."

A charged silence fell as the leader exchanged a glance with C's father. Then, C's father spoke up, his voice measured. "It's a proposition worth considering. But tell me, if you despise Earth's wickedness so intensely, why do you wish to return?"

I sighed, spreading my hands in a gesture of resignation. "Were I alone, I'd gladly remain here. But back on Earth, there's someone waiting for me—my wife, Flora. I implore you, take responsibility. Don't let those who await your leadership be disappointed, and don't allow evil to fester unchecked."

The leader nodded, a solemn promise in his eyes. "We will give your words the consideration they deserve."

I managed a wry smile, knowing well I couldn't compel immediate action. Yet, the leader continued, "You've lingered here long enough. It's time you returned."

I glanced around, feeling the weight of time slip by—less than an hour, yet so much had changed. Though resolved to go back, a part of me yearned to stay, to explore this vast realm. "I wish to linger a while longer," I said. "To see more of this place."

C's father chuckled softly. "This world is seven times the size of Earth. How long do you intend to explore?"

"One month," I declared, a hint of determination in my voice.

D shook his head, "Unless you don't intend to return to Earth, it's best to leave immediately!"

I was momentarily stunned, "Why?"

"You forgot that the time ratio here to Earth is 1:50,000—" D began, and I was suddenly struck by the realization. Speechless, the enormity of it hit me.

A time ratio of 1:50,000 was incredible! An hour here equated to 50,000 hours on Earth. How many days did that make? Nearly six years!

I remembered Flora's panicked face as she rushed toward me when I fell into the box. Six years! While it had been an hour of vibrant experiences for me, they'd been six long, painful years for Flora.

Realizing I couldn't delay any longer, I hurriedly said, "Thank you for reminding me, I must leave!"

With urgency, I moved to the door. Though I craved more knowledge about this place, the thought that a minute here meant over a month on Earth propelled me not just to walk, but to run out.

A, B, C, and D followed swiftly. A peculiar-looking car awaited us. We climbed in, and it traversed the grass and fountain, entering the building. Once again, I found myself in the familiar room, seated under the transparent cover as instructed.

With anxiety peaking, I couldn't hold back my question any longer. "After six years, is my body still intact?"

B sighed, exasperation evident in their voice. "You're hopeless. Still fixated on that 'filthy flesh'!"

I retorted, slightly annoyed, "Don't joke! If that 'filthy flesh' no longer exists, would you have me become a wandering ghost?"

D laughed, "Rest assured, the metal box has preserved your body well!"

Relieved, I gestured for them to proceed. I watched as strands of A's hair rose to touch the glowing crystal, the transparent cover descending. Then, my hair stood on end, and I felt myself exiting this body through innumerable passages. With halos surrounding me, much like when I arrived, I advanced through a light-filled corridor.

Awareness returned, and I opened my eyes to find myself lying in the box. My hair settled, and outside was a strange light. I sensed the box moving, coming to rest in a stone room bathed in soft light. In that moment, I saw Flora!

Her face was ashen, shockingly pale, marked by extreme weariness. As the box moved out, her body trembled. When the cover opened automatically, she shook even more violently.

As I sat up from the box, a strange sound escaped Flora's throat. It became clear that she hadn't left this place since my departure. She must've waited, filled with desperation, only to see me suddenly appear again—no wonder she was so overwhelmed.

To avoid overstimulating her, I refrained from approaching immediately. Watching her rub her eyes with trembling hands, I spoke slowly and calmly, "It's me, I'm back."

Upon hearing my voice, Flora shook violently and rushed toward me. I quickly reached out to steady her, holding her hand firmly.

She stared at me for several minutes, pinching my face to ensure I was real and not an illusion. Once convinced, she quietly said, "You were gone for so long!"

I felt immense guilt and tried to explain my absence wasn't intentional. "It's only been an hour over there," I said.

Flora sighed, "It's been almost six years here."

Swallowing hard, I added, "I realized that when they reminded me. I didn't delay even a minute after that. These days..."

Flora explained, "This has been my home, and the king's been looking out for me. There were times I wanted to give up, but I remembered your promise to return."

"I promised you I'd come back," I reassured her.

As Flora took a deep breath, her body swayed. Her endurance had reached its limit, and she fainted right after exhaling.

I caught her just as a male-female voice announced, "Everything here will be destroyed in ten minutes, please leave quickly!"

With urgency driving my every move, I hoisted Flora onto my back and hurriedly ascended seven flights of stairs to the surface. The oppressive, familiar climate of Earth enveloped us, a stark reminder of the planet we once called home.

Flora regained consciousness as we emerged. Several houses and a troop stationed by the king surrounded us. Their expressions were as if they'd seen a specter when they saw us.

Ignoring their shock, I loudly ordered an immediate retreat.

Once aboard a military vehicle, we drove two or three kilometers away. We heard nothing but saw a towering dust column rise from where the seven-story stone chamber had stood, reaching skyward.

I had the driver stop, and we watched the dust column for about ten minutes until it settled back to the ground.

I knew then that the seven-story stone chamber was gone.

Turning to Flora, I asked, "What was it like when I left?"

Flora exhaled deeply, recalling the terrifying moment. Her face showed traces of shock. "It was so scary! When the transparent cover closed, the whole box moved inward. I rushed over and saw a halo appear in your hair, just like a fairy in a picture!"

I said, "Yes, I traveled there through my hair!"

Flora recounted, "The box moved incredibly fast, disappearing into a secret door in an instant. Once it closed, I tried countless ways to open it, but nothing worked!"

Her words hit me like a jolt. "It's a good thing you didn't succeed. My body was preserved behind that secret door. Opening it might have blocked my return—worse, I might have ended up like Bruce, trapped in the body of an Indian."

Flora's smile was awkward, revealing she hadn't smiled genuinely in six years. "Did you see Bruce over there?" she asked.

"No," I replied.

"What about Randy?" she inquired.

I shook my head, "No, and even if I did, I may not have recognized him. Honestly, I barely recognized myself there."

I recounted my surreal experience to Flora as we sped towards the palace, the landscape blurring into insignificance. Once inside the king's study, his initial shock gave way to rapt attention as I detailed the otherworldly events.

When I concluded, the king's expression was one of weary contemplation. "How long do you think it will take for them to decide?" His question hung in the air, heavy with implication.

I met his gaze, uncertain. "I can only hope it's soon."

The king's sigh was deep, resigned. "Soon? A month? By then, four thousand years might have passed here."

A bitter smile tugged at my lips, mirroring his resignation. His silence spoke volumes, a tacit decision to let the matter rest. With farewells exchanged, Flora and I departed the palace, leaving the mysteries of Nepal behind—but not forgotten.

As we departed, I reflected on the enormity of the situation. The disparity in time made it impossible to predict how soon or if those who had the power to effect change would do so. Yet, despite the uncertainty, I felt a renewed sense of purpose. Flora and I were together again, and with that reunion came hope—a hope that we could, in our way, contribute to making the world a better place, one decision at a time.

# POSTSCRIPT

After returning from "the other side," I find myself pondering why I was so insistent on coming back. If it were solely for Flora, I could have asked them to bring her over as well. I believe that, despite their limited success in "receiving" people over the years, they could achieve it if they focused their efforts on just one person.

Back on Earth, under the vast, mysterious sky, I often gaze up and wonder about that distant planet, knowing it's beyond what the naked eye can see.

Though I don't particularly enjoy everything about Earth, I find myself drawn to the things on "the other side." Yet, after spending millions of years here, Earth feels like home, despite its harsh environment. On "the other side," I felt like a guest, which might be part of why I insisted on returning.

Another reason is my dissatisfaction with "the other side." I don't agree with their attitude towards Earthlings. Evil must be confronted and destroyed, but when will their final judgment come? How long must Earth endure under the rule of evil before they act?

Given the time disparity, A, B, C, and D returned, and for them, only ten days have passed. If we wait for them to decide, as the king suggested, it could take thousands, even tens of thousands of years!

The final judgment of evil and the darker aspects of human nature feels an impossible wait. Earthlings possess both ugly and beautiful traits. Why does the ugly side often prevail, while the beautiful side struggles? Can Earthlings judge their own flaws rather than wait for intervention?

Waiting seems futile. Perhaps the solution lies in self-judgment, but do Earthlings have the opportunity or capacity to do so?

I find myself unable to answer these questions.

If anyone can provide answers, please share them with me.

* * *

In the sacred Amitabha Sutra, the Buddha imparted a profound revelation to the Elder Shariputra. He spoke of a realm lying far to the West, a hundred thousand million Buddha lands away—a world known as Ultimate Bliss. This ethereal domain, also named Sukhavati, is presided over by the venerable Amitabha Buddha, who tirelessly imparts the Dharma with compassion and wisdom.

Sukhavati, born from Amitabha's compassionate vows and boundless merits, is a Pure Land of unparalleled beauty and serenity. This paradise is devoid of pain and troubles, where happiness reigns supreme. The scriptures vividly depict this pure and solemn land: its vast, transparent earth stretches infinitely, untainted by the extremes of climate, and maintaining an eternal, gentle coolness. Golden roads shimmer beneath palatial structures, adorned meticulously with the seven treasures—gold, silver, crystal, agate, pearls, glass, and precious stones.

In the grand hall of this Western Paradise reside the "Three Holy Ones of the West"—Amitabha Buddha, Avalokitesvara, and Mahasthamaprapta Bodhisattva. Together, they impart the teachings of Buddhism to countless souls—friends, relatives, and virtuous beings alike. Seated majestically upon a lotus platform, Amitabha is flanked by his two celestial Bodhisattvas. In the surrounding sky, divine melodies fill the air, played by goddesses and resonating birds, while the trees of color vibrate with harmonious notes, all echoing the supreme truths of the universe—a realm fervently yearned for by the sentient beings of our Saha world.

At the heart of this Pure Land lies a lotus pond of seven treasures, where waters of astonishing merit flow, and countless "subtle and fragrant" lotus blossoms bloom. Those who, in our world, devoutly chant the Buddha's name find their own inscribed upon these sacred lotuses, destined to be reborn from them. This unique and wondrous Buddhist realm stands as a cosmic treasure, embodying the collective beauty of the Buddhas from all directions.

In Sukhavati, the cycle of suffering that binds sentient beings—birth, aging, illness, and death—ceases to exist. Born from lotuses, the inhabitants know not the pains of birth; the ageless tranquility spares them from the ravages of time; their harmonious existence shields them from illness; and with infinite lifespans, they are untouched by death. The worldly sufferings familiar to us—the unfulfilled desires, the presence of foes, the separation from loved ones, and the burdens of the five aggregates—are rendered obsolete.

Within this paradisiacal realm, beings experience unparalleled joy and bliss, their bodies and minds in perfect harmony. The transcendent beauty of Sukhavati defies description.

In this celestial haven, the air itself vibrates with divine wisdom. The teachings of the Buddhas resonate like celestial music, guiding countless souls towards enlightenment. It is a place where the pursuit of spiritual truth reigns supreme, a sanctuary for those seeking liberation and transcendence.

The vivid imagery of Sukhavati paints a picture of hope and redemption, a beacon for all who aspire to break free from the suffering of the mortal world.

* * *

In the sacred teachings, the Buddha provided guidance on how one might seek rebirth in the illustrious Pure Land. He advised that one should hold the Name of Amitabha Buddha in their heart, reciting it with unwavering focus and clarity. This single-hearted devotion ensures that, at the moment of death, Amitabha Buddha himself will come to guide the faithful to rebirth in the Pure Land.

Shakyamuni Buddha underscored the pivotal role of making a vow to be born in this blissful realm and emphasized the necessity of having faith in his words. As an enlightened being, his teachings are a beacon of truth, extending to us the promise of the Pure Land.

Devotees of the Pure Land tradition are well-acquainted with the triad of essential qualities: Faith, Vow, and Practice. These form the cornerstone for those aspiring to be reborn in the Pure Land, as outlined in the Amitabha Sutra, which serves as a foundational text for this spiritual path.

Moreover, Shakyamuni Buddha revealed that the praise for Amitabha Buddha's immeasurable virtues is not his alone. Buddhas from the ten directions join in extolling Amitabha's boundless merit, resonating with the profound commitments encapsulated in Amitabha's 48 Great Vows. Notably, the 17th vow promises that all Buddhas will sing his praises, affirming the universal reverence for his compassionate and transformative power.

* * *

Our conversation unfolded in the quietude of a library, the air thick with intellectual curiosity and spiritual yearning. My friend, a renowned scientist and a seeker of truth, leaned back thoughtfully before responding to my question.

"Ah," he began, a hint of a smile playing on his lips, "the skepticism towards the Western Paradise and Buddhism being superstition is not uncommon, especially in an age driven by empirical evidence and scientific inquiry. But let me share why I walk this path of both science and spirituality."

He paused, gathering his thoughts. "Science, at its core, is a pursuit of understanding the universe through observation, experimentation, and evidence. It seeks to uncover the laws that govern our physical reality. Buddhism, on the other hand, explores the nature of the mind and the universe, offering insights into the metaphysical aspects of existence. To me, they are two sides of the same coin."

I nodded, intrigued by his perspective. "So, how do you reconcile these seemingly disparate paths?"

"Integration," he replied with conviction. "Science provides the tools to understand the external world, while Buddhism offers a profound understanding of the internal world. Both demand rigor and discipline. In my journey, I've found that the teachings of Buddhism, particularly about rebirth and the Pure Land, resonate with the scientific principle of continuity and transformation. It's not about blind belief; it's about exploring these teachings with an open mind and heart."

He leaned forward, his eyes alight with passion. "What motivated me? The quest for truth. As a scientist, I am driven by curiosity, and as a Buddhist practitioner, I am drawn by the promise of inner peace and enlightenment. The concept of returning to Sukhavati, the Pure Land, is not just a mystical notion but a profound metaphor for liberation from the cycle of suffering."

I could see the depth of his conviction as he spoke. "So, you truly believe in the possibility of rebirth in the Pure Land?"

"Absolutely," he affirmed. "It's the culmination of a journey both scientific and spiritual. To return, to be reborn in a realm of bliss, is to transcend the limitations of this world. It is the ultimate synthesis of my life's work and my spiritual aspirations. The Pure Land is a state of being, a return to our true nature. And for me, that is the most beautiful journey of all."

His words lingered in the air, a testament to the harmonious blend of science and spirituality—a dialogue between the empirical and the ethereal, seeking truth in all its forms.

The professor's eyes gleamed with the clarity of someone who has traversed both the scientific and spiritual realms. As he responded to my question, his words were precise, yet imbued with a deep sense of purpose.

"As a scientist," he began, "I am naturally skeptical. My journey into Buddhism was not one of blind faith but of careful investigation and analysis. What sets Buddhism apart from other religions is its empirical approach to understanding human existence and the universe. Unlike religions that posit a supreme deity controlling all, Buddhism invites us to explore the nature of reality through the Buddha's insights into the universe and natural laws."

He paused, allowing the weight of his words to settle. "The Buddha's teachings resonate with the scientific principle of cause and effect. He identified that much of human suffering stems from actions that disrupt the natural order. To alleviate this suffering, one must align with these natural laws. Consider, for instance, the issue of environmental degradation. The smog that now plagues our cities is not a random occurrence; it is the result of human actions—our insatiable greed has upset the delicate balance of nature."

The professor's voice took on a tone of urgency as he continued. "Originally, the air was pure. Trees and forests played a crucial role in maintaining the equilibrium of oxygen and carbon dioxide. But in our pursuit of progress, we've produced excessive carbon emissions and decimated forests, tipping the scales and resulting in today's environmental crisis. This is a tangible example of how deviating from nature's laws leads to suffering—a principle deeply rooted in Buddhist philosophy."

He leaned back, his expression thoughtful. "My motivation to walk this path stems from the realization that Buddhism offers not just a spiritual refuge, but a practical framework for living in harmony with the world. It is a path of returning—returning to a state of balance, both within ourselves and with the environment. The journey to the Pure Land, then, is not merely an abstract concept, but a return to our inherent nature, free from the turmoil we have wrought upon ourselves and our planet."

In his eloquent synthesis of science and Buddhism, the professor conveyed a vision of a life lived in alignment with universal truths—a journey not only towards personal enlightenment but also towards collective healing and balance.

The professor leaned forward, his enthusiasm evident as he bridged the worlds of Buddhism and science with a compelling narrative. "Indeed," he began, "our current advocacy for environmental protection—limiting carbon emissions, conserving forests, and planting trees—reflects a deeper understanding and respect for the natural world. When we align our actions with these natural laws, we move toward a state of balance, and the troubles that plague us begin to dissipate."

He gestured thoughtfully, as if tracing the connections in the air. "What becomes clear is that the principles taught by the Buddha are profoundly aligned with these natural laws. In his teachings and scriptures, the Buddha distilled complex cosmic truths into accessible guidance, showing us how to live in harmony with the universe. This is a path of wisdom that encourages us to adjust our lives according to these timeless principles."

"Modern science, on the other hand," he continued, "seeks to unravel the mysteries of the universe through empirical study—how it began, what laws govern it. Both science and Buddhism are engaged in a quest to understand the universe, albeit through different lenses. They converge on the same ultimate goal: to reveal the truths of existence and guide us towards a richer, more harmonious life."

He smiled, a sense of harmony in his words. "From this perspective, Buddhism and science are not at odds. Rather, they complement each other beautifully. The insights from Buddhist teachings can enrich scientific inquiry, and scientific discoveries can deepen our appreciation of Buddhist wisdom. There's no inherent conflict between the teachings of Buddhism and the advancements of modern science. Both are pathways to understanding, each offering valuable insights into the nature of reality."

"In essence," he concluded, "both paths invite us to look deeply into the world around us and within us, to discover the laws that govern all life, and to live accordingly. This synergy between Buddhism and science holds great promise for addressing the challenges of our time and guiding us toward a more sustainable and enlightened future."

* * *

The professor's eyes sparkled with the excitement of someone on the cusp of revelation, as he addressed the complexities surrounding the belief in Sukhavati, the Pure Land. "I've often pondered why the concept of the Pure Land is so extraordinary," he began, his voice a blend of curiosity and conviction. "At first glance, it might seem like a superstitious notion, beyond the grasp of scientific explanation. How can simply chanting the name 'Amitabha' lead to rebirth in such a realm?"

He leaned forward, his expression earnest. "Consider this: the Pure Land was said to have been created from nothing by the monk Dharmakara after extensive practice. This idea challenges our conventional understanding, yet it invites us to explore the potential of consciousness and intention to manifest realities—a notion gaining traction even in modern physics and cosmology."

"The distance itself, as described in the Amitabha Sutra— 100 trillion Buddha lands away—raises questions about accessibility. But what if this distance is not spatial in the traditional sense? Quantum physics suggests that space and time are not linear, and realms beyond our perception might be closer than we think, existing in parallel dimensions."

He paused, allowing these ideas to sink in. "Many intellectuals struggle with four central questions regarding the Pure Land Method: Was the Pure Land truly created from scratch by Amitabha? Can it accommodate countless beings without overcrowding? Is rebirth as simple as chanting Amitabha's name? And how can we reach a place so incredibly distant?"

The professor's enthusiasm was palpable as he delved into the intricate relationship between modern scientific discoveries and the ancient wisdom encapsulated in the concept of the Pure Land. "Let's tackle the first question," he said, "regarding whether the Pure Land was truly created from scratch by Amitabha Buddha and if it is as wondrous as described. To explore this, we must consider the fascinating intersections between human consciousness and the universe—a topic gaining traction in contemporary scientific discourse."

He continued, "A prevailing idea is that the universe does not exist independently; rather, it is influenced by human consciousness. This concept is largely informed by quantum mechanics, which suggests that the universe as we perceive it is shaped by our observations. Without consciousness, there is no 'real world' as we know it."

"Quantum mechanics," he explained, "reveals that all matter is composed of molecules, which in turn are made up of elementary particles like electrons and quarks. This field of study, which blossomed in the early to mid-twentieth century, has provided insights into the microscopic world that defy our traditional understanding. While it may seem abstract, quantum mechanics has been experimentally validated and is foundational to numerous technological advancements, such as in electronics."

The professor leaned in, clearly fascinated by the profound connections between quantum mechanics and Buddhist philosophy. "Indeed," he continued, "the behavior of particles at the quantum level offers intriguing parallels to the Buddha's teachings on the nature of the universe. When we observe a particle, it 'collapses' into a specific state, a phenomenon that underscores the active role of consciousness in shaping reality. This aligns closely with the Buddhist view that existence is fluid and without inherent permanence—neither born nor destroyed, without origin or destination."

He nodded thoughtfully, drawing the threads of his argument together. "In both quantum mechanics and Buddhism, there is an acknowledgment of the elusive and dynamic nature of reality. When particles are not being observed, they exist in a state of potentiality, much like the Buddhist concept of 'emptiness'—a state where things are not fixed but full of potential."

"This interplay between observer and observed," he continued, "highlights the inseparability of consciousness and the material world. Stephen Hawking's 'Model-dependent Realism' echoes this sentiment. It suggests that our perception of truth is inherently tied to the observer's consciousness. In other words, reality is not an objective, static entity but is shaped by our interactions with it."

He paused, allowing the depth of his words to resonate. "This understanding encourages us to consider the power of the mind not just as a passive recipient of the universe's truths, but as an active participant in creating and perceiving those truths. It invites us to explore the boundaries of consciousness and its capacity to influence reality, much like how Amitabha's vows might shape the Pure Land."

"In essence," he concluded, "by bridging the insights of quantum mechanics with Buddhist philosophy, we gain a richer understanding of the universe's mysteries. It encourages us to remain open-minded and curious, recognizing that both science and spirituality offer valuable perspectives on the nature of existence—perspectives that reveal the profound interconnectedness of all things."

Quantum mechanics reveals the profound impact of human (observer) consciousness, underscoring the inseparability of consciousness and reality. This aligns closely with the "Model-dependent Realism" of the eminent physicist

Stephen Hawking: the nature of truth depends entirely on the observer's consciousness.

The professor further connected this with Stephen Hawking's concept of model-dependent realism, which posits that our understanding of reality is inherently tied to the observer's perspective. "In essence, consciousness and reality are intertwined," he noted.

The professor's excitement was palpable as he delved into the fascinating world of quantum entanglement and its implications for understanding consciousness. "Quantum entanglement," he explained, "is one of the most intriguing phenomena in physics. It describes how particles that have interacted become connected in such a way that their states remain interlinked, regardless of the distance separating them. When one particle is observed and takes on a definite state, its entangled partner instantaneously adjusts its state to match, as if they are communicating across space."

He paused, letting the concept settle in. "This idea of entanglement extends far beyond the microscopic world. We see parallels in everyday life, such as the intuitive connection often reported between twins, where they seem to sense each other's experiences despite being miles apart. This mysterious connection suggests a level of interconnectedness that defies conventional understanding."

The professor continued, "Indeed, scientists Bonnie L. Bassler and E. Peter Greenberg have made groundbreaking discoveries in the field of bacterial communication. They found that bacteria can communicate with their own species and even other species to coordinate and enhance their attack power through a process called 'quorum sensing'. This communication allows bacteria to act collectively, making them more effective in their actions. Current medical research is now focused on disrupting this communication to reduce the lethality of bacteria and ultimately eliminate them. This innovative approach could lead to new therapies to combat bacterial infections and improve health outcomes."

He leaned forward, drawing a connection to the human brain. "Contemporary thinkers like Roger Penrose and Stuart Hameroff propose that our brains operate on similar principles of quantum entanglement. They suggest that the brain contains countless entangled electrons, which exist in a free state until they interact with the external world. This interaction disturbs the electrons, creating specific states that form the basis of our consciousness and thoughts."

"As we perceive the world through sight, sound, and touch," he elaborated, "these brain electrons are perturbed, generating distinct patterns that correspond to our experiences. Other entangled electrons, involved in processes like memory, also adjust accordingly, creating a dynamic and interconnected system that constitutes our conscious experience."

He smiled, clearly enjoying the exploration of these ideas. "When external stimuli cease, these electrons return to their free state, and our thoughts and consciousness may diminish or shift accordingly. This cycle of disturbance and return mirrors the Buddhist view of the mind as a fluid and ever-changing phenomenon, constantly arising and dissolving."

The professor's voice carried the weight of centuries, as if revealing a long-buried secret. "Consider this," he began, his eyes alight with intellectual zeal. "The electrons within our brains are not isolated entities; they share a profound connection with electrons scattered throughout the universe, all born from the same cataclysmic event—the Big Bang. This cosmic bond implies that when the electrons in our brains ignite the spark of consciousness, this information transcends the limits of time and space, spreading instantly across the cosmos."

He paused, letting the weight of his words settle over us. "Visionaries like John Wheeler and Andrei Linde have championed the idea that human consciousness is not a passive observer but a dynamic force shaping reality itself. It weaves through the fabric of our existence, molding our destinies and the world around us. Thus, reality is a subjective tapestry, unique to each observer. The crimson hue I perceive may never mirror the shade seen by others."

The professor leaned in, his voice hushed yet powerful. "Robert Lanza, a towering figure in stem cell research, has dared to challenge conventional wisdom with his theory of 'biocentrism.' He posits that life and consciousness are not mere footnotes in the cosmic narrative but its very heart. They imbue the universe with meaning, reducing time and space to mere constructs of perception."

He gestured broadly, as if embracing the universe itself. "Experiments reveal a hidden symphony within us. When we are suffused with positive energy, our hearts find a steady rhythm, and our minds orchestrate a harmonious alignment of frequencies. Yet, when negativity takes hold, chaos ensues, disrupting this delicate balance."

In the dimly lit study, we sat enthralled, each word a piece of a grand puzzle, inviting us to delve deeper into the enigmatic dance of consciousness and the universe.

The professor's discourse unfolded like an intricate tapestry, weaving together threads of science, philosophy, and spirituality. "Imagine consciousness as a unique energy, vibrating at its own frequency," he explained, his voice steady yet infused with a sense of wonder. "When this energy is amplified, it sets off a cosmic resonance, particularly with energies to which it is entangled. This suggests that a collective consciousness, driven by shared aspirations, holds immense sway over reality."

He paused, allowing the room to absorb the gravity of his words before delving into the complexities of String Theory. "This theory suggests that when numerous elementary particles—electrons, protons, and their kin—align under a unifying force, they resonate in harmony, coalescing into a greater energy field. Einstein's equation, $E=MC^2$, captures this profound transformation, where energy and mass can interchange, manifesting as physical phenomena."

With a deft shift, the professor guided us into the realm of the spiritual. "Consider the figure of Amitabha, a being whose consciousness and vows are said to be immeasurably powerful after countless eons of practice. The possibility of him creating an ideal world from nothingness aligns intriguingly with modern scientific principles. The 'Amitabha Sutra' speaks of birds, wondrous and varied, crafted by Amitabha to disseminate the Dharma's sound."

He continued, drawing connections across the vast tapestry of belief and science. "Sakyamuni Buddha, our esteemed guide, affirmed Amitabha's ability to transform into these magnificent creatures. As more great bodhisattvas and virtuous beings are reborn into the Pure Land, their collective will to construct this perfect realm grows ever stronger. This amalgamation of pure consciousness elevates the Pure Land to an ever more extraordinary state, embodying the profound truth that form is emptiness, and within this emptiness lies boundless potential."

The professor's voice resonated with a mix of curiosity and conviction as he addressed the intriguing question: "Can one truly be reborn in the Pure Land by simply reciting the name of Amitabha Buddha?" He encouraged us to consider the analogy of a television set, which tunes into specific frequencies to receive broadcasts. "Imagine the Pure Land as a cosmic broadcasting station," he suggested, "with Amitabha Buddha's boundless energy traversing the vastness of time and space to reach us here on Earth."

He paused, drawing us into the analogy. "When our teacher, Shakyamuni Buddha, spoke of this energy, he identified its frequency as the sound of 'Amitabha Buddha.' Regardless of language—Mandarin, English, or any other—the essence of these words remains a powerful vibration. Sound, being a form of energy, can create a connection with the Western Paradise's energy field. By chanting 'Amitabha,' we can attune ourselves to this frequency, enhancing our receptivity."

The professor leaned forward, his eyes gleaming with insight. "At the moment of death, the seeds of Amitabha's resonance, stored within our eighth consciousness, may guide our transition, aligning with the Pure Land's energy and facilitating our rebirth there. It's akin to entering a password to access a computer—chanting 'Amitabha' serves as the key to unlocking the gates of the Western Paradise."

He elaborated on the concept of consciousness interacting with the universe. "Research shows that chanting mantras can connect us to specific cosmic energy fields. Thus, it's not far-fetched to believe that chanting 'Amitabha' can establish a connection with the Pure Land's energy."

Addressing the distance to the Pure Land, he acknowledged the challenge from an ordinary perspective. "The Pure Land is described as ten trillion Buddha lands away, seemingly unreachable by conventional means. Yet Einstein's theories suggest otherwise. He taught us that time and space are flexible constructs. The Einstein-Rosen bridge, or wormhole, theoretically allows for travel across vast distances by folding space."

The professor continued, now weaving science with spiritual practice. "Quantum entanglement suggests consciousness can transcend these barriers. To be reborn in the Pure Land, one must cultivate 'faith,' 'willingness,' and 'action.' Scientifically speaking, 'faith' is intense focus, 'willingness' is strong intent, and 'action' is the conscious practice of recitation. Together, they forge a powerful consciousness capable of transcending time and space."

"From a scientific perspective," he continued, "these questions are not insurmountable. Consider the universe's vastness and the possibility of multiverses. The idea of a realm continually receiving beings could align with theories of infinite universes. As for the ease of rebirth, it's about aligning one's consciousness with a higher state, akin to tuning into a frequency rather than physical travel."

He smiled, a gesture of invitation. "I believe that with our evolving understanding of the universe, these questions can be reconciled with scientific principles. I share these thoughts in the hope that those who dismiss Pure Land Practice as mere superstition might reconsider. Science and spirituality are not necessarily at odds; they are different lenses through which we explore the mysteries of existence."

"In the end," he concluded, "the journey to Sukhavati, like many spiritual pursuits, is as much about the transformation of the mind as it is about physical relocation. It's an invitation to expand our understanding and embrace the profound possibilities that lie beyond our immediate perception."

Let's go back. Return home.

www.ingramcontent.com/pod-product-compliance
Lightning Source LLC
Chambersburg PA
CBHW061115310726
48974CB00002B/549